WANT TO KNOW ME?

WANT TO SEE ME?

WANT TO CALL ME?

WANT TO TRUST ME?

WANT TO LOVE ME?

WANT TO MEET ME?

WANT TO

GO PRIVATE?

SARAH DARER LITTMAN

SCHOLASTIC PRESS | NEW YORK

TO THE DEDICATED MEN AND
WOMEN OF THE LAW ENFORCEMENT
COMMUNITY WHO FACE UGLINESS
EVERY DAY IN THE EFFORT TO
KEEP OUR KIDS SAFE

Library of Congress Cataloging-in-Publication Data Available

ISBN 978-0-545-15146-7

10 9 8 7 6 5 4   11 12 13 14 15

Printed in the U.S.A.   23
First edition, August 2011

The text type was set in Avenir Book.
Book design by Phil Falco

PART I

CHAPTER 1
♪ AUGUST 31

"How can you *not* be excited?"

Faith, my best friend since second grade, is lying on the edge of the swimming pool watching the ripples as she trails her slim fingers through the water. "I mean, come on, Abby. We're starting *high school* tomorrow. It'll be so much better than middle school."

"And you know this how?" I wonder aloud.

Faith rolls her eyes.

"Well, for one thing, there are all the new kids from Eastern coming in. It won't just be the same people we've been going to school with, like, *forever*."

"Great. So there will be even *more* Clique Queens to make our lives miserable."

Faith draws her palm through the water, fast, sending a shower of cold droplets over my head. She doesn't get the satisfaction of hearing me shriek, because it actually feels pretty good after an afternoon of baking in the last day of summer sun.

"Why do you have to be so negative?"

"I'm not being negative," I protest, wiping the water from my face. "I'm just . . . ambivalent."

Liar, I think to myself. *What you really are is scared.*

"Ooh, *ambivalent!* You practicing PSAT words already?"

"No. It's just that . . . I guess part of me *is* looking forward to it. But a bigger part of me is just . . . well, scared. About how big Roosevelt is. About getting lost. About how everything is going to be different."

"Different doesn't always mean bad, Abs. Different could also be new and exciting, right?"

That's Faith for you. Miss Always Looking on the Bright Side of Life.

"I guess."

"Well, *I'm* excited. I can't wait. I've already picked out my outfit — I'm going to wear my new denim skirt with that cute Green Girl T-shirt. How do you think I should wear my hair? Up or down?"

"Um . . . I don't know. Down, I guess."

"You could at least *act* as if you cared."

"I *do* care — it's just I haven't even *thought* about what I'm going to wear tomorrow."

"Why not? You're so much prettier than me and you don't do anything about it. Watch, you'll show up to school tomorrow in jeans and some random T-shirt that's too big for you, instead of a cute outfit that shows off your curves." Faith sighs, looking down at her chest, which is on the small side. "At least you *have* curves to show off."

"Oh, stop," I tell her, feeling myself blush. I've always considered my boobs more of a curse than a blessing. "You're starting to sound like Mom and Lily. If I have to listen to one more tag-team lecture from them about how all I need is a fricking makeover, I might just end up murdering someone."

"Well, you can't murder me because I'm your best friend and without me, who would you sit with at lunch?" Faith jokes, wiping her face with her wet hand to cool off. "But seriously, Abby, for once, your mom and Lily are right. You could do with a pre–high school makeover. How about we go upstairs and I try some stuff with your hair?"

"How about we just chill in the basement and watch *The Lord of the Rings* again instead? I need an Aragorn fix."

Faith sighs.

"C'mon, Abby, *please*! This is the *first day of high school* we're talking about. We can watch *Lord of the Rings* anytime. Besides, Legolas is *way* cuter than Aragorn, and you know it."

I don't see the point, but Faith is giving me a pleading puppy dog look with her big, brown eyes and I always have a hard time saying no when she does that.

"Okay. You win. But no putting tons of crap on my face. And afterward I get to see Viggo Mortensen."

Faith smiles, magnanimous in victory. "Only a little crap. Just enough crap to highlight your best features. And afterward I'll *definitely* watch Orlando Bloom."

After what feels like hours but I think is only forty-five minutes, Faith is working what must be the umpteenth hairstyle.

"Come on, Faith. I'm starting to get a headache from all the hair pulling. It's one that only your mom's homemade oatmeal raisin cookies will cure."

"Just a few more minutes," Faith says, twisting two pieces of hair on either side of my head and then pinning them at the back with a large wooden clip. "This one's good. It gets the hair off your face so people can actually see your eyes."

"And that's a good thing? I *like* it when teachers can't tell if I'm awake or asleep in the morning."

"You're determined to be a pain about this, aren't you?" Faith says. Her narrowed eyes glare at my reflection in the mirror.

"No. I just . . . don't see the point. It's not like it's going to make a difference."

"Just wait till I'm finished," Faith argues. "Now look up while I put on this eyeliner."

I tilt my head back slightly and look up at the glow-in-the-dark stickers on the ceiling of Faith's room. They barely look like anything in the daylight, but I still remember the first time I had a sleepover with Faith in second grade. Mrs. Wilson turned off the lights and closed the bedroom door and it was like this magical constellation appeared overhead.

Faith's mom is so cool and artsy; she's like the anti-Mom. She writes articles for craft magazines and is always trying to get us to help her try out new projects, and she never seems to mind the mess we make while we're doing them. I love the random way she dresses, like she doesn't care what people think, and how she just twists her long, dark hair in a bun and sticks a pencil through it. I think I can count on my fingers and toes the number of times I've seen her wearing makeup. She's kind of bemused by Faith's interest in all the girly stuff. *My* mom is religious about getting her "Mom do" trimmed every six weeks and wouldn't be caught dead even coming down for breakfast on weekends without a little mascara and blush. When I came home from that sleepover in second grade and asked if I could put stars on *my* bedroom ceiling, she told me they would ruin the paint.

I feel Faith's breath on my face as she carefully draws the eye pencil across my eyelid. I look down from the ceiling and Faith's tongue is poking out of the corner of her mouth, like it always does when she's concentrating hard. I feel this warm glow in my heart — some things never change. *Or do they?* a nagging voice in my head warns. I wish that voice would shut up. I'm nervous enough already.

"Ta da! Look," Faith says. "And I dare you to tell me you don't like what you see."

I stare at my reflection in Faith's mirror, which has pictures of the two of us stuck around the sides at haphazard angles along with ticket stubs from all the movies and concerts we've been to together. I look *different*. The eyeliner makes my hazel eyes appear bigger and more dramatic, and Faith's put on a pale, almost colorless gloss to make my lips shine. I look older, more like someone who belongs in high school. With my hair up like this, there's nowhere to hide. I feel exposed and, I don't know, vulnerable.

"What's the verdict?" Faith asks. "I think you look really pretty."

"I . . . I just don't know if it's me."

"Of course it's you, silly!" Faith teases, smiling. "It's just called 'you making an effort for a change.'"

I turn to face Faith. "Making an Effort Abby" is giving me the creeps.

"Why is everyone so concerned about making me into something else? Why can't you all just like me the way I am?"

Faith's smile fades into a look of hurt confusion.

"I *do* like you the way you are, Abs. I'm just doing this because . . . you know, 'cause I care about you and I thought, well, you'd want to put your best face forward on our first day of high school. You know, the whole first-impressions-count thing and all that. I'm sorry if you feel like I'm trying to make you into someone you're not."

I feel a wave of guilt for making her feel bad. Faith's the best of best friends, the kind you can count on no matter what. No one understands me like Faith, none of my other friends, my parents, and definitely not my brat of a sister, Lily, who I can't even believe shares the same DNA.

"I'm sorry, Faith. I guess I'm just . . . you know . . ."

"No, Abs, I don't know. Tell me."

I take a deep breath and face "Making an Effort Abby" in the mirror as I make my confession.

"I'm scared."

I turn to look at Faith. "I'm scared about starting high school. I'm scared that things are going to change but I'm just as scared that they're going to be the same. I'm just one big lump of not being able to sleep at night, sick to my stomach, wish the summer would last forever, scared."

Faith's brown eyes glisten, and she envelops me in a hug.

"Everyone's scared of starting high school. If they tell you they're not, they're just full of it. But we were scared of starting middle school and we survived that, didn't we?"

"Yeah, barely. If you call being ragged on by the Clique Queens every day surviving."

Faith frowns.

"Okay, I'll admit, Amanda Armitage and the other Witches of Western did put a kind of a damper on our middle school experience. But it wasn't a *complete* suckfest — we still managed to have *some* fun."

"Yeah, I guess."

"Trust me, Abby. High school will be better. Just wear something nice tomorrow, and do your hair and your eyes like this. Start with a good first impression. Promise?"

Faith holds up her pinkie like she has ever since we met in second grade. I curl mine around hers and mutter, "Pinkie promise," even though I'm pretty sure that it won't make any difference, and I have no confidence that high school will be better.

"What happened to *you*?" Lily says when I get in the car.

"What do you mean?" I ask, reaching to undo Faith's hair clip, so my hair will fall back into its customary place shielding my face.

"Don't, darling, your hair looks very pretty up that way," Mom says, appraising me critically. "Something else is different, too. . . . Wait, it's eyeliner — *finally*, you did something to emphasize your eyes like I've been telling you. Will wonders never cease?"

I feel like an insect under a microscope. I want to wipe off the makeup, mess up my hair, and go back to being my normal self.

"It's the wrong color," Lily says. "Abby should have used gold or brown eyeliner with her eyes, not black. Black makes her look too emo."

"Well, you can always lend her some, Lily."

"No way! I'm not lending her my makeup. She doesn't know how to put it on right. She'll ruin it."

"I don't even *want* to borrow your stupid makeup, okay? Faith was just trying to get me to dress up for the first day of high school."

"Faith's right, Abby," Mom says. "You only get one opportunity to make a first impression."

I'm going to punch the next person who says that to me.

"I've already *made* an impression on most of the people there. It's only the new kids from Eastern. And I've met some of *them* before at church."

"Well, I'm going to lend you *my* makeup," Mom says in her *and that's final* voice. "Because you look very nice, and it's important to put your best foot forward on your first day of high school."

"What!" Lily exclaims. "You never let *me* touch your makeup! And you have all the expensive stuff."

"That, young lady, is because *you* somehow finagle me into buying you plenty of makeup of your own, which you just refused to share with your sister."

"It's still not fair."

Lily sulks in the backseat the entire way home, which normally I would have considered a blessing, except that it means I have to be the one to talk to Mom, and all she wants to do is discuss in detail what I plan to wear tomorrow, like I have the slightest idea or even care.

Mom and Lily decide to make dressing me a joint project, and they invade my room, rummaging through my closet and drawers to pick out potential outfits. I get the impression Lily's purposely trying to make me look like a *Seventeen* magazine reject because she's putting together the most putrid combinations of clothing I've ever seen. My mother finally gives her the *"Lily Ann!"* treatment, and orders her to leave the room.

Mom's trying to convince me to wear this totally preppy outfit that I wouldn't be seen dead in.

"You can't be serious," I tell her. "Face it, Mom, I'm not *you*."

She's starting to get pissed at me, I can tell. Lily would have caved by now. Scratch that. Lily would have come up with some cute little outfit before Mom even walked in the room, instead of being like some sad Bratz doll, who, even at age fourteen, still needs Mommy to dress her, like yours truly.

"Well, I don't see you contributing much to this conversation, Abby, other than saying no to everything. Why don't you pick something out and let *me* say no for a change?"

Great. Way to put myself on the spot. I stare at the clothes on the bed and the clothes in my closet, hoping for inspiration. All I want to do is grab a pair of cargo shorts and my Aragorn T-shirt, but I know that will send Mom into orbit. I will myself to be "Make an Effort Abby," and take a denim skirt and a green spaghetti-strap tank with a white cotton shirt and lay them on the bed. Even though I don't really like wearing skirts that much, I figure it'll get Mom off my case and maybe tomorrow I can switch it for cargo shorts.

Mom smiles approvingly.

"Good. I can see you're starting to think about your appearance."

She goes over to my dresser, where my earrings are mixed in a box with my string bracelets, bangles, and necklaces.

"Darling, I bought you this earring tree," Mom says, starting to hang earrings on the Lucite stand with rows of empty holes. "Why don't you use it? Then you can actually see what you've got so you can accessorize properly."

What Mom fails to understand is that accessorizing properly is pretty low on my list of priorities.

"It's okay, Mom. I'll do that. You've helped me enough for one night."

Mom picks up a pair of pearl earrings that my grandmother gave me as a confirmation present. They practically scream Goody Two-shoes.

"Why don't you wear these tomorrow, honey?"

"Uh . . . maybe. Okay."

At this point I'd agree to wear a freaking nun's habit to get Mom out of my room.

"Well, I'll go start dinner. Make sure you've got all your supplies packed."

"Yeah. Will do."

I'm barely listening to her because I've already opened my laptop and started logging on to ChezTeen.com. It's this new site that's kind of like Second Life but for teens. Faith and I have been on it for a few months now and I like it a lot better than Facebook because you get to design your own avatar and you can use a screen name instead of your real name. And it's like your avatars are actually hanging out together in a real place instead of you just chatting. They even have real musicians give concerts in the Hippodrome. Last month Faith and I saw the *American Idols* tour — or at least our avatars did. Plus, like everyone and their *grandmother* is on Facebook now. My mom made me friend her as a condition of getting an account. At least on ChezTeen.com I have some space to breathe without parental supervision.

I log in and see that Faith's already there. Her screen name is Faithfull205. I'm AbyAngel99.

> Wazzup? I type.
> Did u choose an outfit?

I groan and my fingers hit the keyboard harder than usual.

> Yes, MOM!!!!
> So, what u wearing?
> Jeans skirt, green tank, white shirt.
> Sounds ok.
> Sounds hot!

What? That's not Faith. It's this boy avatar with spiky hair and sunglasses called BlueSkyBoi.

> **AbyAngel99:** Ha Ha
> **BlueSkyBoi:** What about u?
> **Faithfull205:** Denim skirt & Green Girl T-shirt.
> **BlueSkyBoi:** Nice. U guys r like twins.
> **AbyAngel99:** Well, we R BFFs.
> **BlueSkyBoi:** What grade u 2 in?
> **AbyAngel99:** 9th. Starting HS tomorrow.
> **BlueSkyBoi:** Excited?
> **Faithfull205:** Yes. ☺
> **AbyAngel99:** Not so much.
> **BlueSkyBoi:** Why not?

AbyAngel99: IDK. Scared, I guess.

BlueSkyBoi: I survived HS. U will too.

All of a sudden, an MSN chat window opens up. It's Faith.

Faithfull205: He's OLD! R u sure we should talk to him? What if he's a perv?

AbyAngel99: Not that old. Just out of HS & it's not like we're telling him where we LIVE.

Faithfull205: I guess.

We chat with BlueSkyBoi for a little longer. He asks us what are the top ten songs on our iPods. I can't believe when his are almost identical to mine.

AbyAngel99: OMG! We're music twins!

BlueSkyBoi: Or soul mates. ☺

Mom calls me for dinner.

AbyAngel99: GTG.

Faithfull205: See u tomorrow, Abs! xoxo

BlueSkyBoi: Later, soulie ☺

No one's ever called me a soul mate before, and the thought of it being someone I don't even know, some avatar with spiky hair and a leather jacket called BlueSkyBoi is just . . . well, funny.

I'm smiling as I head down to dinner.

CHAPTER 2

My stomach is turning over as Faith and I walk up the steps to Roosevelt High. Everything seems so much bigger here than it did at Western.

"I hope we have the same lunch period," I tell Faith.

"I know," she says, linking her arm through mine. "Otherwise, how will we share cookies?"

I feel weird walking arm in arm, even though last year I wouldn't have thought twice about it. Maybe it's too middle school. We head to the gym, where we're supposed to pick up our schedules, and I manage to extract my arm as we go through the doors. *Whew!*

"I guess we have to go to separate lines," I say. "Looks like I'm in H to P and you're in Q to Z. Does anyone's last name actually begin with Q?"

"Anna Quintana," Faith says.

"Okay, but what about Z?"

"Uh . . . I know, Emilio Zapata!"

"Okay, know-it-all. Go stand in line, and I'll meet you after to compare schedules. We *better* have classes together."

"Don't worry, Abs, we will," Faith says as she heads off to the Q to Z line.

It's sweltering in the gym. I don't know why I let Faith talk me into wearing this stupid hairstyle, with my hair half down my back. I try holding it up in a ponytail to let my neck cool.

"It is so fricking hot in here!"

I turn and find myself looking up into a pair of bright blue eyes, set in a deeply tanned face that's framed by close-cut, dark hair. I swallow, suddenly glad that I bothered to experiment with Mom's extensive makeup selection this morning.

"Uh . . . yeah. You'd think they'd turn up the A/C."

"You didn't go to Eastern, did you?"

"No, Western."

"Thought I didn't recognize you. I'm Nick. Nick Peters."

"Um. Hi. I'm Abby. Abby Johnston."

"Yeah, well, figured it had to be something between H and P, right?" He smiles, and his teeth are blindingly white against his tan.

Maybe Faith's right. Maybe high school won't be so bad after all.

"Nick! Hey, Nicky!"

Amanda Armitage, queen of all Clique Queens and bane of my middle school existence, is coming across the gym, smiling and waving, and I'll bet you my favorite Viggo Mortensen poster that it's not aimed at me. Sure enough, Nick raises an arm and waves back.

"You know Amanda?" I ask him.

"Sure, Mandy and I go way back. Our parents belong to the same country club. She's great."

I take it back. High school sucks. Big-time.

I fake a smile and manage to lie, "Yeah, great," between gritted teeth.

Great at being a total beeyotch. Great at making other people feel like crap.

Fortunately, I'm up next to get my schedule, so I'm saved from any further discussion of the Evil Witch's greatness.

"See you around," I mutter to Nick as I slink away to find Faith.

"Later!" he says, but he barely looks at me. His eyes are on *Mandy.*

Apparently, there's room for more suckage in my life. When Faith and I compare schedules, we find that we're only in one class together, PE, and we don't have the same lunch period.

"How could this happen?" Faith says, sounding like she's about to cry. "We're *always* together. We're like peanut butter and jelly. Ice cream and hot fudge sauce. Hot dogs and mustard —"

"Okay, okay, I get the picture."

Faith gets all quiet like she does whenever I upset her.

"Sorry, Faith." I sigh. "I'm just really freaking out, okay?"

"Me, too, Abs. But we'll meet at the end of the day and tell each other everything, okay? PP?"

Now that we're in high school, we agreed not to pinkie promise in public. But old habits die hard, so Faith said we'd just say "PP" instead.

"Yeah. PP."

"And, Abs?"

"What?"

"You look really pretty today."

I smile, and even though I'm worried about the PDA thing, I can't help hugging her.

"Well, you know, someone whose name begins with F gave me all these lectures about first impressions counting."

Faith laughs and for the first time since second grade, we head our separate ways.

I feel like the ball in an Extreme Pinball game as I try to make my way from science class on one side of the building to math class on the other in the three minutes allowed between classes. Whoever dreamed up these schedules obviously never walked in the hallways when there were actually *people* in them.

I'm a little out of breath when I get to math, but my breathing quickens even more when I see that Nick Peters is sitting at a desk near the back and there are two seats left, one next to him and one in front of him. *It's my lucky day.*

He smiles at me as I put my books down on the one in front of him. I'm afraid if I sit next to him, I'll just gaze at him longingly for the entire class.

"Hey . . . uh . . . Alison, right?"

"Um . . . close. Abby."

"Right, Abby. How's it going so far?"

"Okay. It's a little crazy finding my way around."

"Yeah, I know how that is. But we'll get it, for sure."

"I know. I'm just going to have to improve my sprint times to make it to class before the bell."

Nick laughs and once again, I feel like high school has potential. Until I look up and see Amanda Armitage has just entered the room and is heading for the seat right next to Nick.

"Hey, Nicky! I'm sitting next to you so I can copy all your

answers," she says, tossing her blond hair over her shoulder as she arranges her books on the desk.

Nick grins. "Not so sure you'd want to do that, Mandy. Math isn't my best subject."

"Um . . . it's one of mine," I say, "You know . . . I mean . . . if you ever need help with homework . . . or anything."

Nick glances at me briefly. "Thanks, Ally," he says. "I'll remember that."

He turns back to Mandy.

He could at least remember my freaking name.

I feel like plankton. No, I feel lower than plankton, if there *is* anything lower than plankton, which I can't remember because I feel so miserable. What was the point of putting on all this facecrap and messing with my hair? It hasn't made any difference. People like Amanda Armitage are still going to be on top in high school, and people like me are doomed to a life as pond scum.

Faith and I sit together on the bus home. I just want to forget about my day, but she wants to compare notes.

"There's a really nice girl, Grace, in a few of my classes. I can't wait till you meet her — I think you guys will get along. How about you? Did you meet anyone new?"

I have a dull headache, and I really don't want to relive my day from hell, but there's no way I'm going to get out of it.

"Well, there's this really cute guy, Nick Peters, who's in my math class, but unfortunately he only has eyes for *Mandy* Armitage. Apparently, she's an *old family friend* from the country club and he thinks she's *great.*"

Faith rolls her eyes. "Wow. He must be *seriously* gullible."

"And despite this whole making-an-effort thing, he couldn't even remember my name for more than three minutes. He kept calling me Alison."

Faith manages to look sympathetic for all of three seconds before she bursts out laughing.

"I'm sorry, Alison, I mean Abs. That sucks. But he isn't the only guy at school. This is just Day One. You shouldn't give up on the hair and makeup thing because one idiot didn't remember your name."

I sigh and lean my aching head against the bus window.

"Maybe you're right. But it felt like middle school all over again. Seriously, Faith, do you really think putting this stuff on my face and doing my hair differently is going to turn me into someone new, someone who people like Mandy won't look down on? Someone whose name Nick might actually *remember*?"

Faith takes my hand and squeezes it.

"I don't know for sure, but I mean, what the heck, it can't hurt, can it?"

"I'm not so sure," I mutter.

"Try not to let Amanda get you down, Abs. You know what she's like. What she's *always* been like."

"Yeah. Whatever. I'll try."

"So promise you'll wear makeup again tomorrow?"

"Okay, okay, okay."

When I get home, I go straight up to my room, drop my backpack on the floor, and throw myself on the bed. I watch the afternoon sunlight dapple patterns of stripes and leaves on the ceiling, the dust motes swirling in random patterns that seem to mimic the confusing, uncomfortable feelings I have inside.

There's no homework, so I grab my laptop and log on to ChezTeen.com. Within minutes, I'm surrounded by friends, even though I've never met any of them. There, I can pretend that my first day of school was fantastic, because no one is going to know anything different. I can be anyone I want to be when I'm online and I don't even have to wear makeup.

"So, how was everyone's first day at school?" Mom asks when we're all seated around the dinner table.

"Great!" Lily chirps. "Seventh grade is awesome. I don't know why Abby hated it so much."

My little sister is *such* a freak.

"Mom, Dad, *now* do you believe me that Lily's weird? No one *normal* likes middle school."

"Abby . . ." Mom warns.

"*I* liked middle school, or junior high as it was known then," Dad says.

"Yeah, back when the dinosaurs roamed the earth," Lily says, rolling her eyes.

"Watch it, sprite," Dad tells her. "This dinosaur is the one who pays for your trips to the mall."

The fact that Dad liked middle school just proves my theory. He's not exactly a poster child for Normal. He's obsessed with becoming a millionaire before he's fifty, and when we go on vacation he reads all these business strategy books for fun. *On the beach.* It's so embarrassing. And he's been a serious workaholic ever since he left Strickham and Young, the major accounting firm where he'd worked even before I was born, and started his own practice. A major league workaholic — barely ever home and always totally stressed out. I can't believe he's actually here for dinner tonight. Mom must have read him the riot act about it being the first day of school and ordered him to come spend some face time with Lily and me.

"What about you, Abby?" Mom asks. "How was your first day?"

For a minute, I'm tempted to tell my parents the truth about my first day, how it was basically the same crummy scene as middle school in a bigger building. But I know that if I do, Mom will start listing the thirty zillion ways I need to change in order to be a success, and Lily will join in and that will be the cherry topping on my Cruddy Day Sundae.

So I lie.

"It was fine. Except it sucks because Faith and I aren't in any classes together except gym."

"Omigod!" Lily shrieks, throwing up her arms in exaggerated horror. "How will you *live*?! You guys are joined at the freaking hip!"

"Lily. That's enough," Mom says, giving my sister a stern glance. "Abby, I know that's tough for you, but maybe this is a good thing. It'll force you to branch out and make some new friends."

So now Mom's not happy with my friends, as well as with me?

"What if I'm happy with the friends I've got?"

"It never hurts to make new ones," Dad says. "Who knows where some of these kids might end up in the future? One of them could be the CEO of a Fortune 500 company for all you know."

Trust Dad to bring everything back to business.

"Not everyone has, like, one *special* friend since second grade," Lily says. She does little air quotes when she says *special*, whatever *that's* supposed to mean. "Some of us like to be *popular.*"

I can just imagine Lily and Amanda Armitage having lunch together in the cafeteria, plotting ways to make my life miserable. Not for the first time, I wonder how two people could be raised by the same parents and one end up as a future Clique Queen and the other . . . well, the other end up like me.

"It's not that I expect Abby to become wildly popular overnight," Mom says.

"Yeah, as if!" Lily snorts.

"Lily . . ." Dad warns.

"I just think that you've been such close friends with Faith for so long, it would be good for you to spread your wings a bit and meet some new people. Faith's a wonderful person, but it wouldn't hurt you to meet some . . . different . . . kinds of girls."

So, what, they want to try and turn me into Lily? They want me to start hanging out with Amanda Armitage? Not. Going. To. Happen.

"Okay, okay, I've got the message. You want me to be different. Can we talk about something else?"

Mom and Dad exchange glances.

"It's not that, Abby. Your father and I just want you to expand your horizons. We don't want you to . . . limit yourself unnecessarily."

I stare at my plate, no longer hungry. Why can't my parents just love me the way I am?

"Can I be excused?"

"But you've hardly eaten anything!" Mom says, all worried.

"I'm not that hungry, and I've got some reading I want to do," I lie.

"That's good," Dad says. "Get your studies off on the right foot. Grades really count now that you're in high school."

Sometimes I think my parents majored in cluelessness.

"Mom, can I have some more steak if Abby isn't having any?" Lily asks.

"Sure, sweetie."

I escape to my room and log on to ChezTeen.com. Almost immediately, a chat screen pops up.

BlueSkyBoi: Hey, wut up, soulie?

Soulie? It takes a second or two, but then I realize it's that guy Faith and I were chatting with last night, the one who was my musical "soul mate." I grin and type back:

AbyAngel99: Not much.
BlueSkyBoi: How'd the 1st day go?

I wonder if I should lie to him the same way I've lied to everyone else. But then I figure, *What do I care? It's not like I'm trying to impress him. I don't even know this guy.*

AbyAngel99: It kind of sucked.
BlueSkyBoi: Yeah. HS blows. Did your friend like it? Fairyfall or whatever. You always seem to be online together.

It strikes me as kind of...I don't know...weird that he would notice that, but only for a second. It's true, after all.

AbyAngel99: You mean Faith? I mean, Faithfull205. She's my BFF.

AbyAngel99: And SHE thinks it's great. All these new people to meet and stuff.

BlueSkyBoi: So what made your day such a suckfest?

AbyAngel99: Well, Faith & I aren't in any classes 2gether xcept 4 gym.

AbyAngel99: It's like the 1st time ever since 2nd grade!

BlueSkyBoi: That does suck.

AbyAngel99: And there was this really cute guy but it turns out he's friends with this girl

AbyAngel99: who is the biggest beeyotch EVER

AbyAngel99: & they're both in my math class and he DOESN'T EVEN REMEMBER MY NAME!

BlueSkyBoi: ☹

BlueSkyBoi: I would never 4get ur name.

BlueSkyBoi: If I knew it in the 1st place, that is ;-p

AbyAngel99: LOL! It's Abby.

BlueSkyBoi: I'm Luke.

AbyAngel99: Hi! ☺

BlueSkyBoi: Hi! ☺

BlueSkyBoi: So, this jerk, what's his name?

AbyAngel99: Nick. Nick Peters.

BlueSkyBoi: Well, Nick the Prick is clearly too much of an idiot to know a good thing when he sees it.

"Nick the Prick" makes me giggle. I know Luke's just flattering me, because how would he know if I'm a "good thing" or not? For all he knows, I could be hideously ugly with a really horrible personality. Or a guy even, like they always told us in the Internet Safety lectures at school. I could be some forty-year-old pervert *pretending* to be a teenage girl.

But even though I know it's just a line, it's still good to hear after a day of feeling like plankton. Right now, I'll take my compliments where I can get them. Anything to feel like I'm not the lowest link in the social food chain.

AbyAngel99: LOL!
BlueSkyBoi: I mean it. If I were at ur school, I'd remember everything about u.
BlueSkyBoi: Like, what's ur fave ice cream?
AbyAngel99: Butter pecan.
BlueSkyBoi: ur kidding!
AbyAngel99: no!
BlueSkyBoi: Wow. We srsly *r* soul mates. That's my fave flave 2!
AbyAngel99: ☺
BlueSkyBoi: What's ur fave color?
AbyAngel99: Purple.
BlueSkyBoi: Mine's blue.
AbyAngel99: Duh! BLUEskyboi?
BlueSkyBoi: Hahahaha!

BlueSkyBoi: That's what I like about u. Ur quick. And funny.

"Abby?" My dad is standing in the doorway.

AbyAngel99: GTG P911!
BlueSkyBoi: K

I close my laptop and spin my desk chair around.

"Yeah?"

Dad sits on the edge of my bed.

"So, have you thought about what extracurricular activities you're going to do, honey?" he says. "Because now is when everything starts to count for college."

OMG! I haven't even been in high school for twenty-four hours and my dad's ready to send me off to fricking college?!

"Um . . . Dad? It's my FIRST DAY. I haven't thought about a whole lot besides trying to find my locker and getting to all my classes on time."

A *normal* dad might take this as a clue to back off, but no one, least of all me, would ever accuse *my* dad of being normal.

"Still, angel, you need to start thinking about this stuff. Time flies, and before you know it you'll be filling out college applications. You don't want to be someone who gets turned down even though she has good grades because there are no extracurricular activities on her transcript."

I wish, for once, my dad would care about my *now* instead of my future. Like, in my fantasy dad convo, I'd be talking to him about feeling like social plankton instead of my currently nonexistent extracurricular activities.

"Okay, *okay*. I'll think about it. But can I at least have like *a day or two* to get used to the place first?"

"Sure, honey. Just keep what I said in mind."

That's pretty much the end of our heart-to-heart. He says good night and kisses me on the top of the head. And I'm left sitting at my desk wanting . . . something, I don't know what. Something *more*.

CHAPTER 3

We're on the bus about a month later and Faith is desperately trying to persuade me to audition with her for the drama club's production of *A Midsummer Night's Dream*.

"Try out with me," she urges. "Grace is doing it, too. It'll be fun."

Hearing that Faith's friend Grace is going to the auditions doesn't give me much incentive. I am so sick of hearing about Grace *this* and Grace *that*. All Faith ever talks about is Grace — who's in *all* of Faith's classes. I only get to see Faith in PE and we hardly get to talk there because we're training for the stupid physical fitness test so we have to run laps around the football field. The enormously *large* football field.

But Grace is only part of the reason I'm not exactly falling over myself to do this.

"Faith, you know I hate getting up in front of people. I freak out when I have to do a class presentation. Like I'm really going to be able to speak a part in front of an *entire audience*?"

"C'mon, Abby! Just try. Even if you don't get a part, there are lots of other things you can do, like costumes and sets and lighting and stuff. And we need extracurricular things for college."

"You sound like my dad."

"Well, it's true," she says. "Plus, it's a great way to meet people. And you've been kinda grumpy about the whole making-new-friends thing."

Huh?

"What do you mean, grumpy? I'm not grumpy!"

Faith gives me a sidewise glance.

"No? So why do you get all quiet and distant every time I mention Grace's name?"

I look out of the bus window. *Am I that obvious?*

"See! You're doing it right now."

Faith puts her hand on my arm and I'm forced to meet her gaze.

"Look, Abs, just because I'm becoming friends with Gracie doesn't mean that things have changed with us."

Yes, it does. It feels like you're leaving me behind.

"I wish you'd get to know her better. If you did, you'd really like her. Come on. Promise me you'll stay after school tomorrow and audition with me."

She surreptitiously lifts the pinkie on the hand that rested on my arm and wiggles it, and she bats her eyelids while mouthing, "Pretty please?"

Even though the idea of being on a stage in front of people makes me want to throw up, I move my hand next to Faith's and link pinkies.

"Okay, okay. I'll go. But only because you begged so nicely."

Faith laughs.

"I'll get my mom to pick us up so we don't have to take the late bus. See you tomorrow!"

She grabs her backpack and gets off at her stop, leaving me to worry about what I've just gotten myself into.

After I finish my homework, I log on to ChezTeen.com and go hang out at the ChezNous Café, because this band I like, The Domestix, is giving a live concert there tonight. I check my friends list to see if Faith's online yet, but she isn't. I'm not sure if I want to talk to her right now anyway. The last thing I need is to hear more about Amazing Grace and how awesome it's going to be at the auditions tomorrow, while I'm busy freaking out over making a complete idiot out of myself.

Then a familiar spiky-haired avatar appears. It's that guy, BlueSkyBoi, that I talked to a while back. My "soul mate," Luke.

BlueSkyBoi: Wazzup, Abby?
BlueSkyBoi: Howz the High Skool O'Hell?
AbyAngel99: LOL.
AbyAngel99: Still pretty hellish.
BlueSkyBoi: Did Nick the Prick remember ur name yet?
AbyAngel99: Ha! NO!
AbyAngel99: Yesterday he called me Angelina.
BlueSkyBoi: *snorts*
AbyAngel99: And that was AFTER he copied my homework!
BlueSkyBoi: Wait — ur telling me you let that dickwad who doesn't even remember ur name copy ur homework?!!
AbyAngel99: *hangs head in shame* Yeah.

BlueSkyBoi: Come on, sweetie! Ur too good 4 that!

BlueSkyBoi: Nick the Prick's just using u.

If I think about it, I know he's right. But BlueSkyBoi's never *seen* Nick Peters. He's never felt his heart start to beat faster the minute Nick walks into math class. Or his face start a slow flush when he feels Nick's hand brush his as he hands over his homework for Nick to copy. I have.

AbyAngel99: I know, I know. But . . .

AbyAngel99: He might be a prick but he's just so gorgeous.

BlueSkyBoi: K, now ur makin' me jealous!

AbyAngel99: LOL.

AbyAngel99: K no more talking about N the P.

I think of something to change the subject and then start typing.

AbyAngel99: My BFF Faith wants me to try out for a play w/ her.

BlueSkyBoi: RU gonna do it?

AbyAngel99: Said yes, but I don't want 2.

BlueSkyBoi: Uh . . . So why do it?

Why do it? Because Dad keeps hassling me about extracurriculars? Because Grace is doing it and I'm afraid if I don't, I'm going to be left out? Because maybe Faith won't be my BFF anymore? How pathetically lame does that sound?

AbyAngel99: Cause she's my BFF, duh!

BlueSkyBoi: Yeah, but doesn't mean u have to do EVERYTHING 2gether.

AbyAngel99: Well, it's complicated.

BlueSkyBoi: Complicated, huh?

BlueSkyBoi: WTGP?

Go private? Like a private chat room? I don't usually do private chats with people I don't know in real life. I've had all those Internet Safety talks at school. For all I know, BlueSkyBoi isn't a "boi" at all. He could be some fifty-year-old dude living in his parents' basement in California, or something. But then I figure it's not like I'm ever going to *meet* the guy.

AbyAngel99: K

Chat room name: BlueSkyBoi

BlueSkyBoi: So when's the big audition?

AbyAngel99: Tomorrow. I'm scared.

BlueSkyBoi: Why?

AbyAngel99: Cause I hate to get up in front of peeps.

BlueSkyBoi: And ur trying out for a *play*?!!! ROTFLMAO!

AbyAngel99: Yeah, go figure.

BlueSkyBoi: Srsly, why u doing it then?

I hesitate between truth and excuses, watching the blinking cursor, before typing slowly.

AbyAngel99: Cause . . . if I don't, maybe she'll be BFFs with someone else. This girl Grace.
BlueSkyBoi: She can't be a good BFF if she'd dump u like that.

I feel weird that he's criticizing Faith when he's never met her. It's one thing for me to feel upset with her, but I don't want anyone else saying bad things about her. She's still my best friend . . . I think.

AbyAngel99: She is, really. It's just . . .
BlueSkyBoi: ????
AbyAngel99: High school. Things r changing.
BlueSkyBoi: And not 4 good?
AbyAngel99: IDK. No. At least not 4 me.
BlueSkyBoi: Well, I'll be ur BFF, LOL!
AbyAngel99: LOL.
BlueSkyBoi: Srsly. Tell me what u look like.
AbyAngel99: Brown hair, hazel eyes, abt 5'6".
BlueSkyBoi: Bra size?

I gasp when I read that, because I'm sure he shouldn't be asking. I mean, it's not like most of the guys at school don't ogle my boobs or ping my bra strap whenever they get the chance. It's been that way ever since fifth grade, when I was one of the "early developers," lucky me.

But then, it's not like I'm going to see this guy in the halls at school or anything. He's just words on a screen.

My fingers hesitate for a minute and then I type:

AbyAngel99: 34C

BlueSkyBoi: Nice. I bet the boys at school don't realize how lucky they are.

AbyAngel99: Ha! 2 right!

BlueSkyBoi: If I were there, I'd treat u the way u deserve 2 be treated.

AbyAngel99: How's that?

BlueSkyBoi: Like a queen. Special. Because ur better than all the rest.

My cheeks flush as I read his words, and I can't stop myself from smiling. But I know it's ridiculous, right? He doesn't even know me. He's never even met me. He doesn't know what I look like or anything.

AbyAngel99: Yeah, right.

BlueSkyBoi: I'm serious. I know these things.

AbyAngel99: How? U don't even know me.

BlueSkyBoi: So tell me about urself.

BlueSkyBoi: How old are u?

AbyAngel99: 14. U?

BlueSkyBoi: 27. Does that freak u out?

Does it? Kind of. I guess it would more if I ever thought I was going to meet the guy, but I'm not. He's just someone to talk to online.

AbyAngel99: A little. But not 2 much.

BlueSkyBoi: Good. Cause I like u, Abby.

AbyAngel99: I like u 2.

BlueSkyBoi: ☺

I realize the concert's about to start, and I don't want to miss it.

> **AbyAngel99:** Hey, GTG. The Domestix r about 2 start.
>
> **BlueSkyBoi:** K. But hope to TTY tomorrow 2 see how auditions go.
>
> **AbyAngel99:** K. Bye!

When I meet Faith outside the auditorium the following afternoon, I'm feeling queasy about what lies ahead.

"Do I seriously have to go through with this?"

Faith links her arm through mine and drags me through the doors.

"Yes, you do. Come on, Gracie's already inside, saving us seats. It'll be fun."

I stare at the stage, which is bathed in light. I don't think fun is going to play any part in this.

Faith's friend Grace waves at us from the sixth row. She's tall and slim, with blond hair and blue eyes, and she's wearing big dangly earrings with the laughing and frowning drama masks.

Now I know where this whole try-out-for-drama idea came from.

"Hi, guys! They're going to start soon. You need to sign up on the form at the front there."

Faith drags me down to the front of the auditorium, where a dark-haired boy wearing a DRAMA IS LIFE WITH THE DULL BITS CUT OUT T-shirt sits holding a clipboard and a pen.

"Love your T-shirt," Faith says, smiling at him. "Is this where we sign up to audition?"

"Alfred Hitchcock," the guy says. "The quote, that is, not me. And yes, this is Sign-up Central. Just put your name, grade, e-mail, and phone number down here on this list."

He hands her the clipboard, and Faith lets go of my arm. If I didn't know Faith would kill me for doing it, I'd be sorely tempted to sprint up the aisle and get myself as far away from this whole scene as possible.

"I'm Ted, by the way. Ted Barringer."

"I'm Faith Wilson. And this is Abby Johnston."

Ted nods in my direction and I notice he has green eyes. In fact, if he had round glasses and a scar, he'd be Harry Potter's twin brother.

"Well, ladies, break a leg, as they say. Looks like Mr. Hankins wants to get things rolling."

It doesn't take much for Mr. Hankins to bring the noisy auditorium to quiet. He has a deep voice that projects without a microphone and he explains that everyone is going to be paired up to read the same scene from the play, a girl with a boy.

I'm not sure if I want to be first to get it over with, or last so maybe everyone else will be so outstanding that Mr. Hankins will cast all the parts before they get to me. My mouth tastes bitter, like bile. Why did I let Faith talk me into this? I barely survived the last time I had to give a class presentation to twenty-five kids. There's no way I'm going to be able to get up onstage in front of all these people.

Faith's called first. Grace grabs my hand while Faith's onstage, which feels totally awkward. It's one thing for Faith to give me PDA, but Grace and I barely know each other. I give Grace's hand a quick squeeze, then extract mine and put it as far away from her as I can. We sit listening to Faith run through the lines with a guy named Bob. Or at least trying to listen.

She would be great if you could actually hear *her.* The problem is Faith's voice barely carries to the sixth row, where Grace and I are sitting. Mr. Hankins is at least another ten rows back.

"Thank you," he says, and calls the next pair. Faith comes back to her seat, flushed with excitement.

"How was I? Be honest."

I open my mouth to be honest, the way we always have been with each other, to tell her that she was really good, but that she needs to project more. But before I can speak, Grace hugs Faith and says, "You were fantastic, really good. I'm *sure* you're going to get a part."

Faith seems to radiate with an almost supernatural glow of pride, and I don't want to rain on her parade and have her accuse me of being all negative again, so I'm just like, "Yeah, Grace is right. You're *totally* going to get a part."

She hugs me, and whispers, "So are you."

I shrug and sit there waiting my turn with my stomach churning. Grace is called before me. As much as I hate to admit it, she's good — really good. You honestly believe she's the character, and her voice is so loud she can probably be heard in the back row of the balcony.

"She really knows what she's doing," I whisper to Faith, as Grace nears the end of the scene.

"Yeah, well, she's really into it — she's been to summer acting camp and stuff," Faith says. "I wouldn't be surprised if she gets a lead part, even though she's only a freshman."

"What did you think?" Grace asks when she comes back. "I don't think I projected enough."

"Are you kidding?" I say. "I think they heard you in New Haven."

"She's right," Faith agrees. "You were awesome, Gracie. Don't worry."

"Well, I'm glad it's over," Grace says, flopping into a chair. "I hate waiting around for everyone else to go."

Then, as if she didn't realize that I'm sitting here with my arms folded over my stomach trying not to puke from nerves, she's like:

"Oh, I'm *soooooo* sorry, Abby! I forgot you didn't go yet."

Yeah, right. Sure *you did.*

I watch the next pair read, wishing I were anywhere but here. Faith and Grace are whispering comments about the couple onstage. I can't hear and I don't want to. I just want to go home.

"Abby Johnston and Ted Barringer."

"Lucky you," Faith whispers. "You get to read with that cute guy." She pats me on the back. "Break a leg!"

Graces echoes her. "Break a leg, Abby!"

"With my luck, I really *will* break a leg," I mutter as I get up and head for the stage.

I stand facing the darkness of the auditorium. The script is fluttering in my visibly shaking hands, which I'm trying desperately to keep still with zero success.

"Hey, relax, Abby," Ted says under his breath. "I only bite on Fridays when there's a full moon."

I manage a grimace of a smile. At least he remembered my name, something that Nick Peters can't seem to do after three weeks of copying my math homework.

I can only see the first few rows of faces before the darkness takes over. I know the auditorium isn't even at a fraction of its total capacity, but it still seems like the whole world is watching me, just waiting for me to mess up. My heart beats an irregular rhythm in my chest and I feel dizzy.

"Whenever you're ready," Mr. Hankins says.

How about never?

Ted has the opening lines.

"I love thee not, therefore pursue me not. Where is Lysander and fair Hermia? The one I'll slay, the other slayeth me. Thou told'st me they were stol'n into this wood; And here am I, and wood within this wood, Because I cannot meet my Hermia. Hence! Get thee gone, and follow me no more."

That's my cue. *Speak. Now.*

But the words won't come out. It's as if my vocal cords are frozen, my tongue paralyzed. Ted looks at me and nods, encouraging me to start my lines.

"Y-you d-draw m-me . . ." I stammer.

"Take three deep breaths and then Ted will take it from the top," Mr. Hankins says. He's being nice, but I know I've already blown this.

I breathe in and out deeply three times, but it just makes me feel dizzier.

"You ready?" Ted inquires. He touches my arm lightly.

I nod, although I'm anything but. I hear Ted say his line, but it's as if it's from down a very long hallway, with the sound of ocean waves crashing on either side.

The next thing I know, I'm lying on the floor looking up at Ted's worried face.

"Don't panic, people, I think she just fainted," I hear Mr. Hankins say. He jumps up onto the stage and kneels down next to me, lifts my wrist, and starts taking my pulse. Faith and Grace run up the steps and sit on the floor near my head.

"Are you okay, Abs?" Faith asks, stroking my hair. She looks totally freaked out.

"Your pulse is low," says Mr. Hankins. "Were you feeling dizzy?"

I close my eyes and nod.

He helps me sit up slowly, and makes me rest my head between my knees for a while before helping me to my feet. Faith and Grace rub my back. I just want to get off that stage, away from the spotlights, away from all the eyes watching me make a fool of myself.

"How are you getting home?" Mr. Hankins asks.

"My mom is coming," Faith says. "In fact, she might even be here already."

"Can you help your friend with her stuff?" Mr. Hankins says.

"Of course!" Faith says, putting her arm around my shoulders to support me. I feel like shaking it off. If it weren't for Faith I wouldn't have been here and this wouldn't have happened.

Grace picks up my backpack and together we walk down the aisle of the auditorium toward the front entrance of school. It's the longest, most humiliating walk of my life.

Why'd I even try out for this stupid play? Why did I let Faith talk me into it? Faith knows I'm a basket case when I have to speak in front of people. It's like she didn't even care. All she thinks about these days is being friends with Grace.

"I was so scared when you passed out, Abs, I thought maybe you'd had a heart attack or something," Faith says. "You got all pale and then your eyes rolled back and BAM!"

"I bet you'll have a nasty bump on your head," Grace says. "You should probably put frozen peas on it when you get home."

"Frozen peas?" Faith says.

"Yeah. My mom has a bag of frozen peas that we never eat — she just uses it as an ice pack for whenever someone hurts themselves, because the peas form around whatever hurts."

"Great. So I'll be known as a pea-brained, fainting loser. That's all I need," I say.

Faith hugs me. "Come on, Abs. You are *not* a loser. You just fainted, okay? It's not the end of the world. It could have happened to anyone."

"Yeah, but it didn't happen to anyone. It happened to *me.*"

"It doesn't mean you still can't be involved with the play," Grace says. "You could still be on stage crew or do costumes or lighting."

"Right now, I don't even want to think about the fricking play. I just want to go home."

Grace rolls her eyes and I want to punch her even more than I want to go home.

"Well, lucky for you, Mom's here," Faith says, oblivious to my desire to inflict bodily harm on her buddy. "See you tomorrow, Gracie."

"Listen, Faith, don't tell your mom I fainted, okay?" I tell her as her mom's car pulls up to the curb.

"Why not?"

"Because I don't want my parents to find out."

"But, Abby —"

"Faith, *please.* PP?"

After all, you were the one who got me into this mess in the first place.

The unspoken words hang between us, as I discreetly hold out my pinkie.

Faith hesitates, meeting my gaze with worried eyes, before linking her pinkie with mine.

CHAPTER 4

"How were the auditions?" Mom asks at dinner. I was hoping she'd forgotten. No such luck.

"Fine," I lie.

"What's Abby auditioning for? The Freak Show?" Lily asks.

"Lily, that's not nice," Mom says. "Your sister was auditioning for the school play."

"*Abby*? Have pigs started flying or something?"

"Shut up, Lily!" I snap at her. Times like this you can really understand why Cain killed Abel. I bet you anything Abel was a complete pain in the butt like Lily.

"Girls, that's enough. I'm sick and tired of your constant bickering."

She looks at her watch. "I wonder where your father is. He said he'd be home by six thirty."

"Like he's *ever* home on time," I say. "I thought it was supposed to be *better* to work for yourself than for a big company."

Mom sighs. She looks tired. "It is in some ways. But it's more stressful in others, especially with the economy being what it is. Daddy's having to work out a lot of people's financial messes, and that takes time."

The phone rings.

"I'll get it!" Lily is out of her seat before Mom and I even think of moving — her reflexes highly developed from years of training. If there were a phone-answering medal in the Olympics, she would be a shoo-in for the Gold.

"Oh, hi, Dr. Wilson!" Lily says. "You want to talk to Mom? Okay, I'll get her for you."

I feel my stomach turn over. Why would Faith's dad be calling to speak to Mom?

"Hi, Rudy, how are you? . . . What?" Mom turns and looks at me, concerned. "Goodness, no, she didn't say anything about it. Told me it went *fine* . . . Yes, that does seem to be their answer to everything, doesn't it? . . . Well, is there anything I should do? Do I need to make an appointment with her doctor?"

Doctor? I feel a wave of fury. Faith must have spilled. I can't believe she told.

"Okay, Rudy, I'll keep an eye on her. Thanks for calling. Give my love to Elaine. Bye."

Mom hangs up, sits back down at the table, and gives me a stern look.

"Why didn't you *tell* me you fainted at rehearsal? I *am* your *mother*, as of the last time I checked. So why am I hearing this from Dr. Wilson?"

"Abby *fainted*?" Lily says. "Omigod, what a dork!"

My brain is a swirling mess of anger and confusion.

"I'm *fine*, Mom," I snap. "Stop making such a big deal of it."

"I'm *not* making a big deal, Abby. But if my daughter passes out in school, it's not unreasonable of me to expect to hear about it from *her*, not through the grapevine. . . . Are you even *listening* to me?"

I'm only half listening. All I can think about is that Faith told her dad after promising to keep this secret. She betrayed a pinkie promise, something that's been a sacred ritual between us since we met in second grade. We've *never* broken pinkie promises. *How could she?*

"*Abby!* I'm talking to you!"

"Yes, I heard you. *I'm sorry*, okay? I should have told you. I just didn't think it was such a big deal. Yeah, I fainted, but I was *fine* afterward. I was just . . . you know, all nervous about auditioning. I never should have let Faith talk me into doing it in the first place."

Mom's face softens and she leans across the table to stroke a lock of hair back from my face.

"Sweetie, I think it's great that you tried. Not everyone is cut out to be onstage. You can always work backstage if you want to be involved."

"*No way.* If you think I'm going back there so everyone can laugh at me, forget it!"

"I'm sure they won't be laughing at you, darling."

"Yeah, right," Lily says. She gets up out of her chair and does this really exaggerated swoon onto the kitchen floor. I swear no jury would convict me.

"Lily, that was unhelpful and unkind," Mom snaps. "Apologize to Abby and go to your room!"

"But I haven't had dessert!"

"I don't want dessert," I say quickly. "Lily can help with the dishes and I'll go to my room instead."

Lily starts to protest, but Mom shuts her up with a Look. I stick my tongue out at her as I head out of the kitchen. Serves her right.

I go to my room and shut the door, wishing I could shut one on all the memories of this afternoon's audition fiasco. Anger sweeps over me again as I think of Faith telling, of her promising me she wouldn't, her brown eyes looking into mine as our pinkies linked. I open my laptop to send her an e-mail, but get as far as writing *Faith* before my fingers stop, because what I feel toward her right now is too big and . . . well, scary, to put into words. I mean, Faith and I have argued before, but I've never, ever, felt this gut-wrenching sense of betrayal, wrapped in a fiery cloak of mad. I wish I could call someone to bitch about it but Faith's the person I always call when I have a problem, so I'm left with all these feelings trapped inside.

There's no way I can face doing homework yet, so I log on to ChezTeen to see if there's anything interesting going on to distract me. Over at the ChezNous Café, people are arguing about The Domestix concert the night before — some people, me included, think it rocked and others think it sucked. It's starting to develop into a flame war, so I take my avatar over to the park and walk down to the bandstand by the lake, where this guy John Burik is playing an acoustic guitar and singing sad love songs. I turn up my computer speakers. Even though I'm not normally into that folkie kind of stuff, it suits my mood right now.

BlueSkyBoi: Hey, gorgeous, fancy meeting u here!

It's funny, even though I don't really know him, I'm kind of glad to see BlueSkyBoi. Especially since he's calling me gorgeous. Even if he doesn't really mean it, it feels good after the awful afternoon I've had.

AbyAngel99: Hi.

BlueSky Boi: WTGP?

This time, I don't hesitate.

AbyAngel99: K.

Chat room name: BlueSkyBoi

BlueSkyBoi: How'd the auditions go?

AbyAngel99: Don't ask!

BlueSkyBoi: That bad?

AbyAngel99: Stage fright.

BlueSkyBoi: Uh-oh.

AbyAngel99: Then I fainted.

BlueSkyBoi: :-O !!!!!

AbyAngel99: Yeah & then

I push ENTER and start typing, fast:

Then my friend Faith promised she wouldn't tell anyone but she told her dad and he called my mom.

My finger hesitates above the ENTER key. I feel disloyal telling him about Faith, like I'm betraying her somehow.

BlueSkyBoi: & then what?

Then I remember that *she* betrayed *me.* Faith's the one who persuaded me to do something she knew I'd suck at. Faith's the one who broke a promise. I need to talk and BlueSkyBoi's willing to listen. I press ENTER.

BlueSkyBoi: Harsh. Some friend. Guess u can't trust her anymore.

AbyAngel99: Can't understand y she'd do it.

BlueSkyBoi: Girls can be weird, esp. teen girls. Present company excluded ;-p

AbyAngel99: But she's sposed to be my BFF.

BlueSkyBoi: People change. With friends like that . . .

I sigh as I watch the cursor on the screen. Faith has always been like my true north, the one friend I can always count on, no matter what. If I don't have Faith, then who is there? The screen grows blurry as I fight off tears.

BlueSkyBoi: You ok? Did I upset u?

AbyAngel99: Yes. No. I mean, I'm sad because I feel like

BlueSkyBoi: Like what?

AbyAngel99: IDK, like things are never going to be the same.

BlueSkyBoi: Change is tough.

BlueSkyBoi: But I'm here 4 u, whenever u need me.

He's so sweet. I wipe my eyes with the bottom of my T-shirt, and I wonder what he looks like.

AbyAngel99: Thanx. Ur sweet.

BlueSkyBoi: Eww, sweet. Yuck. ;-p Don't ever call a guy sweet!

AbyAngel99: LOL! Ok, nice but SRSLY macho ;-P

BlueSkyBoi: Better.

BlueSkyBoi: So tell me more abt you. I bet ur really pretty.

I feel like he's reading my mind or something. Maybe we really are soul mates. But on the other hand, I'm glad that we're separated by a computer screen and who knows how many miles, instead of being in the same room. Because this way he can't see me blush when I read his words. This way, he won't be disappointed by the real me. It feels so good to be thought of as pretty.

AbyAngel99: OK, I guess.

BlueSkyBoi: Better than ok, I'm sure.

AbyAngel99: :-p

BlueSkyBoi: U gotta pic?

Ack! I was hoping he wouldn't ask, that I'd be able to drag out his illusion of me as a pretty girl for a while longer. Do I lie and say no? But then I kind of want to see what he looks like, too. Like, I know he's older than me, but does he look *old* old or *young* old? I'm curious enough that I decide to take a chance.

AbyAngel99: Maybe. Depends.

BlueSkyBoi: Depends on what?

AbyAngel99: If u have a pic 2.

BlueSkyBoi: ur a tough customer.

AbyAngel99: So?

BlueSkyBoi: Do I get to see ur pretty face?

AbyAngel99: Do I get to see urs?

BlueSkyBoi: My face isn't "pretty." And I'm not "sweet." ;-p

AbyAngel99: OK, ur srsly handsome macho face ;-p

BlueSkyBoi: That's more like it!

AbyAngel99: Well?

BlueSkyBoi: K, Send urs to redluke27@yahoo .com

AbyAngel99: U send urs first! abbyj209@gmail .com

BlueSkyBoi: K. Sending now . . . tick tock.

I wait impatiently for the incoming mail icon to show up, and feel my heart quicken when I see there's mail from "Luke Redmond." *Hope you like what you see!* reads the message. I open the attachment, anxious to see if Luke looks anything like I pictured him.

He doesn't exactly. He's not blond and blue eyed, like I thought he'd be. Instead, he's got thick, brown hair that curls from underneath a Red Sox hat, which shades his eyes so I can't see them that well, but he has a cute smile, and his Coldplay T-shirt fits well.

"Hello, Luke," I whisper to the picture on the screen.

BlueSkyBoi: Where's my pic?!!

AbyAngel99: Oops, sorry, too busy lookin at urs ☺

AbyAngel99: Will send now.

I quickly scan the photos I've got of myself, trying to figure out which one to send. Most of them are of Faith and me together and I'm so mad at her at the moment I don't want any part of her. Plus, I kind of want to keep Luke to myself. I decide to send a picture Faith took of me at the eighth-grade picnic at Candlewood Lake — right before I went behind a clump of rhododendrons to make out with Roger Hunter. Boy, was that ever a mistake! I'd had a really big crush on him all year, but it turned out he just wanted to try to get to second base. *And* he was a really lousy kisser. But it's a good picture. I'm wearing jeans shorts and a flowery bikini top and these fake Dolce & Gabbana sunglasses that I bought on the street in New York City for ten dollars without noticing they said Dolce & Gabbanana. Lily never let me live that down. But Faith says they make me look like a movie star, especially when I'm doing the pretend-I'm-a-model pose like I'm doing in the picture.

> **AbyAngel99:** On its way.
> **BlueSkyBoi:** So?
> **AbyAngel99:** So . . .
> **BlueSkyBoi:** What did u think?
> **AbyAngel99:** Well . . .
> **BlueSkyBoi:** Yes?
> **AbyAngel99:** Ur pretty cute ☺
> **BlueSkyBoi:** Only pretty cute!? Not the hottest guy u ever saw????? jk.
> **AbyAngel99:** LOL! Maybe 2nd hottest.

I wonder if he's opened the picture of me yet. What if he thinks I'm a total dog and doesn't want to chat with me anymore? It's kind of freaky to send your picture out over the Internet to someone you don't really know and then have to sit waiting for their judgment on how you look. Maybe that's why my aunt Penny, who got divorced two years ago, hates online dating so much. Mom's always nagging her to go back on to Match.com but Aunt Penny says she'd rather have root canal work — without anesthetic.

>**AbyAngel99:** So . . .
>**BlueSkyBoi:** Sew buttons.
>**AbyAngel99:** Ur sew not funny ☹
>**BlueSkyBoi:** Would it help if I said ur the hottest chick I've seen in a long time?

I feel warm all over. I know he's probably lying, but it feels good to hear someone say it anyway.

>**AbyAngel99:** Might help if I actually believed u meant it.
>**BlueSkyBoi:** Srsly, Abby, ur really pretty. I don't know why u don't think so.
>**AbyAngel99:** Maybe cause guys in my hs don't exactly seem to be beating down my door.
>**BlueSkyBoi:** Good! I'd be jealous if they were.

It's strange that Luke's talking like this, all jealous and possessive like he's my boyfriend or something. Strange, but kind of flattering and nice.

>**BlueSkyBoi:** Those guys must be immature idiots. Srsly. If they can't see how cool and hot u are.
>**AbyAngel99:** Cool and hot. Haha!

BlueSkyBoi: U know what I mean ;-p

AbyAngel99: I guess.

BlueSkyBoi: Damn, I GTG. Time for work.

AbyAngel99: Now? What do u do?

BlueSkyBoi: Nothing interesting, believe me.

BlueSkyBoi: Hang in there, gorgeous.

BlueSkyBoi: TTY tomorrow?

AbyAngel99: K.

AbyAngel99: Byes.

I gaze at Luke's picture for a while after he logs off, trying to imagine him in the room with me. I try to imagine what it would be like if he were my age and went to my school, like if it were Luke who sat behind me in math class instead of Nick Peters. I get all depressed at that thought, because then Luke would probably have the hots for Amanda Armitage, just like Nick does, and he'd barely give me a second glance except for when he needed to copy my homework. Oh, yeah, and he'd call me Annabelle or Aggie or something. It's probably a good thing that Luke lives somewhere that we'll never meet in real life. That way I can always imagine the way it could be, rather than be disappointed by the way it is.

But I can't help myself from looking up his profile to see where he lives. BlueSkyBoi . . . age twenty-eight. I thought he said twenty-seven? Anyway, he's from New Jersey, it says. Toms River. I look it up on Google Maps. It's on the Jersey shore, north of Atlantic City. My parents took us to Atlantic City once. Mom and Lily and I hung out on the beach while Dad went to some Boring Accountants Convention. It took us, like, six hours to get there. It was only supposed to take four, but the traffic was awful. And I was stuck in the backseat with Lily whining the whole time. Joy.

I play the I-fainted-yesterday sympathy card with Mom the next morning so she drives me to school, because I don't want to have to sit with Faith on the bus. I know I'm going to have to see Faith sooner or later, but I would rather it be later, because I hate arguments, especially with her, even though I know I've got every right to be mad. Unfortunately, she catches up with me in gym while I'm puffing my way around the track practicing for the god-awful physical fitness test.

"Abs, wait up," Faith calls, jogging just behind me.

If my legs and lungs would allow, I'd quite happily leave Faith in my dust, but if I'm not the world's worst runner, then I'm pretty darned close. In kindergarten I came last in the potato sack *and* the egg-and-spoon races, and things have pretty much gone downhill for me on the athletic front ever since.

When she finally jogs up alongside me, I stare straight ahead like I don't see her.

"Abby, I know you're mad at me and . . . I'm sorry," Faith pants. "The only reason I spoke to my dad was . . . because I was worried about you. It really freaked me out when you . . . fainted. You looked like you were . . . dead, lying there."

I stop jogging and stare at her. "But I . . . was . . . *fine*." I gasp, trying to catch my breath. "You could *see* . . . I was perfectly okay . . . afterward. And you *promised . . . you promised* not to tell . . . *anyone!*"

I start running again, as fast as I can, reinvigorated by a burst of anger. But I hear Faith's footsteps pounding behind me.

"Abs, I know . . . I promised . . . and I'm . . . sorry," she pants as she comes up alongside me again. "I just wanted . . . to ask my dad . . . if you'd really . . . be okay . . . 'cause he's a doctor . . . I didn't know he'd call your mom . . . honest."

I slow down to my regular snail-paced jogging speed, my breath coming in heaves from the effort of sprinting. Faith's face is flushed and sweat beads her forehead. Her eyes plead with me to forgive her, and it looks like she means what she says. But then Luke's words come back me: *Guess u can't trust her anymore . . . People change.* If it wasn't for Faith nagging me to go to those stupid auditions, I wouldn't have been there in the first place. And why had Faith been all over me to go? Because she has a new friend, Grace, and drama is *Grace's* thing.

"Whatever," I pant.

Faith gives me the "let's hug and make up" look, but I'm not having any of it. Things have changed between us, and maybe I'll forgive, but I'm not going to forget.

We finish the lap and walk to the locker room together.

"They're posting the audition results later," Faith says. "I'm really nervous."

"Well, I'm pretty confident I didn't get a part — unless they were casting a dead body."

Faith giggles, assuming that everything is back to normal between us.

"Well, I hope you'll be on stage crew or makeup or something. You've *got* to be involved in the play somehow, even if you aren't acting."

I don't say anything, because I'm not up for one of Faith's full-frontal persuasion barrages. Maybe if I'm lucky, Faith won't get a part and then she'll give up on this whole drama business. But then I feel guilty for wishing that, because it's obvious Faith really wants to be in the play, and even though I'm still mad at her, I can't find it in me to want her to be crushed.

"Gracie and I are meeting right after school to go look at the casting results together. You wanna come?"

I'd rather jam forks in my eyes.

"Uh, sorry, I can't. I have a project I have to work on tonight."

"Already? Wow. That sucks!"

"Yeah. I really lucked out, didn't I?"

"Well, keep your fingers and toes crossed for me," Faith says as we go our separate ways. "I'll call you tonight to let you know what happened."

"Okay," I say. "Well, good luck."

"Don't say good luck! It's bad luck to say good luck in the theater! You're supposed to say 'break a leg.'"

"O-kaaaaay. Well, break a limb or an extremity or whatever."

Faith's laughter follows her down the hall.

I'm finishing my homework when Faith calls to give me the scoop.

"So do you want the good news or the bad news first?" she asks.

"Uh . . . bad news, I guess."

"Well, I didn't get a part."

I'm glad we're on the phone, so Faith can't see my sudden smile.

"Oh, that sucks, Faith," I lie. "I know you really wanted to be in the play. Did Grace get a part?"

"Yes. She's Titania, which is amazing for a freshman, isn't it? She was so psyched!"

"Wow. That's great. So . . . is that the good news?"

"No. I mean, it *is* good news and all, but the really good news is . . . Do you remember that really cute guy? You know, the one you read with? Ted?"

"Um, yeah. It's kind of hard to forget the last person you saw before you face-planted into the stage."

Faith laughs. "Well, he was there when we went to check out the casting results and we got to talking and he didn't get a part either, but he told me that he's going to sign up for stage crew and he thought it would be really cool if I did, too. Can you believe he said that?"

"Uh, no. I mean, yeah. I mean, it seemed like he was kind of . . . you know, flirting with you at the auditions."

"You think so? I was so nervous I guess I didn't notice. I never in a million years thought he'd be interested in me, but I sure noticed he was super cute. . . . I mean those eyes . . . Have you ever seen eyes like that? I mean —"

I kind of tune out Faith's breathless listing of Ted's adorable attributes and log on to ChezTeen.com.

"Abby? Abs, are you listening?"

"Sorry, what? My mom was calling me from downstairs," I lie.

"I was asking if you'll sign up for stage crew with me. I think it'll be really fun. Ted said it's going to be a really elaborate set so they're going to need all the help they can get."

I try desperately to think of a good reason to say no.

"I . . . can't."

There's an awkward pause before Faith asks, "You can't, or you don't want to?"

I don't want to.

"I can't. It'll take up too much time after school and I've got a project to work on."

"But, Abby, you're so smart and you always do well in school. You can manage doing both, I know it. And there are so many cool people involved in the play. Ted says —"

"Faith, I'm not doing it, okay? Just leave it."

The silence down the line is thick and painful. I can almost see Faith's face, the frown lines between her dark brows, and I wonder if maybe I should just give stage crew a try. Maybe if I spend more time with Faith, it'll somehow stop this awful feeling that our friendship is on its way to a slow, painful, and inevitable death. But I just can't face going back into that auditorium where I passed out, center stage. What if everyone laughs at me?

"Okay," Faith says in a quiet voice. "Whatever. It's your choice. I guess I'll see you on the bus tomorrow. Bye."

There's an empty feeling in my chest as I hang up, like a hollowed-out pumpkin. It's as if I've been losing Faith a little each day, and now I've just pushed our relationship over a cliff. I'm in free fall and there's no one there to catch me.

I glance at the blur of my laptop screen through my tears and see that there are two chat messages from Luke that I missed while I was talking to Faith:

BlueSkyBoi: Hey, gorgeous! How wuz ur day?
BlueSkyBoi: ?? U there??

Hoping he's still online, I type in my answer.

AbyAngel99: Sry, wuz on phone. U still there?

I watch the cursor on the chat screen anxiously. I want him to be there so bad. I almost cry with relief when I see the pencil icon that tells me Luke is typing a reply to my message.

> **BlueSkyBoi:** I'm here for u, baby. How goes?
> **AbyAngel99:** Not so good.
> **BlueSkyBoi:** What's up, honey?
> **AbyAngel99:** Faith wants me 2 work stage crew for the play.
> **AbyAngel99:** I said no.
> **AbyAngel99:** Now she's mad.
> **BlueSkyBoi:** Why'd u say no?
> **AbyAngel99:** After passing out in front of everyone? No way!
> **BlueSkyBoi:** Can see that. And wasn't ur friend Faith just doing it to get friendly with that girl, Grace?

I can't believe Luke remembered that. Wow. My own parents don't remember what I tell them about my life from one day to the next. Probably because they're only half listening to me most of the time.

> **AbyAngel99:** Yeah. Plus, now she's crushing on this guy Ted on the crew. I bet I'd just end up being the third wheel.
> **BlueSkyBoi:** Well, I'm kinda glad ur not doing it cause it means you'll have more time 2 talk 2 me.
> **AbyAngel99:** ☺ Me 2, I guess.

BlueSkyBoi: So what do ur parents do?

AbyAngel99: My mom's a dental hygienist and my dad's an accountant.

BlueSkyBoi: Do u get along with them?

AbyAngel99: Okay, I guess. My dad's like a total workaholic right now. He started his own business last year. We hardly ever see him, especially at tax time.

BlueSkyBoi: Brothers and sisters?

AbyAngel99: Younger sister, who is, without a doubt, the Devil's Spawn.

BlueSkyBoi: LOL!

AbyAngel99: Srsly! She's got 666 behind her ear. I checked while she was sleeping.

BlueSkyBoi: Ur too funny, Abby. You've got such a gr8 sense of humor!

AbyAngel99: How bout you? Sis or bros?

BlueSkyBoi: 2 older sisters.

AbyAngel99: Do u get along w them?

The pencil cursor hangs there. I wonder if he's going to answer me. Finally, he types.

BlueSkyBoi: 1, yes. The other . . . not so much.

AbyAngel99: Yeah, well. U can choose ur friends . . .

BlueSkyBoi: Haha! How'd u get 2 be so smart when ur only 14?

BlueSkyBoi: That's what I love about u.

Omigod. He used the L word. No one's ever used the L word to me except my parents and my grandparents. Oh, and Faith, but that doesn't count because that's just best-friend talk.

> **BlueSkyBoi:** Ur so much more mature than other girls ur age. That's why I really enjoy talking to u. I wish we could . . .

"Abby, it's time for dinner."

Mom opens the door and comes into my room and I quickly minimize the chat screen so she can't see my conversation with Luke.

"Can't you knock, Mom? I mean, I could have been changing or something. Aren't I entitled to a little privacy?"

Mom tilts her head and gives me one of those annoying I'm-such-a-cool-understanding-mom smiles.

"I'm sorry, honey. I didn't think. Sometimes I forget that my little girl has . . . *blossomed* into a young woman and doesn't want her mom seeing her in her underwear anymore."

Sheesh. At least she didn't use the words *puberty* and *menstruation*. There was a time when I was afraid to get in the car with her because she kept trying to bring up "my changing body," like I'd actually want to talk about that with *her*.

"It's okay," I say. "Let me just finish this sentence and I'll be down in a minute."

"Don't be long," Mom says. "It's your favorite — spaghetti Bolognese."

As soon as she's gone, I open the chat screen and read:

BlueSkyBoi: . . . talk all the time.
BlueSkyBoi: ?? You still there?

I type, fast and furious.

AbyAngel99: Sorry, had a P911.
BlueSkyBoi: I figured.
AbyAngel99: GTG dinner.
BlueSkyBoi: Bon appetit!
BlueSkyBoi: BTW, u don't talk to anyone about us, do you?
AbyAngel99: No, why?
BlueSkyBoi: People might not understand.
BlueSkyBoi: They don't realize how special u are and that's why . . . Well, I know you've got to go, so I'll save this convo for when we have more time.

I'm not even hungry for dinner now. I just want to know what Luke is going to say to me about "us." But Mom is shouting my name from downstairs.

AbyAngel99: I wish I could talk more now, but I really GTG. Mom's shouting. TTYL.
BlueSkyBoi: I'll be thinking of u. Constantly.
AbyAngel99: Me too. Byes!

I barely taste my dinner, and I toss and turn all night, wondering what Luke was going to say.

CHAPTER 5

♪ OCTOBER 6

I log on before school the next morning to see if Luke's online but he isn't, and there aren't any messages from him either. I was hoping maybe he'd write whatever he was going to say to me in an e-mail. It's driving me crazy trying to guess.

It's also really distracting. I find my thoughts drifting in science and when I look down I've doodled Luke's name in my notes. *Must. Concentrate.*

Ms. Forcier's talking about the characteristics of living things. Wait, I know this. I did the homework. She's already listed:

1. Made of cells
2. Obtain and use energy
3. Grow and develop
4. Respond to the environment

I scribble these down in my notes, next to all my Luke doodles.

"Billy, what's another characteristic of living things?" Ms. Forcier asks.

Billy Fisher is my lab partner. We ended up together after everyone else picked lab partners and we were the only two left without one. In other words, we were the biggest losers in the room. The thing is, he's not the kind of guy you'd think of as a loser. He's really smart and even kind of cute. I like the way he blushes a little whenever Ms. Forcier asks him a question. I guess he's shy or something.

"Uh . . . reproduction."

"Ooooohhhhh," Tyrone says. "Figures you'd remember that one, B."

Most of the class cracks up, and Billy turns even redder.

"Thank you, Tyrone, that's enough commentary," Ms. Forcier says, writing 5. *Reproduction* on the board. "Abby, how about giving me another characteristic?"

I'm trying to visualize the textbook that I read last night, except all I see are Luke's chats. This is bad. Science is usually my best subject. I stare at the list on the board and will myself to remember what I know is in my brain under all the Lukeness.

"Um . . . they adapt to the environment?"

"That's right," Ms. Forcier says, turning to add it to the list on the board.

I glance over at Billy. He grins at me and I mime wiping my brow with relief.

"Didn't you read the chapter?" he asks me after class. "You're usually the first one to raise your hand with the answer when Ms. Forcier asks a question."

"I did. I guess I was having a brain fart or something."

He laughs. "Too many beans for dinner last night, huh?"

"Ha-ha. You're so funny. Not."

But he kind of is. And he's pretty cute when he smiles.

"I've got to get to math," I say.

"Okay, see you around."

Nick Peters is waiting to copy my math homework, as usual. It kind of pisses me off that he's started to expect it. When I said I would help him with math, I didn't mean I would do it for him. I kind of expected him to put in *some* effort.

"Thanks, Angie," he says, handing back my paper. "You rock."

Yeah. *I rock so much you can't even get my fricking name right.*

It drives me crazy how Amanda giggles every time Nick calls me by the wrong name, but she never bothers to correct him. But then, why would she? If they made a movie of our high school, I'd just be "girl in math class" in the credits, where Nick and Mandy would have starring roles.

Glancing down, I realize I'm doodling Luke's name again. I guess thinking about him makes the rest of this seem bearable, because to Luke I'm not just social plankton. To Luke, I'm someone special. I hope he's online when I get home, so I can finally hear what it was he was going to tell me before Mom called me for dinner last night. The suspense is killing me.

I race to check my computer when I get home, but Luke's *still* not online. I go down to have a snack and then force myself to focus on my homework. Well, not entirely. I allow myself to check if he's online every ten minutes, but he's not there. I wonder where he is and what he's doing. I realize he's never really told me all that much about himself.

"Wut up, loser?"

Great. Lily's home.

"Nothing much, spawn o' Satan."

"We learned about sexually transmitted diseases in health today. It was *soooooooo* disgusting. I think I'm warped for life."

"Uh . . . I hate to break this to you, Lily, but you were warped for life before that."

"Like *you're* one to talk! Seriously, though. I am *never, ever* going to have sex. Like, *ever.*"

"Dad'll be psyched to hear that. He won't have to buy a shotgun."

"Whatever. I'm going to get a snack. You better not have finished all the chocolate chip cookies."

The shriek from the kitchen one minute and thirty-five seconds later tells me that Lily's discovered that I have, indeed, finished the chocolate chip cookies. What can I say? I'm stressed out because I need to talk to Luke. She can just sue me.

Dad's not home for dinner, as usual. It seems like we hardly ever see him these days. Even on the weekends, he spends half the time in his home office working, only emerging long enough to ask me what I'm studying and how my grades are doing. Sometimes I feel like telling him I got an F just to get his attention. Yeah, like I'd ever really do that. Being smart is about the only thing I have going for me. It's not like I'm ever going to win a beauty contest or anything. I guess the only way guys like Nick Peters are ever going to look at me is to see if they can copy my homework.

It's so depressing. I wish I could just take some magic pretty pill or something, so I could look like Amanda Armitage. Not that I'd want to be a witch like her. I'd just like to see what it felt like to have a guy like Nick pay attention to me, even if it was only for a day. Or even one math class. Is that *so* much to ask?

Sighing, I log on to ChezTeen. Luke *still* isn't online. Where *is* he? It's driving me crazy. I go into the music store and start talking to a group of people about some of the upcoming concerts. Then an MSN chat pops up from Faith.

> **Faithfull205:** Hola!
> **AbyAngel99:** Hey.
> **Faithfull205:** Wut up?
> **AbyAngel99:** Nothing much. Lily being Satan's spawn.
> **AbyAngel99:** The usual.
> **Faithfull205:** LOL!
> **AbyAngel99:** Wut abt u?
> **Faithfull205:** Stage crew. Crushing on Ted.
> **Faithfull205:** The usual. ☺
> **AbyAngel99:** Wut, he hazn't asked u out yet?
> **Faithfull205:** No. ☹
> **AbyAngel99:** Slacker!
> **Faithfull205:** Yeah. But we talk a lot while we're building stuff.
> **Faithfull205:** Like, he flirts with me and stuff.
> **Faithfull205:** I think.
> **AbyAngel99:** Wut do you mean?
> **Faithfull205:** IDK. Like, how do you know 4 sure when a guy likes you?
> **AbyAngel99:** Ur asking ME?!

But then I think about Luke and how he's always telling me how pretty and smart I am. How he makes me feel special.

AbyAngel99: IDK. I guess maybe if he says nice stuff to u and makes u feel special.

Faithfull205: Ted jokes w/ me a lot. And a lot of times I look up and he's looking at me and he smiles.

AbyAngel99: So, like, he's checking u out?

Faithfull205: I think.

Faithfull205: I know I'm checking him out. ☺

AbyAngel99: U Bad Girl U!

Faithfull205: I know, rite? So anyway, I wuz wondering

Faithfull205: do u want to come for a sleepover this weekend?

Faithfull205: It's been a while.

Faithfull205: & I feel so bad abt my dad calling ur mom.

Faithfull205: Sry again!!!

Part of me wants to go to Faith's more than anything, to see if things can be the way they were before school started. Like if we can turn back time. But there's another part of me that is still really mad at her. And it's probably crazy, but because I haven't heard from Luke, I don't want to be away from my computer. I mean, I'm sure I'll have heard from him by then, but . . . what if I haven't? It'll be hard to explain to Faith why I need to go online every five minutes.

The cursor blinks at me, as if urging me to make a decision. Slowly, I begin to type.

AbyAngel99: Thanks, but I can't.

AbyAngel99: I've got plans.

I'm just hoping she doesn't ask me what they are, because I don't actually have any.

> **Faithfull205:** ☹ That's 2 bad. I miss u.
> **Faithfull205:** We hardly see each other.

That's because you're so wrapped up in Ted and Grace and stage crew and all the stuff you know I can't do. You're the one who changed everything. Not me.

> **AbyAngel99:** Yeah. Well, maybe another time.
> **Faithfull205:** K. Definitely. Well, GTG do homework.
> **AbyAngel99:** K. Bye.

I stare at the screen after Faith signs off, a sudden heaviness in my chest. My cell phone is sitting on my desk and I reach for it to call her back and tell her that I *will* come for the sleepover, after all, but something stops me from pressing the speed dial key with her number. I put the phone back on the desk, and check again to see if Luke's online. When I see he's not, I force myself to turn off the computer and pick up a book to read until I fall asleep. Even after Mom comes and tells me to turn the light out, I can't stop myself from sneaking over to my desk and checking one last time. When Luke's online icon is still set to AWAY, I want to cry. When I get back into bed I give in, and tears of longing and frustration silently soak my pillow.

CHAPTER 6

"Are you okay, Abby?"

Billy is looking at me all worried. I must have completely spaced out.

"Yeah, I'm fine. Just a little tired, that's all."

"You look pretty out of it. Maybe you should go to the nurse or something."

As tempting as it sounds to go down to the nurse and fake a headache so she'd let me lie down for a while, I don't want to risk her calling Mom.

"I'll be okay. So where were we?"

"We're on step four. Here, I'll do this part. You get the petri dishes, okay?"

I go to the front of the room and collect our petri dishes, then set them up on our lab bench. My hands are all trembly, probably because I barely slept last night. Luke better be online tonight to put me out of my misery.

"Okay, here goes nothing," Billy says. He takes a step closer to me and our arms touch. I notice that he's flushed from the neck up. Weird.

We start to label the petri dishes. My hands are shaking so much I manage to drop one. Luckily, it doesn't break, but the lid comes off so I have to go up and get another.

"Are you *sure* you're okay?" Billy asks. "Because you don't seem like your usual bright, funny self."

It takes a moment for his words to pierce through the fogginess in my brain. *Whoa. Hold the phone. Did Billy just say he thinks I'm bright and funny?*

"I . . . uh . . . well . . ." I kind of just stare at him, noticing for the first time how his eyes are a really cool shade of blue.

"And you definitely aren't as quick with the words as you normally are."

He taps lightly on my head with his fist.

"Hello? Is the real Abby home? Can she come out to play?"

I can't help giggling as I push his hand away.

"Stop it, you dork! You're messing up my hair."

"Now that sounds more like the Abby I know," Billy says, grinning. "But I still think I'm going to nominate myself to be in charge of the experiment today, okay? Since you're so out of it, you can just be Lab Flunky to my Evil Genius and take notes. What do you say?"

"I say it sounds good to me. Anything as long as I don't have to think too much."

With Billy in charge, we manage to get through the rest of the experiment without any disasters. I write down what he tells me to, and surreptitiously check the clock, counting down the minutes till class is over.

"So . . . Abby," Billy says, as we're waiting for the bell to ring. "Do you maybe want to get together this weekend and . . . uh . . . study for the science test? And then I thought maybe . . . we could . . . you know . . . uh . . . go see a movie . . . you know . . . or something like that."

My head's spinning from lack of sleep and the unexpectedness of Billy's question.

"I . . . I . . . maybe . . . I . . ."

"Well, I know you're kind of out of it right now, so why don't you, uh, you know, think about it and then when you're a little more with it you could, um, maybe call or text me?"

He takes his pen and scribbles his cell number on my science notebook. I just stand there, nodding like a mute idiot.

"Hope you feel better. Later!" he says, leaving me standing there, dazed.

I wish Faith were on the bus with me on the way home so I could ask her advice. But I bet she's busy backstage in the auditorium working on sets with The Amazing Ted. I rest my head against the window, listening to the hubbub of conversation and the tinny sound coming from the iPod earbuds of the kid in front of me (one case of adult deafness, coming right up) and try to imagine talking to Luke about this. But I get the feeling he'd take it badly. Really badly. This is something I'm going to have to work out for myself.

I log on to ChezTeen.com as soon as I get home, but Luke's *still* not online. What the hell? Maybe he was just bullshitting me when he said I was gorgeous and the "hottest chick he'd ever seen" and stuff like that. Maybe he doesn't really like me at all. I'm struggling to concentrate on my homework, but between the exhaustion and my constant checking of Luke's status, it takes me twice as long as it normally would.

When I'm finally done, I see that Faith's online. I ask her to go into a private chat.

> **Faithfull205:** What's up?
> **AbyAngel99:** Billy Fisher asked me out, kind of.
> **Faithfull205:** OMG!!! Wait — what do u mean "kind of"?
> **AbyAngel99:** He asked me if I wanted to study w/ him tomorrow night and then go to a movie.
> **Faithfull205:** Sounds like a date to me!
> **AbyAngel99:** I guess.
> **Faithfull205:** Soooooooooooooooo . . .
> **Faithfull205:** Is that why u couldn't come 4 a sleepover?

I realize Billy's given me just the excuse I needed for why I said no.

> **AbyAngel99:** Well, yeah. I mean I haven't said yes yet, because I'm not sure if I want to go or not.
> **Faithfull205:** Why wouldn't u go?
> **AbyAngel99:** IDK. I'm too tired to think. I didn't sleep well last night.
> **Faithfull205:** ?

I can't talk to Faith about Luke. *People might not understand about us.* I know *she* won't understand. I just know it.

> **AbyAngel99:** IDK, just one of those nights.

Faithfull205: Well, I think u should say yes. He's cute!

AbyAngel99: IDK. Not sure.

Faithfull205: Y not???????????????

AbyAngel99: I just . . .

Without telling her about Luke, I don't know what to say. So I lie. I'm getting better and better at lying to Faith. It's kind of scary, considering how I never used to lie to her, ever.

AbyAngel99: Just not sure he's my type.

Faithfull205: Waah? But he's cute and nice — what's not to like?

He's not Luke, that's what.

Faithfull205: And anyway, it's only a movie.

AbyAngel99: I bet that's what Mom would say.

Faithfull205: It's rare, but sometimes moms r right.

AbyAngel99: Yeah, very rare. Rarer than a compliment from Amanda Armitage.

Faithfull205: LOL!

Faithfull205: So RU going to say yes??????

AbyAngel99: Maybe.

Faithfull205: What u got to lose?

What have I got to lose? A "relationship" with a guy I've never even met, who I think will be mad if I go out with a guy I actually know.

Maybe Faith's right. Maybe I should say yes to Billy. But I want to hear whatever it was that Luke wanted to say to me first.

> **AbyAngel99:** I'll think about it. I promise.
> **Faithfull205:** K. Think about it & say yes! If u don't, then u HAVE 2 come 4 a sleepover.
> **AbyAngel99:** Whateva, Ms. Bossy.
> **Faithfull205:** I hope Ted asks me out sometime.
> **AbyAngel99:** How r things going?
> **Faithfull205:** He's soooooooooooooooooo cute I can't stand it!
> **AbyAngel99:** O . . . kaaaaaay.
> **Faithfull205:** But we talked the whole time we were waiting for the late bus.
> **AbyAngel99:** Cool. Good sign.
> **Faithfull205:** He's really funny and —

She goes on and on, describing Ted's wonderfulness, and I periodically write "Great" or "Awesome" but after a while I just want to get off, so I tell her my mom's calling me. I log out for half an hour, then go back on briefly to see if Luke is online. He's not.

No luck after dinner, either. I can barely keep my eyes open because I'm so tired from the night before, but I figure maybe he had to work late at whatever he does — he never answered that question when I asked — so I decide to try to stay up at least till eleven.

"Abby, turn off the computer and go to bed!" Mom says. "You fell asleep on the keyboard."

I feel like it's three in the morning, but when I look at the clock it's only ten thirty.

"I thought you said you finished all your homework before dinner," Mom says. "Close that computer and go to sleep!"

"I did. I was just watching some funny videos on YouTube." I close my laptop and yawn. I'm dying to check if Luke IM'ed me, but I don't want to do it with Mom in the room. *Okay, Mom, good night!*

"Did you brush your teeth?"

"*Yeees.*" I groan. "Good night."

"Good night, honey. Sleep well."

She turns off the overhead light and closes the door, leaving it cracked just a little so I can see the night-light in the hallway like she has since I was little and afraid of the dark. Doesn't she realize I'm not that little kid anymore, I'm fourteen? That's one of the things I like about Luke; he treats me like an equal, like a grown-up, not like I'm a little kid with no opinion.

Once Mom's safely down the hall, I open my laptop and check. What I see makes me want to cry, because what I see is nothing. No chat messages, no e-mails. No sign of life from Luke at all. How can he leave me hanging like this? I feel sick to my stomach. Maybe he doesn't care about me after all. Maybe he really thinks I'm ugly and this was all just a game to him — maybe he's been laughing with his twenty-seven-year-old friends about what a gullible idiot I am.

I grab my cell phone and text Billy Fisher that I'll go out with him tomorrow night. Then I cry myself to sleep.

CHAPTER 7

Another day goes by and there's still no sign of Luke. Mom's starting to nag me because I've had no appetite and there are shadows under my eyes from lack of sleep. I've been waking up every few hours to log on to the computer, just to see if there's a message from him, and each time I see there's nothing, I feel like I'm falling into a deep, dark hole, my thoughts spinning crazily, wondering why he isn't there and why he hasn't written to me. Then I cry until I manage to sleep for another hour or so. I'm having a hard time concentrating in class, which I guess isn't surprising because I can barely stay awake.

Meanwhile, I've got this date with Billy tonight. Mom's dropping me off at his house at four thirty so we can study, then we're going to a six fifteen movie, and after, his mom will drive me home. I don't even want to go. I don't want to spend that many hours away from the computer. But then Luke hasn't been online in days. What if he got killed in a car crash? What if he found out he has terminal cancer and only has a month to live?

Or what if he decided that you're just some stupid fourteen-year-old who isn't worth his time? What if he decided he wants to be with a real woman instead of someone whose only experience is kissing Roger Hunter behind some bushes at the eighth-grade picnic?

I log on to my computer again. He's not online. No e-mails, no messages. No nothing. Fighting off tears, I try to figure out what to wear for the date I don't even want to go on with the boy I don't even know if I'm that into.

Jeans and a tank top with a long-sleeved shirt over it, I guess. I figure I at least owe it to Billy to pretend I'm into this, so I put on some makeup and a little spritz of that perfume Aunt Penny got me for Christmas last year, the one that she said the woman at Sephora told her was "all the rage with teen girls." *Great*, I thought when she told me that. *I can smell just like all the Clique Queens, woo-hoo!*

I check my computer one more time before I leave. Still nothing. *Luke, where are you? What did I do? Why aren't you talking to me?*

If I'm honest, I have to admit that Billy cleans up well. He's wearing black jeans and a button-down shirt, and truth be told, he's really pretty cute. I suddenly feel kind of underdressed, like maybe I should have made more of an effort for this study date. I mean WTF? It's not like Luke is sitting around at home checking obsessively to see if *I'm* around, is it?

We sit on the sofa in his family room with our science notes, quizzing each other on convection and radiation and all the other stuff we have to know for the test. Billy's smart; that's one of the reasons I like having him for a lab partner. He can actually do his own homework *and* remember my name, two things Nick Peters *still* hasn't mastered.

"What are some of the properties that characterize a living thing?" Billy asks.

"Um — it has a complex organization composed of one or more cells. It has a metabolism. Like, in other words, it has physical or chemical processes that create and use energy. . . ." I'm ticking off on my fingers as I try to visualize all of the bullet points in the textbook. "Oh, and it's responsive to stimuli in the external environment."

"Good," Billy says, smiling. "Keep going."

"It grows by taking external materials and organizing them into its own structure. Like, I eat doughnuts and get fat."

Billy laughs. "You aren't fat at all, Abby. You look great." He leans a little closer to me. "You smell pretty good, too."

I feel the flush rise up my neck to my cheeks.

"Um, thanks."

"Okay, back to business." Billy grins, leaning back against the cushions. "Give me two more characteristics of living things. I'll give you a hint: You left out the most fun one."

Fun one? I'm picturing the textbook, responsiveness, growth, complex organization, metabolism, responsiveness . . . oh!

I hit Billy. "You are *such* a perv!"

"Who me? What are you talking about?"

"The most fun one? *Reproduction?*"

"Hey, even microorganisms gotta have fun, right?"

"Well, it's a good thing some of us are more *evolved*."

"Ding! Ding! Ding! You've just won the prize for getting all the answers right!"

"So what's my prize?" I ask Billy.

He pretends to think for a moment, but I see him glance at the time on the cable box.

"Your prize is to be escorted to the multiplex by, uh, the amazingly handsome, funny, talented —"

"And modest," I interject.

"And *exceptionally* modest Billy Fisher."

"Well, lucky me." I almost add a sarcastic "NOT," but realize that I've kind of been having fun with Billy, and even better, I haven't thought about Luke in more than an hour. Except, dang, now I have. *Go away, Luke thoughts.*

Billy's mom sticks her head in the doorway from the kitchen.

"If you guys don't want to be late for the movie, you better start packing up the books and get in the car."

Billy sighs.

"It's pretty much impossible to impress your date with how cool you are when your *mom* is driving you."

"Like you were *ever* going to impress me with how cool you were."

He punches me lightly on the arm as we walk to the car.

"Just you wait, Abby Johnston. My coolness will hit you like a tsunami. You will be carried along by its raging power. You will be turned into a freaking icicle by the frostiness of my cool."

I roll my eyes.

"Yeah, whatever, Iceman. Let's just go to the movies, okay?"

If I thought it was awkward having to make conversation with Billy's mom in the car, it's even more weird when it's me and Billy sitting in the back of a darkened movie theater. First, our arms touch on the armrest between us. I quickly move mine away. I wonder if he's going to try to hold my hand. I keep my soda in the hand closest to him so he can't, because I'm not sure if I want him to. Then, I feel his shoulder touching mine, at first lightly, then with increasing pressure, like he's gradually leaning closer to me. Then he moves his hand to the armrest and I'm worrying if the next stop is going to be my knee.

I can't concentrate on the movie because I'm so busy worrying about what Billy's next move is going to be. Although I'm trying to focus on the screen, out of the corner of my eye I see his pinkie finger dangling off the armrest an inch or so above my leg and that's what my brain focuses on. Where will that little piggy go next?

With Luke, I never have to worry about this stuff. I always know where Luke is — he's safely in my computer, where I don't have to deal with real-life hands and pinkie fingers and leaning shoulders and *OMG, is he going to try to kiss me?* thoughts.

Except right now Luke isn't safely in your computer. Right now you have no idea where Luke is, or if he'll ever speak to you again.

The thought brings a lump to my throat. I cannot and will not cry here. Billy will think I'm a total freak and I want him to like me, even if I'm not sure if I want him to *like me*, like me.

Billy's pinkie lands on my knee, a small dot of warmth next to the cold where my soda rests. I glance at him, briefly, but he's staring straight ahead, like he's totally absorbed in the movie, like nothing's happened, like his pinkie hasn't accidentally on purpose strayed into foreign territory.

Slowly, the rest of his fingers follow his Lewis and Clark pinkie onto my knee, and I have to move my cup to the other knee (and hand) to make room for them. Which means that now my right hand is cup-less and kind of hanging around with nothing to do and nowhere to go. It hangs in the air aimlessly for a few seconds until Billy's hand comes over to grasp it and then they both come to rest on my knee, together, entwined.

And there I am sitting in the back of the movie theater holding hands with Billy Fisher, wondering what Luke would think of all this.

What does it matter what Luke thinks? It's not like he cares, right? You haven't spoken to him in days. He's probably ditched you. You were probably some big joke to him. Like, let's play around with some kid's head. Let's pretend that I'm totally into some fourteen-year-old girl and laugh my ass off about it with my friends.

I feel angry all of a sudden, an anger that has nothing to do with the boy I'm sitting next to and everything to do with a person I've never met. That anger makes me want to get back at Luke. To hurt him the way he's hurt me.

I rest my head on Billy's shoulder, and feel him take a deep breath before he rests his head on top of mine. His thumb strokes the back of my hand, gently. *Billy, Billy, Billy*, I think. *No more Luke. Forget Luke. Delete Luke from your brain. From now on it's Billy all the way. Well, not ALL the way. But this is okay.*

The problem is, Luke's words keep popping into my head.

"Ur the hottest chick I've seen in long time . . . Srsly, Abby, ur really pretty. I don't know why u don't think so . . . I'd be jealous . . ."

Must. Shut. Him. Out. I close my eyes and will myself to think of anything other than Luke. Puppies. Flowers. The characteristics of living things. Billy. Mom better not ask me what this movie was about because I haven't got any clue at all. I'll have to read the summary on IMDb.com.

And then I feel Billy's breath on the side of my face. *Oh shit, he's going to kiss me.* Sure enough, his lips graze my cheek and then his free hand takes my chin and turns my face toward him and then he's kissing my lips. I've still got my eyes and my mouth closed but he opens his mouth and I can feel his tongue pushing against my teeth.

I'd be jealous . . .

I relax my mouth and we're kissing and it's a lot nicer than it was with Roger Hunter behind the bushes at the eighth-grade picnic. A whole lot nicer. Billy's mouth tastes like popcorn and Twizzlers, and he isn't trying to suffocate me with his tongue like Roger did.

"You smell sooooo good, Abby," Billy whispers when he comes up for air. "It's driving me crazy."

Maybe that little bottle of stuff from Sephora is Amanda Armitage's secret. I wonder if I wear this stuff to math class on Monday, if Nick Peters will magically remember my name. I don't think Billy's going to be forgetting it any time soon.

We spend the rest of the movie making out. At one point his hand starts to creep upward from my knee but I put my hand on top of his and keep it locked there. I'm not ready to do anything more than kiss.

When the movie ends and the lights start to come on, I pull away from him.

"I've got to go to the bathroom," I say, and I trip over people in our row who are sitting there like lumps just reading the credits. *What's so important, dude? Do you really need to know the name of the key grip and the best boy?*

My reflection in the bathroom mirror doesn't look any different, except my lip gloss is totally kissed off, but I feel strange and I'm not sure what I'm going to see in Billy's face when I come out of the bathroom and what he'll see in mine.

What I see is him standing there with his hands in his pockets, and his face smiling this cute, shy smile that gets really bright when he sees me.

I wonder if he can sense the confusion I'm feeling right now. If he knows that while I was feeling his lips on my mouth I kept hearing Luke's words in my head. No, he can't know that. If he did, he wouldn't be smiling at me like that.

"Hey," he says, taking my hand.

"Hey."

"Good movie, huh?"

I look at him and roll my eyes.

"Um, yeah. What little I remember of it."

"Well, I took the precaution of reading up on the plot," he says. "You know, just in case."

I pull my hand away from his.

"What, you *expected* this to happen?"

Billy's cheeks flush red. "Of course not, Abby! Jeez. But . . . I mean . . . I *hoped*. You can't blame a guy for hoping."

I guess I can't.

"Okay, so what was this movie we just saw all about, exactly?"

Unfortunately, my parents are in the family room watching a movie when Billy's mom drops me at home, so I get the third degree.

"How was your date, honey?" Mom asks.

"She had a date?" Dad says. "How come I didn't know about

this? I'm supposed to meet the boy first with a shotgun in hand to scare him off."

"OMG, Dad, get a life!"

"Yes, Rick dear, get a life. The Cro-Magnon era ended years ago." Mom laughs. "So, Abby, tell me about the movie."

I repeat everything Billy told me about the movie, and fortunately Mom and Dad sound convinced that I actually saw it.

"He took you to see *that movie* on a date?" Dad says, shaking his head. "I tell you, kids these days . . ."

"And how did it go with your young man?" Mom asks, nudging Dad to be quiet.

"Good, I guess. And will you stop with the my-young-man stuff?"

"That's it? That's all we get? 'Good, I guess'?" Dad complains.

Someone save me from my parents.

I roll my eyes. "I'm going to my room. See you in the morning."

"I guess that's all we're getting," I hear Mom say as I head upstairs. I'm lucky Lily's at a sleepover or else she'd probably be interrogating me, too.

My laptop sings its siren call as soon as I walk in my room. I make a conscious effort to ignore it. I decide to give myself one of Lily's face masks, even though I'm convinced they don't do anything except make you look really stupid while they're on your face, and then I take a blissfully long shower, since I know Lily's not around to complain about me using up all the hot water.

As the steam slowly clears to reveal my mirrored reflection, I try to figure out what it is that Billy finds attractive about me. *Ur the hottest chick I've seen in long time. . . .* I wonder if Billy thinks I'm hot. I wonder if Luke really thought I was the hottest chick he'd seen in a long time or if that was just a typical guy line, the kind of thing he'd say to any girl.

All I can see is my usual self, which doesn't seem that hot at all. I mean, yeah, I've always had a bigger chest than most girls my age, which wasn't exactly a picnic in fifth grade when I was the first one to get a bra and somehow it became common knowledge and a mark of pride for all the boys to ping my bra strap. I guess my hair isn't that bad — it's long and auburn. But I'm no Amanda Armitage and I know it. And all the boys know it, too.

But Billy Fisher seems to like me. *Like me,* like me. I close my eyes and think about kissing him, and run my hands over my body. But then I open them and see myself in the mirror and feel like a total freak. I can't put my pajamas on fast enough to cover me all up.

Then I'm back in my room and the computer is beckoning. This time I give in, taking it to my bed and logging on.

Almost as soon as I get on to ChezTeen.com, I see a spiky-haired, leather-jacketed avatar and my heartbeat quickens.

BlueSkyBoi: Hey, baby!
AbyAngel99: Where've u been?!!
BlueSkyBoi: Y? Did u miss me? ;-)

I feel like throwing something at the computer screen. How can he be so . . . casual about the fact that he just dropped off the face of the freaking earth for three days! I decide I'm not going to give him the satisfaction of letting him know how I basically lost it when he disappeared from my life with no warning. No, he's not going to hear one peep about sleepless nights and lack of appetite or checking his online status every five minutes. Nuh-uh.

AbyAngel99: No, not at all. Been too busy.

BlueSkyBoi: Busy doing what?

AbyAngel99: Stuff.

He asks me to go private, and I agree right away.
Chat room name: BlueSkyBoi

BlueSkyBoi: Stuff like what?

AbyAngel99: U know. School. Studying 4 science test.

Might as well take this all the way. I take a deep breath and type.

AbyAngel99: Going on a date.

I watch the pencil icon that shows he's typing, waiting to see his response.

BlueSkyBoi: A date? With a guy?

AbyAngel99: No, with an alien zombie unicorn. ;-p Duh!

BlueSkyBoi: :-l U 2-timing me?

BlueSkyBoi: I told u, I'm the jealous type.

Yes, you did tell me. And after all the misery I felt over the last few days wondering why you weren't speaking to me, it's kind of good to know that I'm making you suffer a little, too.

AbyAngel99: Well, it's not like u were around.

BlueSkyBoi: So the minute I turn my back ur off with another guy?

AbyAngel99: Where were u anyway?

BlueSkyBoi: I had to work late and then I had a stomach flu. Been puking my guts out for the last few days. Not a pretty sight, let me tell u.

I feel kind of guilty for thinking so badly of him.

AbyAngel99: Poor baby.

BlueSkyBoi: Yeah, coulda done with a hot nurse like u.

BlueSkyBoi: So tell me about this guy.

BlueSkyBoi: Who is he?

AbyAngel99: He's a guy from my science class.

BlueSkyBoi: Have u gone out with him before?

AbyAngel99: No, this was the 1st time.

BlueSkyBoi: What did u do?

AbyAngel99: We studied 4 our science test then went to the movies.

BlueSkyBoi: I mean what did u *do*? Did Science Boy get lucky?

AbyAngel99: Depends what u mean by lucky.

BlueSkyBoi: Did he kiss u?

I hesitate before answering. Part of me wants to tell him that it's none of his business. But I kind of like the fact that he's so jealous. It makes me feel, I don't know, powerful, after the last few days of feeling like crap, and it's almost like I'm compelled to spill.

AbyAngel99: Yes.

BlueSkyBoi: Did he feel ur tits?

AbyAngel99: No!

BlueSkyBoi: Did he try to get in ur pants?

AbyAngel99: NO!

BlueSkyBoi: Did he fuck u?

What? We went to the freaking *movies!* Plus, I'm *fourteen years old.* Sheesh!

AbyAngel99: OMG No!!! I said we went to the *movies!!* Not that any of this is ur business.

BlueSkyBoi: What do u mean, none of my business?

BlueSkyBoi: I thought *I* was ur main man.

AbyAngel99: Yeah, well, u weren't around. I didn't know what happened.

BlueSkyBoi: So u DID miss me!

AbyAngel99: I guess.

BlueSkyBoi: A lot?

AbyAngel99: Maybe.

BlueSkyBoi: Even while u were making out with Science Boy?

Do I admit that his words echoed in my head even as I locked lips with Billy? Do I want to give Luke that satisfaction after all that pain he put me through?

But it's not like he was ditching me intentionally. The poor guy was sick. I mean, he's been puking his guts out for the last few days. I guess I should cut him a *little* slack, right?

AbyAngel99: Yeah. Even then.

BlueSkyBoi: I feel better already.

AbyAngel99: ☺

BlueSkyBoi: U gonna make me feel even better?

AbyAngel99: IDK. How?

BlueSkyBoi: Tell me ur my girl.

I feel bathed in warmth, like someone's wrapped me in a snuggly fleece blanket. Luke doesn't think I'm just a stupid fourteen-year-old. He wants me to be his girl.

AbyAngel99: I'm ur girl.

BlueSkyBoi: ☺

AbyAngel99: Does that mean ur my guy?

BlueSkyBoi: Does it ever! In fact, I want to send u something to prove it.

AbyAngel99: What?

BlueSkyBoi: A cell fone, so we can talk without anyone giving us a hard time. I want to hear ur voice, baby. I want to be able to talk to u all the time.

AbyAngel99: But I already have a cell.

BlueSkyBoi: But this will be our private fone — just between u and me.

BlueSkyBoi: Also, I want to give u one of those cool fones that plays music so I can put special playlists on for u since we're musical soulies. ☺

I'm sure my parents would totally freak if they knew I was accepting presents from someone I just know from the

Internet. But I've always wanted a cool phone. My parents got me the basic one that comes for free and just makes and receives calls and takes a zillion keystrokes just to send one text because "it's only for emergencies." Guess who has a smart phone . . . yeah, Amanda Armitage. She got an iPhone, like, the minute they came out. My *parents* wouldn't even get one for themselves, and there was Amanda all "Oh, I'll just call *insert witchy friend's name* on my *iPhone*."

> **AbyAngel99:** Cool!
> **BlueSkyBoi:** So u need to give me ur address. But do u get to the mail before ur parents? We don't want them to see it.
> **AbyAngel99:** No problem. My mom and dad both work and I get home from school b4 my sister.
> **BlueSkyBoi:** Awesome. So what's ur addy?

I hesitate for second before giving him my address. We've had so many talks at school about Internet Safety and they always go on and on about never giving out any personal details about yourself online, *blah, blah, blah.* But I've been talking to Luke for a while now and I'm pretty sure he's not some stalker pervert dude. So I go ahead and tell him. I'm so psyched to get my phone. I just wish I didn't have to keep it a secret. It would be so cool to be able to whip it out in front of everyone and show it off.

> **BlueSkyBoi:** Great. I'll get it in the mail on Monday. So watch out 4 it!
> **AbyAngel99:** I will! I'm sooooo excited!

BlueSkyBoi: Me 2. Can't wait to hear ur voice. ☺

BlueSkyBoi: How bout giving me something to keep me happy in the meantime?

AbyAngel99: Like what?

BlueSkyBoi: Like a pic of u.

AbyAngel99: ok.

BlueSkyBoi: Topless

I gasp when I read that, but he's still typing.

BlueSkyBoi: It'll make me feel less jealous of Science Boy.

BlueSkyBoi: Prove to me ur really my girl.

I don't know what to do. I really am Luke's girl, but no one's ever seen my boobs, ever. Well, yeah, Faith has. And my mom, but even she hasn't recently. But no guy. But I don't want him to disappear on me again. And I don't want him to change his mind about sending me the cell phone.

AbyAngel99: I . . . guess.

BlueSkyBoi: OMG, baby, ur making me the happiest guy alive!

I open Photo Booth and slowly take off my pajama top. The cool air puckers my skin and I cross my arms over my breasts, feeling more naked and exposed than I ever have in my life, even though I still have my pajama bottoms on. But I know Luke doesn't want a picture of my arms. He wants to see what's underneath them.

So taking a deep breath, I lower my arms and press the camera button. It counts down, beeping, three, two, one, and the photo snaps. It's so weird to see a picture of myself, my breasts exposed. I have to make sure I delete it as soon as I send it to Luke, because the last thing I need is for anyone, especially my parents, to see it.

It feels kind of like stepping off a ledge as I press SEND. And then I sit there, anxiously waiting for Luke's reaction. It doesn't take long.

> **BlueSkyBoi:** Jesus, Abby, look at u. U r gorgeous, baby. U r just so incredibly beautiful.

I guess he liked it.

> **BlueSkyBoi:** U cannot believe how hard I am rite now looking at u.
> **BlueSkyBoi:** I could break a freaking door down with my cock.

His words are exciting and scary at the same time. They make me feel older, more grown-up, powerful. But at the same time, part of me wants to run downstairs and snuggle up on the sofa between my parents and watch a movie and eat popcorn like a little girl. I've had enough for one night.

> **AbyAngel99:** My parents are calling. I GTG.
> **BlueSkyBoi:** Ok, baby. Listen, u should put a pword on ur computer if u don't have 1.
> **AbyAngel99:** Ok.

AbyAngel99: Gnite!

BlueSkyBoi: Sweet dreams, baby — I know mine
will be.

I delete the photo, shut down my computer, and curl up in bed. I think this has been the most screwed-up night of my life. I don't know what to think about anything anymore. I don't know how I'm going to face Billy on Monday. Life is so confusing right now. But at least I can look forward to getting Luke's cell phone.

CHAPTER 8

♪ OCTOBER 10

I never thought I'd be happy about a test, but I'm so, so glad that we have one in science on Monday. I hang out in the girls' bathroom in between classes so I have just enough time to slide into my seat right before class starts. All Billy can do is smile at me with a warm look in his blue eyes, and mouth, "Hi," before Ms. Forcier hands out the test papers. I give him a quick smile in return, and turn my attention to the test. I just hope I do okay on it. I can't say I was exactly one hundred percent focused on studying yesterday after what happened with Luke.

When we were sitting in church on Sunday morning I felt like somehow the pastor could tell that the previous night I'd gone to the movies and made out with one guy and then come home and sent a picture of myself topless to another. I could have sworn he kept shooting me disapproving looks during the service.

What was I thinking? How could I have sent Luke that picture? I'm never going to do that again, I swore to myself as I sat in the pew, blushing at the memory of his words, and praying for forgiveness for even thinking about that kind of stuff in church.

I stayed off-line all that day and all night, even though part of me was desperate to talk to Luke. He was becoming like, I don't know, like a drug almost. I craved talking to him, and when I wasn't talking to him I was thinking about the last time we chatted or the next time I'd be able to chat with him.

Now I've got the test in front of me and of course the first question is about the characteristics of living things, which sends me back to Billy's sofa on Saturday night as he quizzed me: *You look great. . . . You smell pretty good, too. . . . You left out the most fun one.*

I won't turn around and look at him. I'm going to stay focused on this test and when the test is over, I'm going to leave this classroom as fast as I can so I don't have to talk to him. How can I face him now?

Billy finishes his test before me. Everyone does. I'm the last person left, because even though science is one of my best subjects, and I know this stuff, I can't concentrate. I keep thinking about the picture I sent to Luke. I keep hearing the words he used to describe how excited it made him.

I barely manage to finish by the time the bell rings. Ms. Forcier asks me if everything is okay when I hand her my test.

"You look a little . . . under the weather today, Abby. How are you feeling?"

More confused than I ever have in my life, thanks. But I would seriously rather die than talk to a teacher about it.

Still, she's handing me an excuse on a platter.

"I've kinda got a headache. I think I might be getting a cold or something."

"Do you need a pass to the nurse?"

The thought of escaping to the nurse's office and just being able to lie down and stare at the wall for a while is pretty tempting. But I don't want to get behind on my work, especially with tests coming up in my other classes.

"No, thanks, it's okay. I can always go there and get some ibuprofen during lunch if it doesn't go away."

"Well, feel better," she says, giving me a concerned smile.

Billy practically pounces on me the minute I walk out of the classroom, startling me so much that I let out a cry of surprise.

"Sorry," he says, standing a little closer to me than I want him to in school where people can see us. He smells nice, a clean soapy smell that reminds me of the movie and the warmth of his kisses. I feel color rising in my cheeks. "I just really wanted to talk to you; you know, to tell you how much fun I had on Saturday and . . ."

Luckily, I'm saved by the bell.

"I've got to run — I'm late for math," I say, already a few paces down the hall.

Billy looks back at me, crestfallen, and says, "Okay, later."

I'm practically running down the hall on the way to math, hoping I don't get in trouble for being late without a pass. With every step I hear Luke's words in my head. . . .

Did Science Boy get lucky? . . . Did he feel ur tits? . . . I told u I'm the jealous type. . . . Prove to me ur really my girl. . . .

By the time I get to math, two minutes late, I really *am* starting to get a headache. Especially after seeing the smirk on Amanda Armitage's face when Mr. Evans threatens me with a detention. Fortunately, he lets me off with a warning because I'm a straight-A student in his class and I'm normally really punctual.

"Hey, Angie, where you been?" Nick whispers. "I need your homework."

My head feels like it's going to explode. Luke wouldn't treat me like this. Luke has *always* remembered my name, ever since the first time I told it to him. Luke thinks I'm beautiful — and not just beautiful, but that I'm *hot*. Nick Peters may be drop-dead gorgeous, but he's too freaking stupid to do his own math homework, and he thinks Amanda Armitage is a great girl. Well, I've had it with him. I've got a *real man* who likes me.

Turning around, I hiss, "It's Abby, asshole, and do your own homework from now on." Then I turn back to the board.

I hear him and Amanda whispering behind me, but I ignore them. Whatever. I don't care about them. Nick's so immature compared to Luke. Who needs some random high school jerk when you've got a mature guy who thinks you're hot?

That night, Luke asks me if I have a webcam so we can video chat. I tell him there's one built into my computer.

> **BlueSkyBoi:** Well, what are we waiting for?
> **AbyAngel99:** I don't know. Nothing, I guess. Hold on a sec.

I throw on a bathrobe over my camisole and pajama bottoms and make sure my hair looks okay. Then I click on the video icon so he can see me, and wait for him to start his.

When Luke turns his on, his face is half in shadow. I put in my earbuds, so no one at my house can hear the conversation.

"Hey, baby," he says. "How's it going?"

His voice is different than I thought it would be. It's not as deep and he has an accent — I'm not sure exactly what kind. It's not New York, from around here . . . maybe Boston? But he's from New Jersey — I don't know. I'm not so good at accents.

"Okay, I guess."

"It's great to hear your voice, finally," he says. "You sound as beautiful as you look."

I feel myself blushing. Why can't I ever hear him say something nice about me without turning dorkishly pink?

"Aw, you're blushing," he says. "That's so cute."

That only makes me blush more.

"How was your test?"

"I don't know. I kind of had problems concentrating."

"What was on your mind? Not Science Boy, I hope."

"Well, him a bit. But you, mostly."

"You normally get good grades, right?"

"Yeah. Especially in science. And in math."

"So you're smart and beautiful. Wow. How'd I get so lucky?"

"I'm just worried if I get a bad grade on this, my parents are going to freak. Especially my dad. It's like if I don't get A's, it's the end of the world or something."

"It's tough when your parents expect you to be perfect all the time."

"It wouldn't be so bad except he's not like that with Lily. Like, she doesn't get nearly as good grades as I do, but I don't hear my parents giving her the kind of grief they give me."

"I can relate, baby. My parents were way harder on me than they were on my sisters."

"It's so unfair."

"Word. But I wanna hear more about you, honey. Did you see that guy today? Science Boy?"

"Yeah. I saw him when I took the test."

Luke makes a pouting face and it makes me laugh.

"I'm glad you find making me jealous so amusing," he says, but he doesn't look all that happy. He actually looks kind of pissed. I want to make him feel better.

"I'm just kidding, honest. I barely spoke to Billy. I was trying to avoid him, if you want to know the truth."

"Yeah?" he says, looking at me intently through the computer screen. "Why's that, Abby?"

"Because . . . because I'm . . . you're . . ."

I feel embarrassed saying the words, particularly now that I can see his eyes and I'm not just typing them into a chat box.

"Because you're my girl?" he says, his voice low and husky.

Without saying a word, I just nod my head.

"I can't tell you how happy that makes me," he continues. "Do you want to see how happy that makes me? Do you, baby?"

I'm not sure what exactly he means, but his voice pours into my ears like liquid caramel, soft and comforting but exciting at the same time.

"Yeah, I guess."

He stands up, slowly, and puts his hands on the zipper of his jeans, where I notice there's a bulge that looks like someone stuck a cucumber in his pants. That can't be his . . . thing, can it? He undoes the button and then his fly and then slides his jeans down. He's wearing those tight boxer-brief things, like the guy in the Calvin Klein commercial, and I realize it's definitely not a cucumber.

Luke touches the bulge and then smiles straight at me.

"Now it's your turn, sweetheart. Take off that robe. You're all covered up. I want to see those gorgeous tits of yours."

My mouth feels dry all of a sudden and I swallow, hard. But I do what he says. I untie my belt and slide the bathrobe off my shoulders and onto the bed. I hear Luke's breathing quicken in my ears.

"Now take your shirt off, baby."

He sees me hesitating and says, "Do it, baby. Do it for me. Because I love you, honey. Because you're my girl."

First, I make sure to lock my bedroom door and I have to take the earbuds out to do that. I pull my camisole over my head, but when I emerge from the fabric I see Luke's eyes staring at me from my screen with so much heat it feels like they'll burn through me. I start to cover myself with my hands and I see his lips move and his head shaking, no. Placing the earbuds back in, I hear: "No, baby, no, don't cover yourself. Don't ever be ashamed. You are the most beautiful girl I have ever seen. Look, sweetheart, look what you do to me."

He pulls down his briefs and OMG, there on the screen in his hand is the first penis I have ever seen — well, except for the line drawings in the movies we saw in health about the reproductive process. It's so big and angry-looking. I can't believe that something like that would ever fit inside a woman's body. Like maybe inside of me someday when I'm older. It's so . . . freaky.

Luke's voice becomes more and more breathy as he slowly starts to stroke himself.

"Oh, sweetheart, you should see your face right now. Don't be scared, Abby angel. It won't bite you. . . . I won't bite you. I would never do anything to hurt you, beautiful. . . . I love you. . . . Do you love me, baby?"

I'm filled with so many strange sensations. My breasts feel heavy, almost like Luke's eyes on them has made them grow bigger and more womanly. I can't believe that I, plain old Abby Johnston, could be so exciting to anyone. Is this love? I don't know, but it's way more powerful than anything I've been feeling for Billy.

"Um . . . yes. I think maybe I do."

"Oh, baby, show me. Show me you love me, honey."

"How?"

"Touch yourself. Go on, let me see you touching your pussy, baby."

My *what*? Does he mean . . . he can't mean . . . down *there*? No, I can't. I can't do that. *No way*. It's so embarrassing. I'll die. I already feel like my face is going to catch fire, it's turning so red.

"Remember what I said, sweetheart. Nothing to be ashamed about. You're a beautiful girl. Any guy would get turned on looking at you. And I'm getting extra turned on because I know how smart and wonderful you are, as well as gorgeous. I tell you, I'm rock hard now. It's killing me, you're such a knockout."

He breathes deeply into my ears, and groans as he strokes himself.

"*Please*, baby, I'm begging. Make me the happiest man alive. Let me see you touch yourself."

With trembling hands, I pull down my pajama bottoms. I hear Luke groan, "*Yes*," softly in my ears. And then I touch myself — there. While Luke is watching, like a hawk watching a mouse it's going to eat for dinner.

I feel exposed and shy but also these weird feelings like I've never felt before. Strange and exciting, but so incredibly embarrassing. My cheeks are on fire, but there's an unfamiliar heat in other places, too.

"Oh, baby, you are so adorable. Do you feel it, too? Are you getting hot for me, honey? Tell me, Abby."

"I . . . I don't know."

"Doesn't it feel good, baby? I want my girl to feel as good as she's making me feel right now."

It's hard to describe how I'm feeling, because these sensations are so new and . . . different.

"Talk to me, Abby, tell me it's good for you."

"It feels . . . good."

His breath is getting shorter and shorter, brief pants, interjected with "open your legs wider" and "oh, baby" and "that's my girl" or just groans until his face contorts like he's in pain and he lets out one big, *"OH, YEAH!*

"Oh, baby, you are amazing," he says. "I can't believe how —"

"Abby? *Abby!* Why is your door locked?"

Shit, that's Mom!

"Hold on!"

I slam the laptop shut and throw on my bathrobe, stuff my pajamas under my bed, and wrap a towel around my head. Then I race to the door and open it.

"Sorry, Mom. I was just in the middle of getting dressed after my shower."

"Are you feeling okay, honey? You look flushed."

She reaches a hand to my forehead. Her fingers feel cool against my skin.

"You are a little warm, but that could just be from the shower. Maybe you should take some Tylenol before you go to bed, just in case."

If Mom had the slightest idea of anything, she'd realize I need a lot more than Tylenol. But as usual, she doesn't. Have the slightest idea of anything, that is.

"Sure, Mom. I'll take some as soon as I'm in my pajamas."

"Have you done all your homework?"

"Yes," I lie. I actually still have five more math problems to do, but got a little, um, distracted by Luke.

"Okay. Well, good night, honey. Get to bed soon, in case you're coming down with something."

"What's Abby coming down with?" Lily says, sticking her head out of her room. "I don't want to get any of her germs."

I step toward her and fake a cough.

"*Mom!* Did you see that? Abby is trying to give me the plague."

My mother rolls her eyes.

"Abby, that was uncalled for, and Lily, your sister does *not* have the plague. Besides, you're supposed to be in bed, and if you were there, Abby couldn't have coughed on you."

"Figures you'd take Abby's side," Lily grumbles, slinking back into her room and slamming the door shut.

Mom sighs. "It's been a long day. I'm going to take a nice hot bath," she says. "Don't forget to take the Tylenol."

"Okay, good night."

I go back into my room and quickly throw my pajamas back on. Then I open my laptop to see if Luke's still online.

AbyAngel99: Sorry I had to go. Had parental 911.
BlueSkyBoi: It's okay. I figured. But . . . I didn't get to tell you.
BlueSkyBoi: I love you, baby.
AbyAngel99: ☺

BlueSkyBoi: Hope u get the phone soon so I can talk & txt u all the time.

AbyAngel99: Will check as soon as I get home from school.

BlueSkyBoi: It's a pay as u go phone so let me know when u need more minutes.

AbyAngel99: Ok.

BlueSkyBoi: My number is programmed in. Txt me when u get it.

I don't want to break the connection I have with Luke. I wish I could chat with him all night. But it's already late, and I really need to finish those stupid math problems.

AbyAngel99: I will. I GTG. Have to finish my homework.

BlueSkyBoi: That's my smart girl. Okay. See u tomorrow.

BlueSkyBoi: Sweet dreams, Abby angel.

I shut my computer and bury it under a pillow, hoping to blot out any thoughts of Luke while I finish my math problems. Yeah, right. Like *that's* possible. Images of his face and . . . well, other things . . . keep flashing through my head. It's well past midnight before I finish what would normally have taken me twenty minutes. Even then I have trouble getting to sleep.

CHAPTER 9

It feels like I'm drifting on a cloud the whole week in school. I keep hearing Luke's voice in my ear telling me "I love you, baby" and the intense sound of his breath as he told me how beautiful I was and how much he wanted me. It doesn't even bother me when I pass Amanda Armitage and a bunch of her friends in the hall and they look at me and start giggling after I've walked by. Normally, I'd get all paranoid worrying about what they were saying, like if my clothes were all wrong or my butt looked big in the jeans I was wearing or I was having a Bad Hair Day of epic proportions. But it's like Luke has cast a protective spell around me with his words; none of the idiots at my school can hurt me because I know he loves me. And he's a mature guy, not some stupid teen Clique Queen.

I find myself doodling *Abby Redmond* in the margin of my Spanish notebook. I know I'm getting totally carried away with that, but I've just never felt this way about anyone before. Luke understands me so well. Maybe he's right and we really are soul mates. It won't really matter about him being so much older than me when I'm older. Look at Tom Cruise and Katie Holmes. Or Jay-Z and Beyoncé.

Science lab forces me off my cloud with a bump. Not just because we're working with chemicals, but because Billy keeps looking at me with a question in his eyes. A question that I don't want him to ask out loud because I don't really want to have to answer it. Because I like Billy, I really do. He's a nice guy, and he's smart and cute. Faith keeps asking me when I'm going out with him again. I keep saying, "I don't know, he hasn't asked me." I don't tell her that's because I keep running away before he gets a chance, and signing off MSN the minute I see he's online so he can't chat with me. Like, I guess the thing I should do is just say, "Hey, Billy, it was fun but . . ." and make up some lame excuse. But I don't want to do that.

"So, how are things with my favorite lab partner?" Billy says.

"You mean your *only* lab partner?"

He grins.

"My favorite only lab partner then, Ms. Picky."

I stick my tongue out at him. "Fine."

"So, whatcha doing this weekend?"

Oh, no. Please don't do this.

"Um . . . I'm not sure."

"Oh. 'Cause I was just wondering if . . ."

"Wait. Don't we have to add the substrate?"

Billy looks confused for a second, then he realizes that I'm talking about the experiment and looks at the sheet.

"Oh, yeah."

Meanwhile I'm totally freaking out. Because . . . OMG, it's so confusing. Like, I'm Luke's girl, right? He's the one who loves me and understands me and who makes me feel all these . . . things . . . that I've never felt before. He treats me like an equal even though I'm just a kid and he's this grown-up guy, like he actually respects my opinions, which is something my parents would never do. But Billy is standing right here next to me. Even though I've "done things" with Luke that I'd never in a million years think about doing with Billy, I've actually *kissed* Billy. I actually spent practically a whole movie making out with Billy. And it was kind of fun, too.

"So, like, I was wondering if you maybe wanted to see another movie or something this weekend," Billy says, talking really fast like he's afraid I'm going to interrupt him again, and keeping his eyes on the experiment instead of looking at me.

My thoughts are spinning around so fast I feel like my head's going to explode. Pictures of Billy's adorable grin outside the movie theater, the way his lips felt when we kissed. And Luke. *:-l U 2-timing me? I told u, I'm the jealous type.* The strange sensations I felt when he had me touch myself on the webcam, how he makes me feel so grown-up and desirable.

I can't do it. I can't two-time Luke. He'd be too upset.

But how would he find out?

I'd know. And I'd feel guilty.

"Uh, gosh I'm sorry. I forgot. We're going away this weekend," I lie. "Family reunion. Sorry."

Yeah, right. Like I even see Dad at the moment. Just having him come home for dinner a few times a week would be enough of a family reunion for me.

"Oh. That's cool. Well, maybe another time."

Billy's cheeks are flushed and he finally looks over at me. Now that I see the hopefulness in his eyes, I feel bad about lying. I'm turning into such a Liar, Liar, Pants on Fire these days. I never used to be like this.

"Yeah, sure. Another time."

After I say that I curse myself. Because I can't do it another time. I can't do it ever, at least while I'm still Luke's girl. And as far as I'm concerned, I want to be Luke's girl forever.

That night, Luke asks me about my day.

> **AbyAngel99:** Okay, I guess.
> **AbyAngel99:** Billy asked me out again.
> **BlueSkyBoi:** :-l
> **BlueSkyBoi:** Fucking Science Boy. I want to kill him.
> **BlueSkyBoi:** What did u say?
> **AbyAngel99:** No, of course!
> **BlueSkyBoi:** ☺
> **BlueSkyBoi:** I'm happy, of course, but why?
> **BlueSkyBoi:** Out of curiosity . . .
> **AbyAngel99:** Duh! Because I'm ur girl, silly!
> **BlueSkyBoi:** Darling, u just made me a v. happy guy.
> **AbyAngel99:** ☺
> **BlueSkyBoi:** I don't deserve u, honey.
> **AbyAngel99:** ??
> **BlueSkyBoi:** Seriously, ur so smart and funny and gorgeous
> **BlueSkyBoi:** and me . . . well, I'm nothing special.
> **BlueSkyBoi:** Ur too good for me, baby.
> **AbyAngel99:** No I'm not.
> **AbyAngel99:** I love u.
> **BlueSkyBoi:** I love u 2, baby.

AbyAngel99: U understand me better than anyone.

AbyAngel99: Even Faith.

BlueSkyBoi: Ur so amazing, Abby. I'm so lucky I found u.

AbyAngel99: ☺

BlueSkyBoi: I just wish we could run away to an island somewhere where no one would care that I'm older than u and we could live 2gether and be happy.

I picture the Abby Redmond doodles in my notebook. Maybe they aren't so crazy after all. Maybe there is a future for Luke and me. Like when I'm older.

AbyAngel99: Yeah, that would be cool.

AbyAngel99: Maybe someday.

BlueSkyBoi: I'm so jealous of Science Boy.

AbyAngel99: Why? I said no!

BlueSkyBoi: Yeah. But he's the lucky guy who's tasted those sweet lips of urs. Not me.

OMG, that's so romantic! And it's kind of cute that he's jealous of Billy. Especially since there's nothing to be jealous of. Well, okay, maybe there's a little, if I'm honest. But nothing really. Nothing that I'm going to *act* on. Because I'm loyal to my guy.

BlueSkyBoi: Hey, baby, I need to see ur face. Turn on ur webcam.

I shiver, wondering if my face is all Luke is going to want to see. But I turn on my webcam anyway.

> **BlueSkyBoi:** Wow. I almost forgot how gorgeous u are. I can't believe how lucky I am.
> **AbyAngel99:** Lucky Luke!
> **BlueSkyBoi:** ☺
> **BlueSkyBoi:** So, Angel, are u going to make me even more lucky?
> **AbyAngel99:** How?
> **BlueSkyBoi:** Show me some more of ur beautiful body, baby.

Okay, I think. I'll show him more of my body. I lean back and hold up my foot to the screen.

> **AbyAngel99:** That's a part of my body u haven't seen before ;-)
> **BlueSkyBoi:** LOL! That's why I love u, baby. Ur smart, gorgeous, AND u have a sense of humor!
> **AbyAngel99:** I've just got it all, ha ha.
> **BlueSkyBoi:** U sure do. How 'bout showing me some more? Maybe put on some music and do me a little striptease since ur in a teasing mood?

I feel weird about doing it, and he can see it in my face.

> **BlueSkyBoi:** Remember, honey, there's nothing to be ashamed about. Ur beautiful. And it's just u & me. Me and my gorgeous, sexy girl.

Just me and Luke. Me and my guy. I guess it can't do any harm, right?

AbyAngel99: K. But I get to choose the music.
BlueSkyBoi: Anything u want, baby.

I grab my iPod and search till I find the song I want. Then I stick it in my speaker and as soon as I hear the music begin I start dancing in front of my webcam.

Let's have some fun this beat is sick
I wanna take a ride on your disco stick

I sing along with Lady Gaga as I slowly take off my sweater and move my hips to the heavy beat. I glance at my laptop screen and see Luke is rubbing his crotch, slowly, as he watches me.

Hold me and love me, just wanna touch you for a minute

By this time I'm down to my bra and panties. Luke has his jeans open and he's taken his thing out and is stroking it. I keep dancing without taking anything else off, singing along to the words.

BlueSkyBoi: C'mon, baby. I wanna see every inch of ur sweet skin.
BlueSkyBoi: I dream about u all day and all night, Abby.
BlueSkyBoi: Can't stop thinkin' abt u, sugar.
AbyAngel99: K

I take off my bra and then my panties. I throw them at the webcam, playfully, and they cover it. Luke won't like that. I hurry to take them off so he can see me again.

> **BlueSkyBoi:** Missed u there. OMG, u make me so hard, Abby.
> **BlueSkyBoi:** Let me see u touch yourself. I love that, baby. It drives me crazy.

Touching myself with Luke watching is so embarrassing, but it's also kind of . . . I don't know . . . exciting, I guess. The way he looks at me makes me feel incredible, because I can tell that he's just so, soooo, into me.

> *Daddy I'm so sorry, I'm so s-s-sorry yeah we just*
> *like to party, like to p-p-party yeah*
> *Bang, bang, we're beautiful and dirty rich.*

I might not be rich, but I definitely feel beautiful when I'm with Luke. No one's ever told me I'm hot and gorgeous and sexy and all that stuff. Not before him. It's like he's Prince Charming on a webcam.

All of a sudden he erupts like a fleshy volcano, and I see his lips move as he groans. I throw on my bathrobe and lean over to type.

> **AbyAngel99:** Did u like it?

I see him reach for some tissues to wipe his hands. He does up his jeans and comes closer to the keyboard and the camera, so he can type more easily and I can see him smiling.

BlueSkyBoi: Did I like it? Baby, I LOVED it!

AbyAngel99: ☺

BlueSkyBoi: And I love u, sweet girl.

BlueSkyBoi: Promise me that u are mine

BlueSkyBoi: all mine

BlueSkyBoi: that u won't go out with Science Boy

BlueSkyBoi: or let him see

BlueSkyBoi: or touch

BlueSkyBoi: what's mine

BlueSkyBoi: especially when I can't do it.

He loves me. He really loves me. He loves me so much he wants to keep me all to himself. I have to make sure I'm really strong when I'm with Billy. No more wavering over his cute smile. Because Luke is my guy.

AbyAngel99: I promise.

BlueSkyBoi: Well, good night, princess. Sweet dreams. U definitely gave me some. I'm gonna be thinking abt u all nite!

BlueSkyBoi: And all day 2morrow, too ;-)

CHAPTER 10
♪ OCTOBER 14

Faith waves at me, all excited, as I get on the bus the next morning. She looks so disgustingly cheerful I feel like throwing her a punch and going to sit at the back of the bus. But instead I sit down next to her.

"Guess what?" she asks, almost before my butt hits the seat.

"What?"

"Ted asked me out! We're going to see this independent movie on Saturday. He's into that kind of thing. Ted says they're more interesting than the usual bourgeois Hollywood stuff."

"The what?"

"Bourgeois Hollywood stuff. You know, the typical commercial films they show at the multiplex filled with homages to material goods."

Huh?

"What's wrong with 'bourgeois films' all of a sudden? You seemed to really enjoy them not so long ago. Aren't you the same girl who watched the entire Lord of the Rings trilogy with me seven times, just so she could drool over Orlando Bloom?"

At least Faith hasn't been *completely* brainwashed by The Amazing Ted. She manages to blush.

"I don't think there's anything *wrong* with bourgeois films. In fact, it was really embarrassing — I had to ask Ted what he meant when he started talking about them. I didn't have a clue!"

"So what are you going to see, exactly?"

"I'm not sure. Some French movie with subtitles."

"I guess you won't be making out then. Not if you have to read the subtitles."

"Abby!" Faith punches my arm. "Who says we're going to make out?" She leans over and whispers in my ear. "Not that I wouldn't mind, though. Ted is sooooooooo hot."

Her breath in my ear makes me shiver slightly, but maybe it's just because her words remind me of Luke.

"You should memorize the IMDb synopsis before you go, just in case," I tell her.

"That's a great idea," she says. "Why didn't I think of that?"

"Probably because you aren't a guy. Billy Fisher is the one who told me *that* trick."

"So what's going on with you two? Are you going out again? Billy told Mike Landau, who told Emily Tunick, who told Gracie, that you were giving him the cold shoulder. I thought you liked him."

Wow. That school grapevine works pretty fast.

"I *do* like him. I'm just not sure, you know, if I *like* him." I hesitate for a moment, trying to decide if I should tell Faith about Luke. I mean not *everything*, obviously. He said to keep us a secret. But I feel like he's too important a part of my life to stay totally hidden. Plus, maybe it'll get back to Billy through the grapevine and get me off the hook. "And, well . . . I'm kind of seeing someone else."

Faith turns to me wide-eyed. "Seriously? You never said anything! Who?"

"You don't know him. He . . . goes to another school. He doesn't live around here."

"Wow. How did you meet him?"

Oh, snap! Can't say the Internet. Faith will freak.

"Um . . . do you remember the church retreat I went to while you were on vacation with your family this summer? I met him there."

"But you never said anything about him! How come I'm just hearing about this now? I'm your BFF, remember?"

I remember. You're the one who doesn't seem to remember.

"Well, because nothing happened at the retreat. But we've been e-mailing back and forth since then, and we kind of hit it off."

"That's great, Abby!" Faith says. "He must be a nice guy if you met him at a church thing."

I wonder what Faith would think of Luke if I told her the truth. I'm not sure I want to know. Maybe he's right about keeping us a secret.

As we're pulling up at school, Faith drops the bombshell on me.

"Maybe when he comes to visit we can double-date!"

I try to imagine Luke hanging out with me and Ted and Faith at Starbucks or Panera or Urban Pizzeria. Does not compute.

"Yeah, maybe," I mumble over my shoulder as we get off the bus.

When hell freezes over.

Ms. Forcier hands back the science tests. When she gets to my desk, she places it facedown, and gives me a questioning look before moving on.

Uh-oh.

I lift the top edge of the paper and take a peek at my grade. I got a seventy-one — a C-minus — and Ms. Forcier's written *SEE ME AFTER CLASS!* in big red letters. It's the lowest grade I've earned in science, ever. OMFG. My parents are going to *freak*. No, "freaking" is an understatement. They're going to lose it to the infinite power.

"How'd it go, Abby?" Billy asks me. "Did our study session pay off?"

Why can't he just leave me alone right now?

"Not exactly."

"Oh, no! That sucks. 'Cause you were totally the best good luck charm ever."

He shows me his paper, which has a big red A+ at the top. *I hate him. Why does he have to flaunt it?*

I force my face into a smile and lie through gritted teeth. "Awesome. Glad I could help."

He smiles. "Do you want to *help* again this weekend?"

"I . . . can't. I've got plans this weekend. Family reunion, remember?"

Billy shrinks in such sudden dejection. He looks like a balloon that someone just let the air out of to make a fart sound.

"Oh, yeah. I forgot. Well, maybe the weekend after then."

"Yeah. Maybe."

Or maybe not. I turn back to my lousy C-minus test that I'm embarrassed to let anyone see.

After class, Billy tries to talk to me again, but I tell him I have to speak to Ms. Forcier.

"Later then," he says, shuffling away awkwardly. I feel kind of bad, but not as bad as I do when Ms. Forcier starts asking me about the test.

"Abby, I'm concerned about this test result. It's not up to your usual standard of work. Didn't you study?"

"No, I studied."

She looks me straight in the eye, as if to see if I'm lying, which I'm not. I *did* study.

Looking over the test, I can't believe I got so many answers wrong. Answers I totally knew. It's like I was just . . . in Lala Land. *Or in LukeWorld.*

"Is there something going on that might be causing problems with your schoolwork? Anything you might want to talk about?"

I look down at the big red C-minus circled on my test paper.

"No. Nothing."

"Are you sure?"

I messed up one test, okay? Why does she have to act like I'm some Major League Problem Child all of a sudden?

"Yeah, I'm sure."

"Okay. Well, let me know if you need any help. You're one of my brightest students, Abby, and I'd hate to see your grades suffer because you're not studying for tests."

As I slink out of the classroom, I think, *I've got to concentrate.* But all day in school, it's impossible because the only thing on my mind is getting home to check the mailbox to see if my gift from Luke has arrived.

The box is postmarked BOSTON, MA, which seems strange, since Luke's from New Jersey. But I figure maybe he was visiting family over the weekend or traveling on business or something. I still don't even know what he does.

I race inside to the kitchen, get a knife, and open the outer box. Then I take it up to my room and shut the door so I can examine my present in private. Even though Lily isn't home yet, I don't want to risk her walking in on me and blabbing about this to Mom and Dad.

The phone is awesome. It's red and has a real texting keyboard. Just like Luke promised, there's a built-in MP3 player, too. I turn it on, and immediately there are already five text messages, one from the phone company and four from a number I don't know, but when I go to my inbox, they're all from Luke.

> **Hey, baby, welcome to ur new phone!**
> **Text me NOW.**
> **Let's make sweet music!**
> **Luke n Abby 4ever.**

I find my earbuds and plug them into the phone. Luke's already made me four playlists, Sweet, Sexy, Hot, and Sensual. I'm not really sure what Sensual is supposed to be about, so I try that one.

> *Baby, I'm hot just like an oven, I need some lovin'* . . .
> *When I get that feeling, I need sexual healing* . . .

I'm slow dancing around the room to this song, which is old and kind of corny, if you want to know the truth — more like something my parents would listen to. But it's sweet that Luke took the time to make me all these playlists. No one's ever done that for me before.

Thx for the fone. I LUV it! I text him.
Listening 2 one of playlists now.

It's only a minute or two before the phone rings.

"Hey, gorgeous. Now I get to speak to you on the top secret Abby line. Just for you and me."

"It's such a cool phone, Luke. Thank you *sooooo* much!"

"Just make sure you don't go showing it to all your friends, okay?"

"I won't. Even if I wish I could just happen to whip it out in front of Amanda Armitage, just so she'd shut up about her iPhone."

He laughs.

"Maybe someday I can get you one of those. But in the meantime, this will have to do."

I love the thought of getting an iPhone someday, but I don't want Luke to think that I'm all about the presents.

"It'll more than do. It's awesome. I love it."

"So have you listened to any of my playlists yet?"

"I started listening to the Sensual one."

"Good. Maybe when you're listening to it you can touch yourself in front of the webcam for me."

"I . . . guess."

"What are you wearing now?"

"Jeans. A shirt."

"What kind of underwear?"

"A bra. Bikini underpants."

"You should get a thong."

"But they go up your butt."

"Maybe, baby, but they're really hot. I bet you'd look great in one. Maybe I'll send you a few. What size are you?"

"Small, I guess."

"Abby, where'd you get that cell phone?"

Oh, crud! Lily's home. How come I didn't hear her come in the front door? Because I was listening to the music with stupid ear-buds in, that's why.

"Oh, Faith, I've got to go, Lily's home. See you tomorrow."

"Okay, I'll IM you later," Luke says, and hangs up.

"Haven't you ever heard of *knocking*?" I ask Lily.

"I've heard of it. But I didn't want to damage my knuckles. So. Where'd you get it?"

She's leaning against the doorjamb, her arms crossed over her chest, and it's clear she's not going anywhere till she gets an answer.

"I couldn't find mine, so Gracie lent me hers."

"Who's Gracie? And why would she be stupid enough to do that?"

"She's a friend of mine and Faith's and because she's *nice*, not a selfish brat like you, that's why."

"Well, you better not lose it like you lost yours. Dad's gonna be really pissed when he finds out."

"I haven't lost it. It's probably in my locker or something. I just couldn't find it when I needed it and Gracie didn't need hers because her family is going to their cabin in upstate New York for the weekend and they don't have cell service up there. I'm giving it back to her at school on Monday. Anyway, it's none of your business, so why don't you go squeeze that zit that's erupting on your nose?"

Ha! I know I've faked her out because she immediately touches the end of her nose with her fingertips, a worried expression on her face, and then rushes into the bathroom and slams the door.

That was a really close call. I just hope Lily keeps her mouth shut and doesn't say anything to Mom and Dad.

I text Luke a quick message apologizing for having to hang up on him, and then hide his cell phone in my backpack next to the phone my parents gave me, which is in its usual place in the front pocket. Like I'd actually lose it. *Sheesh.* It's incredible how Lily thinks the worst about me, when I'm like twenty times more responsible than she is.

Time to do homework. When I take the books out of my backpack, my C-minus test falls out. I hide it in the back of my closet, where no one will ever find it.

Mom brings home Chinese food for dinner because she's too tired to cook and Dad's going to be late, surprise, surprise.

Lily opens her big fat mouth over the sesame noodles.

"Abby lost her cell phone."

Mom gives me a sharp look.

"Is that true?"

"No, of course it's not true. I just left it in my locker by accident."

"Abby was talking on this really fancy phone when I got home from school. She *said* it was her friend Gracie's," the Lily Monster says.

"Why were you using someone else's cell phone?" Mom asks. She sounds really ticked off. If I had killer vision, Lily would be totally dead. She *would* have to bring this up when Mom is tired from work and already grumpy.

"I realized I'd left mine in my locker and Grace said she didn't need hers over the weekend so she lent it to me in case I had an emergency. Seriously, what's the big deal?"

"The big deal, Abby, is that you need to be more responsible with your own cell phone. I certainly wouldn't want you lending the phone that your father and I pay for to anyone else, and I'm sure this Grace's parents wouldn't be happy to know that she's handing her phone out like this. I've a good mind to call them and tell them."

Oh, crud.

"No, Mom, don't! I'll give it back to her on Monday, okay? She's away all weekend and doesn't need it. Why are you making such a big deal about this? I leave my phone in my locker one time and you're acting like I've committed this huge crime!"

Mom takes another bite of sesame noodles while I sit there freaking at the thought of her calling Grace's parents and finding out that I've lied.

"Well, make sure you give it back to her first thing Monday. I don't want you borrowing other people's phones, or lending them yours. And make sure you remember to bring yours home — those school lockers aren't safe — and if it gets stolen, the replacement is coming out of your allowance. Is that clear?"

"Crystal. Can I eat now?"

My sister has been busy stuffing her face with sweet and sour chicken the whole time Mom's been freaking on me. I want to empty the carton of it over her snitchy little head.

"Lily, leave some of that for your father and Abby," Mom says.

"Do I have to? It's so good!"

"Yes, you do have to, you selfish brat!"

Mom slams down her knife and fork.

"Okay, that's enough. I've had a long day at work and I really don't need to come home to the two of you bickering. I don't want to hear another word from either of you unless it's civil."

We eat the rest of dinner in total silence, except for the sound of Lily's chewing, which drives me crazy, but I can't say anything or else Mom will lose it again.

CHAPTER 11

Over the next month, I spend most of my evenings on the computer with Luke, or talking to him on my secret cell phone. My parents want me to watch a movie with them tonight, but Luke and I have a webcam date so I say no.

I try to ignore the crushed expression on my dad's face as I turn to walk out of the family room, and the cloak of guilt that wraps itself around me as I walk up the stairs. But I shrug it off as I close and lock the door to my room. I mean, it's not like Dad's been around at all lately. And now that he's finally making an appearance I'm supposed to drop everything just so he can spend some "quality time" with me? Yeah, right. While Dad's been doing his workaholic thing, coming home only to give me grief if I'm not getting straight A's, Luke's the one who's been there for me every night, listening to my problems. Unlike my parents, he knows — and remembers — what's going on in my life. So I'm not about to give up my evening with him to watch some lame movie with Mom and Dad. Just not happening.

* * *

It's Sunday night a few weeks later and I've got a big math test the next day. I've got serious studying to do because I've been spending so much time talking or video chatting with Luke that I've gotten way behind with schoolwork. Luckily, my parents didn't find out about the C-minus in science or I would be in deep doo-doo. But I can't afford to mess up anymore, especially in math, which is supposed to be one of my best subjects.

To avoid any temptation, I keep my laptop closed and on my desk, while I sit on my bed with my math books, studying. I even turn off Luke's cell, although it's charging under my bed, where no one can see it. But it's a struggle to stay focused on geometry. I miss talking to Luke. The evening feels empty without him.

Mom comes in at eleven.

"Honey, lights out now. You've been studying for hours and you need to get a good night's sleep."

"Yeah, okay," I say, getting up to go brush my teeth.

Mom brushes my hair back from my face as I pass her on the way to the bathroom.

"Good night, sweetheart. Sleep tight."

I automatically say, "Don't let the bedbugs bite," because it's this ritual we did when I was little.

It's so weird. One minute she's expecting so much of me like I'm a grown-up, and the next minute we're doing baby nighty-night rituals like I'm five years old again. Whatever.

When I get back to my room I turn on Luke's cell and there are six text messages from him, asking me where I am and telling me that he loves me and misses me and he's worried about me. Even though I'm supposed to be going to sleep and I know I've got a big test tomorrow, I can't stop myself from firing up my laptop to see if Luke's online. I'm so psyched when I see that he is.

> **BlueSkyBoi:** Hey, baby, where were u?
> **BlueSkyBoi:** I was worried abt u.
> **AbyAngel99:** I wuz studying. Got big math test 2morrow. Got 2 do well.
> **BlueSkyBoi:** My smart girl.
> **BlueSkyBoi:** I luv how motivated u r.
> **AbyAngel99:** Well, I'm kinda behind on stuff.
> **AbyAngel99:** Been talkin 2 u 2 much.
> **BlueSkyBoi:** ☹
> **BlueSkyBoi:** That's not good.
> **BlueSkyBoi:** I don't want to be a bad influence on u.
> **BlueSkyBoi:** Maybe we should stop talking 4 a while.

My heart feels like it misses a beat when I read that. Without Luke, there would be this huge, scary void in my life. I think about him all the time, and talking to him is the one thing I look forward to every day. Now that Faith is totally wrapped up in the play and with the most awesomely amazing Ted, I'd have no one if it weren't for Luke. He's my love. He's my best friend. He's my everything.

> **AbyAngel99:** NO!!!
> **AbyAngel99:** It's okay.
> **AbyAngel99:** I'll catch up.

AbyAngel99: I just have 2 get more organized and stuff.

BlueSkyBoi: r u sure?

BlueSkyBoi: The last thing I want 2 do is screw up my girl's life.

BlueSkyBoi: I luv u so much, Abby.

BlueSkyBoi: I only want wut's best 4 u.

AbyAngel99: Then keep talking 2 me

AbyAngel99: cause u are wut's best 4 me!!

BlueSkyBoi: If ur sure that's wut u want.

AbyAngel99: I'm sure.

BlueSkyBoi: Good. Cause I think abt u all the time.

BlueSkyBoi: Not a minute goes by when u aren't on my mind.

BlueSkyBoi: Wait — did I say a minute?

BlueSkyBoi: I meant a second.

It's a relief to know that Luke thinks about me as much as I think about him. I was almost starting to think that I was getting kind of . . . I don't know . . . obsessed. But if he feels the same way about me, then it must be normal, right? Maybe this is just how people are when they're in love with each other.

AbyAngel99: It's like that 4 me 2.

BlueSkyBoi: So . . . it's late

BlueSkyBoi: and u have a test.

BlueSkyBoi: I guess u have 2 go to bed.

BlueSkyBoi: Wish I could be there with u.

AbyAngel99: me 2

BlueSkyBoi: So . . . can I kiss u good night?

AbyAngel99: ☺ But . . . I can stay up 4 a little while longer.

BlueSkyBoi: Are u sure?

AbyAngel99: Yeah. I'm sure.

I end up staying up with Luke until three in the morning. And undressing for him in front of the webcam while we whisper to each other on our secret cell phone.

When my alarm goes off at six fifteen a.m., I realize that probably hadn't been the smartest decision I ever made in my life. My eyelids feel weighted down and my head pounds with one of those killer headaches I get sometimes when I don't get enough sleep. I drag myself to the bathroom for a shower and look in the mirror. Argh. I am definitely not in optimal math-test-taking form.

Down in the kitchen I put an extra teaspoon of instant coffee in my cup, hoping it'll give me a boost. It just makes the coffee taste like crap. I have to put in twice as much sugar so I can drink it.

"What's with you? You look like you need a Black and Decker beauty kit this morning," Lily says when she comes into the kitchen.

"Yeah, good morning to you, too, Cruella De Asshole."

Of course, Mom comes in and hears what *I* said, not what Lily said, so *I'm* the one who gets in trouble. Story of my life.

"Abigail Johnston! What on earth has come over you?" she shouts. "How *dare* you use that kind of language in this house! Apologize to your sister *right now*!"

Mom stomps over to the fridge to get out the Coffee-mate. "I really don't need this first thing in the morning."

Like I do?

"Sorry, Lily," I say with as little sincerity as I can muster.

She sticks her tongue out at me as soon as Mom turns her back to fill her travel coffee mug. For like the nine zillionth time, I wonder how we can possibly be related.

Amanda Armitage looks twice as gorgeous and put together as usual, as if to contrast with my *Close Encounters with a Zombie* look.

"Hey, Ally, are you feeling okay?" Nick asks me when I sit down. "You don't look so hot."

Oh, great. Thanks for pointing that out.

I hear Amanda snickering. I'm tempted to say that I've got the bubonic plague and it's really, really contagious. And then sneeze on them.

But I'm too tired. I just want to get this fricking test over with and this whole day at school over with so I can go home and get into bed and nap. I'm actually thinking of my pillow more than I'm thinking about Luke, that's how tired I am.

Mr. Evans hands out the test papers and I pinch the inside of my elbow to try and make myself more alert.

For the first fifteen minutes I'm able to concentrate, mostly. But then I feel myself blinking constantly as my eyelids get heavier and heavier, and the numbers start to swim on the page in front of me. I pinch myself again, hard, but it doesn't seem to do much good.

The next thing I know is that I wake up with a start as my

pencil rolls on the floor. I bend down to pick it up and as I do so I glance up at the clock near the door. What I see scares me wide awake. There are only five minutes left in the period and I've still got half the test to finish.

I sit up and pull the paper toward me. I've written total gobbledygook for the last answer, and have to do that question again. *Shit, shit, shit!* I'm going to fail this test.

People start going up to hand in their papers, but I'm frantically trying to answer the questions. The worst is, I know this stuff. If I hadn't fallen asleep for half of the period, I'd have done okay. Nick Peters passes by my desk to hand in his paper. I can't believe I'm finishing a test after Nick Copies-My-Homework-and-Can't-Even-Remember-My-Name Peters.

When Mr. Evans calls "time" and tells everyone to put their pencils down, there are five questions I didn't even get to. I am so royally screwed.

I can't look Mr. Evans in the eye when I hand him my paper because I know I've done so badly. I've never gotten below an eighty-nine on anything in this class. This test is going to bring my average *way* down.

There's no way I can face gym. Basketball. Running up and down the gym with people shouting at me to shoot or pass or to be better at defense. As I head down there, I'm trying to work out my excuse to go to the nurse.

"Hey, Abs! OMG, what's the matter? You look terrible!" Faith says as she meets me in the hallway on the way to the gym.

Do I go with period pains or headache and possible virus?

"Yeah, I don't feel so great," I say, putting on a feeble *I'm sick* voice. "I've got a really bad headache and I feel kind of achy."

"You should go to the nurse," Faith says. "You definitely don't want to be playing basketball. I'll go ask Ms. Carlucci for a pass."

I sit down on the bleachers and look pathetic, which isn't too hard because I feel like total crap and as bad as taking that math test was, I know that the moment I get it back is going to feel even worse.

Ms. Carlucci comes over with Faith.

"You're not feeling well, Johnston?"

"No. I've got a really bad headache and my muscles ache."

She gives me the eagle eye *Are you sure you're not faking this?* stare, takes in the shadows under my eyes and the pasty white pallor of my skin, and decides that I'm genuine enough for a pass, which she scribbles off and hands to Faith.

"Wilson, you can take her to the nurse, but I want you to come straight back here."

"Sure thing, Ms. C. I will."

As she walks away, Ms. Carlucci lets out a loud blast of her whistle, which feels like a knife splitting my brain in half. I swear she did it on purpose, just in case I was faking.

Is it any wonder I hate gym?

Faith and I walk down the hall in awkward silence. We used to always have so much to say to each other. But now . . . well, so much of what I would want to tell her is secret, a private little world that's only inhabited by Luke and me.

"Um . . . how are things going with the play?" I ask her.

"Great! We're making good progress with the sets. We're starting to look for props. My mom's been taking Ted and me to

Goodwill on the weekends to hunt for things we need. It's actually kind of fun. Have you ever been there?"

"Only to drop off stuff for donations."

"We should go sometime. Grace came with me yesterday and she got this really cool retro jacket for five bucks."

Part of me is miffed that Faith didn't even bother to ask me to go. But then I probably wouldn't have gone anyway.

I force down the hurt part, the one that's whining, *Why didn't she invite me?*

"So things are going well with you and Ted?"

Faith's eyes get this faraway look, and she has this goofy half smile on her face.

"Better than well. I swear, Abby, I never thought . . . well, he's just so different . . . you know, from other guys. He's smart and funny and . . . like, we really *talk* about stuff. *Really* talk, the way you and I do."

Or used to. When I still mattered in your life.

But then I have Luke, who I can talk to about anything. Anything and everything. Luke, who never accuses me of being "negative." Who listens and supports me, no matter what I say or do.

"That's great," I tell Faith, but I'm starting to drift into LukeWorld.

"How's your boyfriend?" Faith asks.

What boyfriend? I think, panicked. *I never told her about Luke.*

"I'm not seeing Billy Fisher anymore," I tell her. "I mean he's a nice guy and all, but that was kind of a one-time thing."

Faith gives me this strange look, like I've suddenly sprouted donkey ears or something.

"I know that. You told me. I'm talking about the guy you met at the retreat. *Whateverhisnameis.*"

Oops. I totally forgot about that.

"Oh, yeah. He's good. We talk a lot on the phone and stuff, and we're hoping to get together someday soon. It's hard, you know, because he doesn't live near here."

I know she wants to ask me more questions, but luckily for me, we're at the nurse's office.

"Thanks for walking with me," I tell her. "You better get back before Ms. C makes you drop and give her twenty."

"Yeah, right," Faith says. "I hope you feel better, Abs."

She turns to go but then turns back and says, "And let's try to have a sleepover soon, okay? I miss you."

I wonder if she really *does* miss me, what with Ted and Grace and stage crew and her trips to Goodwill to find props that she didn't invite me on. But she's giving me the puppy dog look.

"Yeah. Let's make a date. I've . . . missed you, too."

On Tuesday, Mr. Evans hands back the tests. My heart is beating so loud I'm sure Nick and Amanda can hear it as Mr. Evans walks toward my desk. He puts the paper facedown. I don't even want to turn it over because I know it's going to be bad. Like maybe a C-minus or something.

I take a deep breath and flip the edge up so I can see my grade. *What?* It's even worse than I thought. I got a D. I've never, ever, in my entire life, got a grade that bad in anything, much less math, which is supposed to be one of my best subjects. Underneath the grade, Mr. Evans has written *SEE ME!!!* in big red letters, underlined three times.

I am so dead.

Even Nick fricking Peters did better than me. I hear him telling Amanda that he got a C-plus. Which for him is like an A. Amanda got a B. I think I'm going to throw up.

Being smart is what I have. It's what I do. And now I'm screwing up in what's supposed to be my best class?

It feels like the longest period ever, and it just kills me as Mr. Evans goes over the test, because I *know* this stuff. If I hadn't been so tired . . . if I hadn't been up half the night talking to Luke . . . if I hadn't been so . . . fricking . . . *stupid.*

When the bell rings, I stay at my desk until the room is mostly empty, then I drag myself up to the front of the room and stand in front of Mr. Evans's desk.

"So, Abby. What's up with you?"

"I . . . well . . . I . . ."

"Did you study for this test?"

"Yes, I did. I know all this stuff, really, I do."

"So then what happened?"

"I think . . . I just wasn't feeling well that day. I could barely keep my eyes open and . . ."

Mr. Evans looks at me like he's trying to weigh my words for truth.

"I'd like you to get one of your parents to sign this test and then you can return it to me tomorrow."

"But . . . I thought you only did that if kids failed."

"I like parents to be aware when there are any out-of-the-ordinary test results, so they can help their kids get back on track. Is that a problem for you?"

Yes. Because my parents are going to kill me.

"No. I'll give it to you tomorrow."

Mr. Evans gives me a sympathetic smile.

"Don't worry, Abby. You're a good student. I'm sure you'll do better next time. And you can always do some extra-credit work to bring your grade up."

"Okay, thanks. See you tomorrow."

If I'm still alive . . .

I'm doing my homework in my room listening to music on Luke's cell phone with my earbuds in, when Lily comes in. Without knocking, of course. I slide my backpack over the phone so she can't see it, but forget that my math test was underneath it.

"Holy crap!!!!" Lily shouts, picking up the test and waving it around. "Amazing Abby got a D on a math test?!!! Dad is going to flip his lid!!"

I rip the earbuds out and yell at her. "Give it back, you brat! It's none of your business. What are you doing in here anyway? *Get out!*"

"I came to tell you that Mom called and said she's bringing Chinese food home for dinner. I guess I better call her back and tell her to pick up a side order of whup-ass for you."

"Don't even think about telling her, Lily. I'll kill you. I really will."

Lily tosses the test back on my bed and saunters toward the door.

"Oooh. I'm *soooo* scared, D is for Dumbass."

I pick up my sneaker and throw it at her, but she's already turned the corner into the hallway, and anyway, my aim sucks so the sneaker just hits the door frame. She better not tell Mom. It's bad enough that I have to do it.

*　　*　　*

When Mom gets home, I hear her shouting my name almost as soon as she walks in the door, and she sounds seriously pissed.

I shove the test in my back pocket and go down to the kitchen, where she's taking the Chinese food out of the plastic bags and putting it on the table.

"Abigail, I believe you have something to tell me?"

I know I'm in serious trouble when she calls me Abigail. *I'm going to kill Lily, the evil little snitch.*

I take the test out of my pocket and hand it to her. "You have to sign this."

She looks at the grade and then stares at me in anger and disbelief.

"What on *earth* is going on with you, Abby?"

"Come on, Mom. Everyone has bad days. Even you."

"Don't you talk back to me, Abby. This is about *you*. Doing well in school is your job, and getting a D on a test is not part of the job description."

"It's *one test*. I've gotten A's on all my quizzes and homework assignments in math and —"

"Well, that's all the more reason I want to know what's going on with you. Is it that boy, what's his name . . . Bobby?"

Nice to know my mom is about as clued into my life as Nick Peters.

"His name's *Billy*, and no, it has nothing to do with him."

"That's how it goes with girls your age — you waste all your time mooning over some guy while he's focusing on his grades and getting into a good college."

She is so clueless. How can she lump me with "girls my age"? I'm nothing like them. I get *good grades*. It's just one frickin' D! I'm so mad I can't stop myself.

"Is that what happened with you?" I ask her.

Mom's always been sensitive because Dad went to Cornell and she went to Albany State. Not that Albany State isn't a good school or anything, but as long as I can remember, my parents have both been telling me to work hard so I can get into an Ivy League school like my dad did.

The flush starts around my mother's neckline and moves upward until her entire face is bright red.

"You have just got yourself grounded, *missy*. And you can hand over that computer of yours. You waste way too much time IM'ing with your friends when you're supposed to be doing your homework and that's part of the problem. From now on, I will hand you the computer when I get home from work, and you can do your homework in the kitchen under my supervision."

"But, Mom —"

She holds up her hand to shut me up.

"Abigail, I don't want to hear another word out of you right now. Just go upstairs and get me your computer. *NOW!*"

"*I HATE YOU!*" I scream as I stomp up the stairs. I'm so angry that I can hear the blood rushing through my ears. No computer means no video chats with Luke. There's no way I can chat with him in the kitchen under my mother's eagle eye, with Lily the Super Snoop hanging over my shoulder. This sucks big-time. I feel like knocking my mother's china vase over as I come back downstairs clutching my precious laptop to my chest. I'm so glad Luke told me to put the password on it, so at least I know my mom can't snoop while it's confiscated.

I hand it to her without a word, grab the signed test from the kitchen table, and turn to go back upstairs.

"Abby," she says as I reach the kitchen door. I stop, but don't look at her. "Abby, what is going on?"

"Nothing, except you getting on my case for no reason at all."

She starts to say something else, but I ignore her and go back to my room, slamming the door shut behind me. I take the precaution of locking it and then I take Luke's cell phone out and dial his number. He answers on the third ring.

"Hey, gorgeous, how're you doing?"

I didn't plan to lose it, but I'm so upset and angry about what's happened tonight that I burst into tears.

"Whoa, baby, what's the matter?"

"M-my m-mom. She's such a bitch. I h-hate her!" I hiccup. "S-she t-took m-my computer away."

I hear Luke's quick intake of breath.

"You put a password on that sucker, right?"

"Y-yes."

"Good . . . What made her confiscate it?"

"I got a D on m-my m-math test. My teacher made me get the t-test signed by parents, and my mom totally f-freaked. She s-said that it's because I've been s-spending too much time online."

"Man, that's harsh! What's her problem? So it's not because she suspects anything about us?"

"No, n-nothing like *that*. In fact, she accused me of *m-mooning* over Billy, that guy from my science class."

"You don't, do you?"

"Moon over Billy? Of course not!"

"Good. 'Cause you're all mine, baby. Every sweet inch of you."

"Don't worry. I don't care about Billy. He's nothing like you, Luke. He's just . . . Billy, this kid in my class. But, Luke, I'm scared."

"What are you scared about, honey?"

"My dad's going to kill me when he gets home. He's gonna go totally ballistic. He's like a nut about my grades and every-thing. And I've never messed up like this before."

I hear Luke's laughter in my ear. "Messed up? Getting a D on a test? Wow, he's really hard on you if that's considered 'messing up.' Think of all the things you could be doing to mess up!"

"I know, seriously? Like I could be doing drugs or, like, I don't know, stealing stuff, and I don't do any of that. I'm like Miss Goody Two-shoes Gets Good Grades except for this one time."

"Well, . . . and I'm just thinking out loud here . . . maybe you need to teach your parents a lesson."

"What do you mean? How?"

"So, you know you're saying how you're the perfect kid all the time and they're still giving you all this shit?"

"Yes, but . . ."

"Well, what if you actually gave them something to really worry about for a change? Just to put things into perspective."

My heart starts beating faster, and my voice drops almost to a whisper.

"What do you mean?"

"You know I've been dying to meet you, Abby. So what if you and I went away on a trip together for a few days? It would . . . give us a chance to . . . get to know each other better, and it would teach your parents a lesson about what's really important. You know, teach your dad that he shouldn't go ballistic on you just for something stupid like getting a D on a math test. And teach your mom that she needs to accept you for who you are, instead of trying to make you into someone you're not. "

My throat goes dry and I'm not sure I can speak. *Meet Luke? Go away with him for a few days?*

His voice continues, low and soothing in my ear. "Baby, you know I would never do anything to hurt you, don't you? I love you. You're the most special girl in the world. I hate hearing that your parents are treating you so badly. You deserve better. Forget that, you deserve the best. The best of everything, sweetheart, and I want to give it to you."

I feel my heart expanding in my chest, swelling with love from the sound of Luke's words. No one has ever loved me the way he does. No one has ever seen the real me the way Luke can. I want to cuddle up in his arms and put my head on his chest.

"So . . . how would we do that?" I whisper.

"I could come get you," he says. "You could pretend to go to school, but then sneak away to . . . let's see. Is there a mall you could get to?"

I think about the possibilities.

"I could sneak out after homeroom and take a bus to the Galleria."

"The Galleria. Let me just look that up online. . . . Is that the one that's near the I-84 exit?"

"Yeah."

"Good. So, what time is homeroom, and about what time do you think you'd get to the Galleria?"

"Homeroom is at seven thirty and . . ."

"Wow! I forgot how early they make you get up in high school."

"Yeah, right? It's torture."

"Okay, so what time do you think you'd get to the Galleria?"

"I think maybe eight fifteen. Or maybe eight thirty. But I don't think it opens till nine thirty."

"Well, maybe you should stay in school till later, then. I don't want my girl hanging around an empty mall. It's safer if we meet when the mall is crowded."

I wonder why it's safer when the mall is crowded, but I tell Luke I can leave after science and meet him at the mall at eleven thirty.

"Let's meet at the food court," he says. "What's your favorite place there?"

"Cookie Madness," I tell him. "They make the *best* chocolate chip cookies ever."

"Only the best for my best girl," Luke says. "So. I'll see you tomorrow, beautiful. At the Galleria, at Cookie Madness. Eleven thirty. If there are any problems, call me or text me, okay?"

"Okay . . . Um . . . what should I pack? Like for how long and stuff?"

"Just enough clothes for a few days. And don't worry, baby. If you forget anything, we can stop and buy it."

I hesitate for a second, then ask, "Luke . . . are you sure you'll recognize me?"

"Of course, baby! Your beautiful face is engraved on my mind. And I'll be wearing my Red Sox hat and a leather jacket, so you'll know it's me. Don't walk off with just any guy in a Red Sox hat, okay?"

I laugh. "Of course I won't. My mom always taught me not to talk to strangers."

He laughs, too.

"I can't wait to finally see you, baby. I've been dreaming about this."

I want to see him, too, but I'm also nervous. Still. My parents deserve it. Luke's right. They're being such assholes. Maybe if I just go away with him for a few days, they'll be more chill when I come back.

"I'll see you tomorrow."

We hang up and I hide his phone in my backpack again. I'm so glad I have it. Otherwise I would have been so screwed when Mom confiscated my laptop. I would have been totally cut off from my Luke Lifeline. And we never would have been able to arrange this amazing plan.

I take all my schoolbooks out of my backpack, except for the ones I'll need for the first few periods. But then I pack some underwear and socks and some T-shirts and a sweater. Tomorrow morning I'll make sure to pack my toothbrush and toothpaste and some makeup. For Luke, I don't mind making an effort. For Luke, I actually *want* to.

The thought of meeting Luke tomorrow gives me courage when I hear Dad shouting for me to come downstairs.

I H8 my parents! H8 H8 H8 H8 them!!! I text Luke as soon as I get back to my room after getting bawled out by Dad.

Dad is such a #$%!
Can't wait 2 CU 2morrow! Xo

I roll up another T-shirt and stuff it into my backpack, then I hear the ping that Luke's texted me back.

I can't wait, either. Send me a pic 2 keep me going.

By now I know what Luke wants, and I want to make him happy by giving it to him, because he's the only one who really cares about me. So I take off my shirt and bra, stand in front of the mirror with Luke's cell phone and, pretending that the mirror is Luke, make like I'm giving it a kiss. I snap a picture and then send it to him, making sure to delete it from the phone as soon as it's sent. Then I get my bathrobe and get ready to go take a shower. Right before I'm about to unlock my door, he texts back.

> OMG, AbyAngel Ur so hot! U make me hard as
> a rock, baby.
> Can't wait 2 kiss u all over . . .

I feel weird reading that. *All* over? Like *every*where? But I love that I can make him so happy just by sending him a picture. It's so much easier than working my butt off to make my parents happy and having them be mad at me anyway.

Luke's phone gets hidden away in my backpack, and I unlock my door to go take a shower. Mom is coming up the stairs, looking like the Grim Reaper.

"Abigail Victoria, you are grounded for the next two weeks. Your father and I will revisit this at the end of two weeks and see if your grades have picked up and if your behavior has improved. If not, you will stay grounded. Understand?"

Normally, I'd be crushed by this. Normally, I'd protest, I'd cry, I'd rail against how unfair they're being. But right now, I don't care. Because I'm thinking, *Tomorrow, I'll be gone. And you are going to be sorry.*

So I just shrug my shoulders and continue to the bathroom.

"Abby, wait . . ." Mom says.

I turn to face her. She stands there looking at me with this pleading expression on her face.

"What's come over you, Abby? Why are you being like this?"

Why am I *being like this*? Tears well up in my eyes when my mother asks me that, because it just shows me that Luke's right. I want to tell her that the reason I'm *being like this* is because this is who I am, and ask her why she can't just love me this way.

But instead I just say, "Whatever," and go lock myself in the bathroom, where I cry in the shower and imagine what it's going to be like when I finally meet Luke tomorrow.

CHAPTER 12
♪ DECEMBER 7

I'm up at five the next morning. Well, it's not like I wake up, because I didn't really sleep a whole lot, just dozed fitfully between weird dreams and waking imaginings of my meeting with Luke. It's hard to imagine anything beyond our initial encounter — that's just this big unknown. But I know it will all be good, because Luke really loves me. And in a few days, I can come home and hopefully my parents will realize that I'm not just some straight-A machine — that I'm a thinking human being with feelings, and that once in a while even perfect Abby might get a stupid D on a frickin' math test and *it's not the end of the world*. I mean, sure they're going to freak out and be really pissed. I'm sure they'll totally ground me. But wait — *I already AM grounded* so it's not like I've got a whole lot to lose, is it? Once my parents get over the initial freak-out and being mad at me, though, I think they'll see that some little kid wouldn't have been able to arrange all this — that this kind of planning takes brains and . . . I don't know . . . *maturity*. They'll realize that they need to start treating me like a grown-up instead of a kid. They'll realize they need to start treating me the way Luke does.

I put more thought into my outfit for meeting Luke than I did for the first day of school, because I actually *care* about this first impression. Not that he hasn't already seen me on video chat, but I don't want him to be disappointed when he sees me in real life. I wear my tight, skinny-leg jeans and a green sweater that's soft to the touch and that Faith says brings out the color of my eyes. I even put on makeup and a spritz of perfume that I stole from my mother's bathroom. I don't want to wear the stuff Aunt Penny got me, because it reminds me of Billy. I tuck the makeup and Mom's perfume into my backpack and head downstairs for breakfast. I want to be out the door early.

I'm too nervous to really eat much, but I figure I'd better down something. Lily comes into the kitchen just as I'm taking the last Eggo waffle out of the package.

"Hey! I was going to have that!" she whines.

"You snooze, you lose," I tell her. "Have a Pop-Tart."

"But I don't like them! *You* have the Pop-Tart."

"Um, no. I got here first. The Eggo is mine."

The funny thing is, I don't even *want* the stupid waffle. But there's no way I'm going to let Evil Snitch-Face have it. I'm going to make myself eat it just to spite her.

I manage about half before I feel like I'm going to barf and I end up throwing the rest away, which provokes even more whining from Lily about how I should have let her eat it. Tough. Maybe she should have thought about that before being such a pain in the butt all the time.

My backpack is pretty stuffed, but I squeeze in a Nutri-Grain bar, just in case I get hungry later. I'm just about to go out the door when Dad walks into the kitchen.

"You leaving already?" he says.

"Yeah — I don't want to have to run for the bus."

He comes over and gives me a kiss good-bye. I stand there stiffly, because I'm still mad at him.

"Have a good day, sweetheart. And hang in there. You're my smart girl. I know you can do better if you just put your mind to it."

Dad hugs me, and sniffs.

"You smell nice. I like that perfume, honey."

You should. You bought it for Mom.

"Thanks. Bye, Dad."

As I walk away from the house, away from my dad and my mom and even my brat of a sister, I feel like I'm sitting at the top of a really tall roller coaster, about to careen down at full speed. It hits me that I'm going to meet this guy Luke, who I love, but don't really know except for on the Internet. But what I have with Luke seems more real to me than anything in my so-called "real" life. He understands me better than my parents; he knows me better than my friends. Sometimes I think Luke knows me better than I know myself.

Faith waves to me when I get on the bus. I haven't been sitting with her all the time lately, because sometimes I just can't stand to hear her going on about Ted and how *amazing* and *intellectual* he is. Like, I get it, you've got a boyfriend. Or how *fun* Gracie is. Like, I get it. I'm not fun. But today, I want to be with her, because . . . well, because. Because no matter what, she's Faith, and it's hard to remember when she wasn't my best friend.

I accidentally put my backpack down on her leg when I sit next to her.

"What have you *got* in there, Abs? Rocks?"

"No. Just my math and science books. I have tests coming up in both subjects, so I took them home to study."

I realize right after I say it that Faith has Mr. Evans for math, too, so she'll know I'm lying about the math test because she just took the same one I got the D on. (She got a B-plus. I lied and told her I got the same.) But luckily, she doesn't seem to notice, because she's too busy admiring my outfit.

"You look so pretty today, Abby! I love that sweater on you. It really brings out the green in your eyes."

"Yeah. I think you've mentioned that once or twice before."

"And you're wearing makeup, too!"

"Well, you know. Might as well make a good one hundredth — or whatever it is — impression."

Faith laughs.

"That's true. So how are things going with Church Retreat Guy?"

If only you knew . . .

"Things are going really well, actually. Who knows? Maybe sometime we can double-date."

Now that I'm actually going to meet Luke, maybe this isn't such a crazy possibility. Is it? Now that we're going to be real-life boyfriend and girlfriend we can do things like go to the movies and stuff, like Ted and Faith do. Like I did with Billy that one time.

"Oh, Abby, that would be so awesome! I would love that. We hardly ever get to hang out these days. I miss you."

She looks at me like she really means it. I feel like telling her that I've been here all along, that it's her who's been off doing all these other things and leaving me behind. But what's the point? I'm meeting Luke today and I don't want to spoil my mood. I want to leave Faith on good terms.

"I miss you, too. Let's try to spend some more time together — maybe when the play's over or something."

"Yeah, it's been so crazy busy with rehearsals and stuff. But when it's over, definitely."

When we get to school, I wave good-bye to Faith, but instead of turning to go to my locker right away, I stand and watch her go down the hall until she's swallowed up by the hordes of other students. Part of me wants to run after her and confide what I'm *really* doing today. But then I remember how she told her dad about how I fainted at the auditions after she promised not to. Luke's right. I can't trust Faith the way I used to. I can't really trust anyone except for him.

The morning drags so slowly I want to scream. Normally in homeroom, I'm barely awake, but today I'm sitting up straight watching the clock, my foot tapping.

"What's got into you, Johnston?" Tyrone asks me. "You drink too much coffee this morning?"

It's as good an excuse as any for the wired sensation that's running through my veins.

I hold out my hands, so he can see how they're trembling. Little does he know it's got nothing to do with caffeine.

"Yeah. Those extra-large Dunkaccinos will do it every time."

"Girl, you're gonna give yourself a heart attack if you keep that up," Ty warns me.

We both laugh as the bell rings for first period.

I suffer through Spanish and art, then it's finally science. Billy's already there, reading the handout on the desk about our experiment. He looks up and smiles at me when I put my textbook down. I realized when I got to my locker this morning that, like a moron, I left my science notebook at home on my desk. I guess I wasn't exactly thinking so clearly this morning when I left.

"You look really pretty today," Billy says. I notice he's checking out my sweater.

Why do I blush when he says stuff like that, even though I'm going to meet Luke as soon as this period's over?

"Uh . . . thanks, I guess. So, does the experiment look complicated today? Please say no, because I've had too much caffeine and my hands are all shaky."

I hold them out for him to see. He grasps my hands to still them. His palms are warm and dry.

"Wow, Abby, your hands are freezing!"

He starts to rub them, one at a time.

I'm the jealous type.

I pull my hand away quickly.

"Thanks. I'm fine, really. Just . . . uh . . . bad circulation, you know."

Grabbing the lab handout, I start to read it intently. Or pretend to read it, because it's hard to concentrate on anything right now.

"Luckily for you, there's no pouring and measuring today," Billy says.

"Too right," I agree, although I don't look at him when I say it. I'm afraid to. I glance at the clock quickly. I just have another forty minutes to live through and then I am so out of here.

Billy's right. The lab does look pretty easy today. We're just taking swabs of things and putting them on petri dishes to see what bacteria grow.

We have to take one from the inside of each other's mouths. Can you spell a-w-k-w-a-r-d?

"I wish I'd remembered to use Listerine this morning," Billy jokes before I take his swab.

"Yeah, it's safer to kiss a dog than to kiss a human, you know. Fewer bacteria in their mouths. I saw it on *MythBusters*."

"Maybe," Billy says. "But I'd just like to remind you that I don't eat my own poop or lick my private parts."

Then, as if he just realizes what he's said, he turns bright red. I crack up.

"Just open your mouth so I can take a swab, okay?"

He nods, and opens wide.

I swab his cheek and wipe the cotton bud across the petri dish, then close it and label it — *Billy Fisher 12/7.*

"Do you have a train to catch?" Billy asks.

"What?"

"You keep looking at the clock every thirty seconds. I was just wondering if you had a train to catch."

Not a train. A bus.

I fake a laugh.

"Good one. No, I just didn't eat much for breakfast, so I'm counting down until lunch."

Billy takes a step closer to me and whispers, "I've got a Snickers bar. Do you want me to sneak you some?"

Even though I was lying about the lunch thing, the thought of chocolate sounds pretty good.

"Yes, please!"

He surreptitiously slides the candy bar out from his binder, unwraps it under the lab desk, breaks off a piece, and hands it to me under the desk. I drop my pencil and bend down, stuff it in my mouth, and chew.

I'm half giggling while I'm chewing because this is so naughty. We're not supposed to eat in the classrooms and especially not stuff with peanuts in case someone has an allergy. Billy's already stood up and continued with the experiment, but his hand reaches down and gently brushes over my hair. I almost choke.

I'm the jealous type.

Doesn't he understand that I'm Luke's now? That in — I glance up at the clock again — just over an hour I'm going to meet the man I love for the very first time?

I swallow the rest of the Snickers and stand up.

"Come on, let's go swab the water fountain," I say, determined to be all business. I'm going to focus on the experiment until this never-ending period is over.

When the bell rings for the end of science, I want to scream with relief. At last, it's time to go, time to go meet the man who loves me.

"Hey, Abby —"

"Sorry, Billy, can't talk now, I've got a math quiz," I tell him, trying to ignore the hurt, confused look on his face as I practically run out of the classroom to my locker. I dump my books and grab my backpack and then head down toward the gym, which is the best place to sneak out of the building without getting caught. I hear the bell ring just as I shut the door behind me. It feels like everyone is watching me as I walk away from the school toward the street, and I keep expecting some administrator to call me back, but nothing happens. I get to the bus stop and stand there, waiting for the bus, my stomach turning over from nerves.

I turn off my parents' cell phone because I don't want to hear from them, and I turn on Luke's. I text him that I'm on my way. Just as the bus arrives he texts me back:

Can't wait to see u, baby!

Staring out of the bus window, I'm trying to see Luke in my mind. Will he look like he did on my screen? Will it feel right when we meet each other, or awkward? I'm excited, but suddenly, I'm crazy nervous. What if he doesn't like me in real life?

By the time I get off at the Galleria stop, I'm all sweaty, so I go to the first ladies' room I see to freshen up before I meet Luke. I take off my coat and wash under my arms with a paper towel, then put on more deodorant and another spritz of Mom's perfume. I make sure my makeup looks okay and brush my hair. Then, figuring this is the best it's going to get, I head up to Cookie Madness.

He's not there.

My heart sinks. Maybe he got caught in traffic or he went to the men's room. I decide to buy two cookies, one for me and one for him. I buy myself a milk to go with mine, but I don't know if Luke likes milk. I realize there's a lot we don't know about each other. But I guess we'll have a chance to find out now that we're going to meet, finally.

I sit down at the table and nibble at my cookie, but I'm too nervous to be really hungry. Every so often, I scan the food court, but I don't see him.

Then I get a text.

> Hey, baby. I'm in the car waiting 4 u.
> Take elevator by Macys to P2.
> I'm in blue Ford Focus.

I text him back **K. CU in a few,** grab my cookies and backpack, and head for Macy's.

It takes me a few minutes to find the elevator, because I'm so used to taking the escalators. But I finally do. A woman with a baby in a stroller gets into the elevator with me.

"Can you press P2?" she says.

"Sure. That's where I'm going."

I smile at the baby. She gives me this adorable gummy grin and babbles, "A ba ba ga ga." It almost sounds like she's trying to say Abby.

"She's really cute," I say. "How old is she?"

"Six months," the lady tells me. "Her name's Samantha."

"Bye-bye, Samantha!" I wave when we get to P2. I get out first and put my hand in front of the door so it doesn't close. Samantha waves her chubby little fist back at me as her mom wheels her out of the elevator.

I see Luke's blue car outside the glass doors to the elevator area. My lips feel dry again so I reach into my coat pocket to reapply my ChapStick. I feel like I'm in a dream as I walk toward the car, my heart thudding against the wall of my chest. I can see the outline of Luke's profile. He's wearing the Red Sox hat, just like he said he would. One of the songs from his "Sexy" music mix is playing on the car stereo.

I open the car door. I can hear Samantha babbling behind me.

"Hey, beautiful," Luke says, smiling at me. There are a few

more lines on his face than I noticed on the computer screen, but other than that, he's the same Luke. The car smells faintly of cigarette smoke.

He pats the seat next to him.

I'm about to get in when someone calls, "Hold on! Wait!"

I turn around. It's Samantha's mom.

"Is this your glove?" she asks, holding up one of my blue wool gloves from Old Navy. "I think it fell out of your pocket."

"Oh, thanks!" I tell her. Samantha is giving me a big grin showing off her three teeth. I touch her waving hand and for an instant feel her warm, velvety soft skin. "Bye-bye, cutie-pie!"

Her mom smiles at me, and glances at the car briefly, before pushing the stroller away.

I look back in the car. Luke's hunched down, his hat farther over his face than it was before.

"I bought you a cookie," I tell him. I feel like a total dork the minute the words leave my mouth.

"Well, isn't that sweet? And you're even more gorgeous in person," he says. "Why don't you hop in and we can get to know each other better?"

I want to say that we already know each other, we love each other, but I guess he just means in real life. I throw my backpack in the backseat and take my place in the front. Then I shut the door and he drives away.

CHAPTER 13
LILY ♪ DECEMBER 7 10:00 P.M.

Abby's gone and it's all my fault.

When I got home from school this afternoon there was, like, this weird emptiness. It's not like Abby's usually there welcoming me home with milk and cookies or anything, like Shelley Adkin's mom does, except Shelley's mom gives her "healthy snacks" instead of cookies. But this afternoon the house was super quiet — none of that "Baw, baw, I'm so depressed" emo music blaring from Abby's room like it usually is. I called out, "Abby? Abs, are you home?" but — nothing. I looked around the kitchen to see if there was a note but there wasn't.

At first I was mad, like, why didn't anyone tell me that Abby was staying after school and I'd be coming home to an empty house? It's not like I *need* Abby there — I'm in seventh grade and I took the babysitting class so I can babysit little kids myself if I want. It's just I like to know what's what. I guess I'm like Dad that way.

I got myself a snack and watched TV for a while, and then I sat at the kitchen table and started my homework. Mom called me at about five, to tell me she had to pick up a few things at the grocery store on the way home and she'd be home about a quarter to six.

"Where's Abby?" I asked her.

"What do you mean?" Mom said.

"She's not home. Did she stay after school or something?"

At first Mom was more mad than scared. "Well, she didn't say anything to *me* about staying after school. And she's *supposed* to be grounded."

"Well, she's not here."

"I'll call Mrs. Wilson on my way to the supermarket. Abby's probably over there. And now she's going to be even more grounded. I'll see you later. Finish your homework!"

She hung up and I went back to my homework, although I was doing it in front of the TV, something my parents consider a serious no-no. They don't think I can do two things at once, but that's just because they're old and they don't know how to multitask.

Fifteen minutes later, Mom called back. She sounded kind of . . . stressed.

"Lily, I keep calling Abby's cell and it just goes straight to voice mail. And I called the Wilsons' — Faith says she hasn't seen Abby since the bus this morning. She wasn't in gym class. Faith thought maybe Abby was at the nurse, so she didn't think anything of it. . . . Oh, Lord, where has that girl got to? I'm going to kill her, I really am."

"Mom . . . do you think . . . Like, could someone have kidnapped her or something?"

"I'm sure Abby is fine, honey. She's just being irresponsible and forgot to call." She said it like she was trying to convince herself as well as me. "I'll be home in five minutes. Forget the groceries. See you soon."

I couldn't concentrate on my homework after that. I kept imagining all the terrible things that could be happening to Abby. I'm not going to pretend that there haven't been plenty of times that I've imagined doing some pretty awful things to Abby myself — but that's because she's such a weirdo and I wish she were more fun and normal like Jeanine's sister. I mean, Mom's probably right. I bet Abby's just being an irresponsible jerk and is over at one of her weirdo friends' houses. But what if she isn't? The thought that she might be out there somewhere, who knows where, with some stranger who might —

When I heard Mom's car pull into the driveway, I unlocked the front door and threw myself into her arms, crying, before she even walked in the door. She hugged me, hard, and I felt her shoulders heave like she was crying, too, but when I lifted my head she was already pulling herself together into Take Charge Mom mode.

"Come on, Lily. Calm down. I'm going to go inside and call the police. I called Dad and he's going to wrap things up at the office and come home early."

That got me scared. Dad coming home early? They must have been more worried than Mom was letting on.

Mom threw her coat on the table, a sign of her distress. Normally, she hangs it up before she does anything, then heads straight to the kettle to put the water on for a cup of tea. It's like her after-work ritual. She grabbed the phone and then started muttering to herself.

"Do I dial 911? Is this an emergency or should I dial the non-emergency number?"

"It's an emergency, Mom!" I said. "Someone could be, like, *killing* Abby right this very minute."

Mom lost it.

"NO ONE IS KILLING ABBY!" she shouted at me. "ABBY IS GOING TO BE FINE!"

I stared at her, wide eyed.

How do you know? is what I thought.

"Okay, okay, I'm sorry" is what I said. "But I still think you should call 911."

It was like Mom was determined to keep it from being a crisis, like the force of her will could keep anything bad from happening to Abby.

"No, I don't want to burden the 911 system. I'm going to call the nonemergency number. Like I said, Abby's probably just being disobedient. I'll bet anything she's gone to a friend's house and forgot to call."

"Abby doesn't have that many friends. And why isn't she answering her cell?"

"I don't know. Maybe she forgot to charge it and the battery died. Or maybe she's still mad at me because Dad and I grounded her, so she's not picking up when I call. Or . . . wait a minute — what about that boy she went on the date with? What was his name?"

"Jimmy. No . . . Billy. I can't remember his last name. Faith will know."

"Right. I'll call the Wilsons again."

Faith told my mom that Billy's last name was Fisher. Mom looked up his number in the student directory and called his house. I was so glad it wasn't someone *I'd* gone out on a date with — can you imagine the embarrassment of having your mom call the guy you're crushing on to ask him where you are? I'd die. But then, I wouldn't do what Abby's done. I wouldn't disappear and not tell anyone where I was and not answer my cell.

"Hello, Mrs. Fisher, this is Kate Johnston, Abby's mother. Billy and Abby are in the same science class. . . . Yes, that's right. I think they went to the movies a month or two back? I was just wondering if by any chance Abby happened to be over there? She's not home and she isn't answering her cell. . . . No?"

I could almost see Mom deflate as she said the word *no*. I think she was really counting on Abby being at Billy Fisher's so she didn't have to call the police.

"Well, thank you for your time. Have a good evening."

She hung up, took a deep breath, and called information, asking for the police nonemergency number. Mom was busy explaining about Abby being missing when Dad walked in.

"Is Abby home yet?"

"No — and Mom's on the phone with the police."

Dad paled, and he practically collapsed into one of the kitchen chairs, his briefcase dropping from his hand to the kitchen floor with a loud thump.

"I've called her best friend, who said she saw Abby on the school bus this morning but that she wasn't in gym class, which is later in the day. . . . Yes, I've tried calling her cell several times, but I think it must be turned off because it keeps going straight to voice mail. . . . But Abby is usually very responsible — if she's going to be late she always calls. . . . I see. So, if she's not home, and we haven't heard from her by eight o'clock, I should call you back. But . . . yes, I understand. Okay, thank you, Officer."

Mom hung up the phone and slumped into the nearest chair.

"Kate, don't tell me they aren't doing anything," Dad said. "Are you telling me my daughter is out there somewhere and the police, whose salaries are paid by *my taxes*, aren't going to *get off their asses and go look for her*? I'm going to call them back and give them a piece of my mind!"

Even when he's losing it, Dad never forgets to remind you who pays the bills.

Dad got up and reached for the phone, but Mom grabbed it before he could get there.

"*No*, Rick. Don't antagonize them. We need their help and this is the usual procedure. Right now the best thing we can do is call around to the people who know Abby, and look through her room to see if there are any clues to where she might be."

"But, Kate, my daughter —"

"Rick, she's *my* daughter, too. If you want to help, call Elaine Wilson back and get Faith to help you make a list of all Abby's friends. Then use the school directory and call them."

The look on Dad's face said he didn't agree, but he would do it anyway.

"Okay. Just give me the phone already."

Mom handed it to him and turned her gaze to me.

"Lily, you come upstairs with me. We're going to go through Abby's room and see if we can find anything that might tell us where she is."

I couldn't believe my ears. *Mom was going to let* me *go through Abby's stuff?* If I needed any proof that the world was turned upside down, this was it. Abby would *freak* if she knew. That's if she ever gets home again to find out. But it serves her right for putting us through this.

We went upstairs to Abby's room.

"I'll take her closet and bedside table, you take the desk," Mom said.

There was the same weird stillness in Abby's room that had been there earlier. I've snooped in Abby's room before and it's always been kind of nerve-racking because I've felt her presence even when I've known she was staying at Faith's overnight. But this time, it was like even though all her normal Abby things were there, the room was devoid of some essential Abby-ness. And that made me scared. So scared that my hands were shaking as I opened her desk drawers and started going through her stuff.

Her drawers were so much neater than mine. Abby's really organized and particular like Dad. I think that's why he loves her more. All my life it's been "your sister, Abby, this" and "your sister, Abby, that" and "Abby got an A in that class" from Dad. I wonder what he's thinking now about my shining example of a sister. But I know if something's happened to her, I'd never live up to her in his eyes, and — I had to stop for a minute to give myself a silent pep talk:

Don't think about this. Abby's fine. She's a stupid, selfish idiot for coming home late and forgetting to call and making Mom and Dad and me crazy and scared and worried, but right now she is absolutely rootin' tootin' one hundred percent F-I-N-E fine.

If I ever pulled an Abby and someone had to go through my stuff (which I'd *hate*), they'd barely be able to get the drawers open, they're stuffed so full with notes and makeup and nail polish and old issues of *Seventeen* and *Girls' Life*.

But Abby's drawers weren't like that.

Drawer Number 1: Pens, pencils, highlighter, pencil sharpener, cool fake sushi eraser, which I was tempted to steal because I deserved it after what she was putting me through, ruler, calculator. *Boooooring.*

Drawer Number 2: Nail file, a few rubber bracelets, purple nail polish, black nail polish. *OMG, could she get any MORE emo?* Clear lip gloss. *Come on, Abby, live a little!*

This is such a waste of time.

Other than the fake sushi eraser, I didn't find anything remotely interesting, and definitely nothing that might tell us where Abby went. Although — what a blind idiot! Sitting right in front of me on the middle of her desk were her *schoolbooks*. The ones she was *supposed* to have taken to *school* that morning.

So the whole time Abby was in the kitchen stealing my breakfast, she knew she was going to walk out and leave us. And whatever she had in her backpack, it sure wasn't books.

I was so mad, I reached into the drawer for her fake sushi eraser and put it in my pocket. *Serves her right for being such a big fat Eggo-scarfing liar.*

"Mom, Abby didn't take her books to school today. They're right here on her desk."

My mother was looking in Abby's closet. She had this seriously awful look on her face when she turned to me, like she'd finally started to realize that something really, really bad might be happening here. Like, *hello, Mom!*

I started looking through Abby's notebooks. The top one was labeled *Science* and it had *Billy Fisher* and a phone number scribbled across the top. That was the guy she had that date with. But if she's not with him and she's not with Faith, then who the heck is she with?

"What's this?" Mom said, pulling a piece of paper out from the back of Abby's closet. "I can't believe it! She got a C-minus on a science test and she didn't even tell us? She made it sound like the D she got in math was a one-off!"

Wow. Perfect Abby really *had* fallen off her pedestal.

"Wait till your father sees this," Mom muttered.

I flipped through the science notebook to see if Abby drew or doodled like regular people. Forms of Energy, *Boring!* Nature and Properties of Earth Materials, *Dullness!* Characteristics of Living Matter, *Oh, look, Abby finally doodled something . . . a flower, cute!* Energy Transfer and Transformation, *Zzzzzzzzzzz . . . Wait!*

The margins of Abby's notebook gradually did become filled with doodles and they were all of the same thing — a name that I'd never heard her mention, ever. Luke. She'd drawn *Abby and Luke* entwined with elaborate flowers and, yuck, she'd signed her name Abby Redmond like she was daydreaming about *marrying* the guy. *Abby?* Quickly, I paged through her other notebooks and found the same thing — pages of margin doodles devoted to this Luke Redmond guy.

"Mom? I don't know . . . but . . . I think maybe Abby might have met someone."

"What makes you think that?" she said, coming over.

I showed her the notebook.

"Who is this Luke Redmond person?" Mom asked. "Has Abby ever mentioned him to you?"

"Are you *kidding*? *Abby* talk to *me* about *anything*?"

Mom grabbed another of Abby's notebooks and started flipping through the pages, all frantic.

"His name's all over this one, too. Who *is* this guy? Why haven't we ever heard about him?"

"Ask Faith. Maybe she knows."

"I will. Right now."

Mom grabbed the notebooks and we headed back to the kitchen. She showed Dad the doodles.

"Kate, do you think she . . . she wouldn't . . ."

"Dammit, Rick, I don't know! I don't know anything right now!"

Now it was Mom who sounded like she was about to lose it.

"Give me the phone. I need to call the Wilsons again."

When she got Faith on the phone, it turned out Faith had never heard of Luke, either. But apparently, Abby had been talking about some mystery guy she met at the church retreat she went to last summer in the Berkshires, and said maybe someday she and Faith could double-date.

"Do you think this church retreat person could be Luke Redmond?" Mom asked. "And, Faith . . . Abby didn't take her books to school today. Do you think she might have . . . she didn't say anything to you about . . . going to meet him, did she? You aren't covering for her, are you? This is really serious."

I think Mom would have been happy if Faith had just said, "Okay, yeah, I'm sorry, I was covering for her and this is where they went," as long as it meant she knew where Abby was. But she didn't. From what I could hear, Faith just started crying and said she wasn't covering for Abby. She said she had no idea where Abby was, honest, and she wished like anything that she did. Mom's face went as pale as death. I started crying, too.

"I'm sorry, Faith, you're Abby's best friend and I had to ask," Mom said, a tremor in her voice. "Thanks for all your help. Tell your mom I'll keep you posted."

She hung up the phone and covered her face with her hands.

"That's it," Dad said. "I'm calling the police again."

Mom didn't argue with him this time, and that made me cry harder.

Dad called the number Mom had written down on the yellow pad by the phone.

"Is this Officer Carozza? My wife spoke to you earlier about our daughter, Abby. Abigail Johnston. She's still missing and you need to get on it. I . . . What? . . . Yes, we've tried calling her friends. Nobody knows anything, other than she took the bus to school in the morning but wasn't there for gym halfway through the day. No, she's not answering her cell phone. Yes . . . I . . . You'll come out now? Okay, we're here. . . . Yes, of course, we'll call right away if we hear from her. See you shortly."

Dad gave him the address and hung up. He slumped into the nearest chair.

"He says he'll be here in fifteen minutes. He's going to need .to ask us background questions about Abby."

"Maybe I should make dinner," Mom said, but she didn't move and none of us were hungry anyway. We all just sat there, listening to the clock tick every never-ending second and watching the phone that didn't ring with Abby's call.

When the doorbell rang, it made me jump.

"I'll get it," I said, but Dad stopped me.

"You stay here, Lily," he said. "Let me get this."

I sank back into the chair, frustrated. I was sick of sitting around doing nothing. Mom was sitting there like a freaking zombie, staring at the phone as if she could will it to ring by using some mad psychic skills she'd never told us about. But the phone just hung there on the wall. No ringing. No Abby.

"Kate, this is Officer Carozza," Dad said, coming into the kitchen with the police officer, who was complete with handcuffs and a gun on his belt. I'd never seen a real gun so close up before. It freaked me out.

"Good evening, ma'am," Officer Carozza said.

Mom went from zombie to Martha Stewart mode in the blink of an eye.

"Can I get you something to drink?" she said.

"No, thank you. I just need to ask you a few questions."

"Oh . . . Okay," Mom said. "Why don't you have a seat?"

Officer Carozza sat at the table and took out a notebook and pen.

He asked a bunch of stuff Mom and Dad had already said on the phone, like Abby's full name and address and date of birth and stuff. I could tell that Dad was getting annoyed. I was wondering when the officer was going to get to the finding-Abby part myself.

"So Abigail normally comes home on time?" Officer Carozza asked.

"Always," Mom said. "She's very responsible. And if she were going to be late, she would call. She has a cell phone."

"What's her number?"

Mom gave him the number.

"You've tried calling it?"

"I've been trying constantly. It keeps going straight to voice mail, so it's either turned off or the battery's dead."

"That's too bad," Officer Carozza said. "If it's turned on, we can get the cell company to ping the phone to see which cell towers it's responding to and get some idea of the child's general location."

"There's no way to do it if the phone is off?" Dad asked. Knowing Dad, he probably thought there had to be some technological fix for everything.

"No, I'm afraid not. And you've called all her friends? Any likely place where she might be hanging out?"

"Yes, Officer," Dad said. He was losing his struggle to remain patient. "I told you that on the phone."

Mom gave Dad a *Shut up and don't make the policeman mad* look, which Dad ignored.

"When did you realize Abigail was missing?"

I spoke up.

"Abby's usually here when I get home from school," I told him. "But when I got home —"

"What time was that?" Officer Carozza asked.

"About twenty past three," I said. "Well, she wasn't here. I didn't freak out at first — I thought maybe she'd stayed after school and no one told me, because, like no one ever tells me anything, but when Mom called me at five to say she was on the way home, she didn't know about Abby either."

"To be honest, Officer, I was angry with her at first, because she's supposed to be grounded," Mom said.

"Grounded? So Abby was in trouble? Did you fight with her?"

"She got a D on her math test," Mom said. "Math is one of her best subjects. It's not like her to do so badly."

"Abby is an honor student," Dad bragged. He couldn't resist the opportunity to talk about how smart Abby is, even when she might be off with some crazy person.

"So you've noticed some slippage in her grades recently?" Officer Carozza asked.

"I guess you could say that. Even more than we'd realized, Rick," Mom said. "I just found a science test from eight weeks ago where she'd gotten a C-minus, hidden in the back of her closet."

"Are you kidding me?" Dad said. He sounded really mad. If Abby were to walk in the door then, I'm not sure if he would have been more relieved to see her home or mad about the science test.

"We thought it was because she was spending too much time chatting with her friends on her computer while she was supposed to be doing homework," Mom explained. "So last night we took her laptop away."

It was like suddenly someone turned on a switch inside Officer Carozza as he looked up from his notes.

"Does Abby spend a lot of time online?"

"Quite a bit, yes," Mom said. "Enough that I think it was starting to affect her grades, at least."

"Do you know what sites she was on? Did she have a MySpace or Facebook profile?"

"She definitely has a Facebook," I said. "Not MySpace, I don't think. But, Mom, tell him about the notebooks."

"When Abby went to school this morning she left what looks like most of her schoolbooks on her desk," Mom said. "But Lily says her backpack looked full, so . . . maybe . . . could she have been *planning* to go?"

"Kate, you can't possibly believe that Abby would be stupid and irresponsible enough to run away —"

"Mr. Johnston, if she's been engaging with an Internet predator, then nothing would surprise me," Officer Carozza said. "I'm not saying that's the case here, but whenever a kid has been active online we have to consider the possibility."

"*Internet predator?*" Dad said, his face turning gray. "Abby? No . . ."

"She wrote some guy's name in all her notebooks," I blurted out, since no one else seemed to be telling Officer Carozza this and it seemed kinda like something he should know. "Look here."

I opened her science notebook to the first of the Luke Redmond doodles, then turned a few pages for him so he could see that she had been carried away enough about the guy to experiment with "Abby Redmond" signatures. *Yuck.*

"It's like this in her other notebooks, too."

Officer Carozza stood up.

"I'm going to place a call to our Youth Division, and get one of our detectives out here as soon as possible. Did you say you had Abby's computer?"

"Yes," Mom said. "I've got it hidden up in my closet."

"We'll want to take that down to headquarters and get our forensic guys on it to see what sites Abby's been on and who she's been talking to. Do you know her passwords?"

"I . . . no. We don't," Mom said. "Is that a problem?"

"It depends on the site," Officer Carozza said. "Let's just go one step at a time."

Mom ran upstairs to get Abby's laptop. Dad looked at me across the table and said, "Lily, I want you to write down the password to every single Internet account you have right now."

It was so unfair.

"What? Just because there's some remote possibility that Abby might have been stupid enough to run off with some freak, you're going to start snooping through my e-mails?"

"We recommend that all parents have their kids' passwords. Just in case," said Officer Carozza. "It's a wild world out there."

"Yeah, I know, we've been having the Internet Safety talk at school every year since, like, fourth grade or something. But I'm not like Abby. I only talk to my *friends.*"

He just gave me this *Yeah, right, I've heard that one before* look, as Mom came into the kitchen with Abby's laptop. She turned it on, but as soon as it booted up, instead of the usual emo band picture, there was a password screen.

"Since when has Abby had a password to get into her computer?" Mom asked. "I'm sure she never used to have one — did she, Rick?"

Dad stared at the screen helplessly, shaking his head.

"Don't worry, Mrs. Johnston. The forensic team won't have any trouble getting what we need off here, password or no password. That's what they do."

He took out a plastic bag and put Abby's laptop in it, and got my dad to sign something.

"I'll get this down to the computer forensic guys. I'm not sure what their caseload's like at the moment. It might take them a little while to get to it. But it'll definitely give us some clues about what we're dealing with here. In the meantime, let us know if you hear anything. I also want to get a list from you, Mrs. Johnston, of the names and phone numbers of Abby's close friends. I'll have the officers on the next shift set up appointments for them to be interviewed at their homes first thing in the morning before they go to school. And you'll probably get a call from one of our Youth Division detectives later tonight."

"Officer, what are the chances . . ." Dad started to ask but then he covered his face with his hands.

My heart felt like it was playing hopscotch while I waited to hear the policeman's answer.

"Mr. Johnston, we'll do everything we can to bring Abby back home safely," he said.

Which told us absolutely zip about her chances.

OMG, Abby, where are you?

I was just finishing my homework after getting home from stage crew when Mom called up to me saying that Mrs. Johnston was on the phone asking about Abby. I'd wondered where she was during gym, because she was on the bus this morning. She even sat next to me, which has been a touch-and-go thing lately. Some days she just smiles at me and then goes to sit by herself in an empty seat, like sitting by herself is better than sitting next to me, which really hurts, if you want to know the truth. I don't know what's going on with her. Well, *obviously*, I don't know what's going on with her, if she's disappeared without saying a word to me about it. There was a time when we didn't do anything without telling each other. And this . . . this is so . . . so *major*. It's like I don't know Abby anymore. How could she be so thoughtless?

It's almost midnight now and I can't sleep. I'm trying to remember everything and anything I can think of that might help them find Abby. Mrs. Johnston called about eleven p.m. and said a policeman is coming tomorrow morning to interview me. I'm nervous because I've never, ever in my whole life been interviewed by the police before. I mean it's not like I've done anything wrong, but still. It's the *police*.

Instead of lying here tossing and turning, looking at the glow-in-the-dark stars on the ceiling (Abby always loved those), I get out of bed and find a notebook and a pen. I'm going to make a list.

I think back to this morning when Abby got on the bus. I close my eyes and visualize her. What was she wearing? I remember thinking that she looked really pretty, like she'd made an effort. She'd put makeup on and everything, just like the first day of school. And she was wearing a cute sweater — green, I think, because it brought out that color in her eyes. Abby has those cool hazel eyes that change color depending on what she's wearing.

1. Wearing makeup. Green sweater. Jeans.

What else? Okay, she sat next to me, which has been iffy recently, but I don't think the police want to hear about all the ups and downs of our friendship. They'd probably get all "typical adolescent girl stuff" on me. But then I think of something else:

2. Seemed happier than she has recently.

Because she did. Abby's been such a . . . well, I hate to say it about my best friend, but I have to be honest here . . . *downer* since we started high school. But this morning she was, like, all bubbly and talkative and, oh, there's another thing:

3. She talked about her mysterious boyfriend, Church Retreat Guy.

She said that things were going "really well" and maybe sometime Teddy and I could double-date with them. I got all excited because she's been so secretive about the guy. I said, "Oh, Abs, that would be so cool. I'm dying to meet him!"

I wonder if she's run away to meet him somewhere. But that would be so unlike Abby. It's so dangerous and stupid. She's *way* too smart for that. And she would have told me. I can't believe she would do something that major without telling me.

But she *has* done something without telling me. She's disappeared, without telling anyone, not even me, where she's gone. *Why, Abby? Why? Couldn't you have trusted me?*

Then I remember how angry Abby was when I told Dad about her fainting at the auditions. How even though she said she forgave me, things weren't quite the same between us after that.

I only did it because I was worried about you, Abby. Because you're my best friend. Because I care.

What else did we talk about? I'm trying to remember every word in case there is a hidden clue, but it was *morning* and I'm not fully functional till halfway through first period. Oh, yes —

4. Backpack was heavy.

I only noticed because when she sat down next to me she accidentally half put it on my leg and I made a joke about her having rocks in it. She said she had both her math and science books in it because she was studying for tests. I'm such an *idiot*! I should have realized she was lying about the math test because we both have Mr. Evans and we just *had* a test. There isn't another one till right before Christmas break. I mean, Abby's a good student and all, but even she doesn't start studying *this* far out. If only I'd realized.

But then what would I have done? Said, "Abs, you're full of it? There's no math test? What's *really* in there?"

Would she have told me the truth? Would I have been able to stop her? If I'd been a better friend, could I have kept her safe?

Probably not. She probably would have just given me a dirty look and moved to another seat. Like I said, things have been kind of awkward between us recently. But I can't help thinking that there must have been something I could have said or done or noticed that would have stopped her.

I fall asleep with the light on and my face planted on the notepad, the thought running on a constant loop in my head that, somehow, I might have been able to keep my friend safe.

I'm *soooo* tired. I'm tired of hearing the same questions over and over and over. Detective Larson from the Youth Division is here with Officer Gans. I had to tell them all the same stuff I told Officer Carozza. I don't get it. Why can't they just talk to each other or read each other's notes or something?

The same questions: What happened when you got home? Did you try calling her cell phone? Have you called her friends? Is Abby normally reliable? Have you noticed any change in her recently? Have her grades slipped at all? Does she spend a lot of time online?

But then Detective Larson lobs out one we haven't heard before:

"Mr. and Mrs. Johnston, is Abby promiscuous?"

I'm not sure what *promiscuous* means, but the question sure pisses Dad off. His face turns bright red and he half rises out of his chair, shouting, *"How dare you!"* before Mom puts her hand on his arm to push him back down and shut him up.

"Detective, Abby has barely been on any dates," Mom says. "She's a good girl. She went on a church retreat last summer."

"And she is *not* promiscuous," Dad growls, his arms crossed firmly across his chest.

Okaay . . . So I'm guessing promiscuous *means being all slutty and stuff. Nah. Not Abby. She's too busy being a boring nerd with no life. Wait. I don't mean no life. Please let her have a life. Even if it is a boring, nerdy one.*

"And you fought the night before she left about . . . grades, was it?"

"That's right," Mom says. She sounds as tired as I feel. "She brought down her math test for me to sign because she'd gotten a D. I know it might not sound like the end of the world, Detective, but if you knew Abby — math is one of her best subjects and she normally gets A's and A-pluses. So for her to get a D, well . . ."

"So her grades have been slipping. Have you noticed that Abby seemed less involved with the family recently?"

"I haven't noticed that," Dad says.

"Well, *you* wouldn't," I say. "*You're* never here."

I see the detective's pen move across his pad. If my father had killer vision, I'd be seriously dead right now.

Mom steps in to keep World War III from breaking out.

"My husband started his own accounting firm a year ago, so he's been working very long hours." She smiles at the detective. "You know how it is."

He nods but keeps writing.

"Abby was very angry last night. She said . . . she . . ."

Mom puts her hand over her eyes.

"She said she . . . hated me."

Her shoulders heave with suppressed sobs. Dad puts his arm around her and murmurs something I can't hear.

"Detective, is it my fault she's gone?" Mom asks. "If anything happens to her, I don't know what I'll do."

"Of course it's not your fault, Kate," Dad says. "Don't say that."

Mom thinks it's her fault. Dad doesn't seem to think it's his fault, not at all. But deep down, in a place I don't want to go, or let some police officer pry, I know it's because of me, and I don't know how I'm going to live in this family if something really bad happens to Abby.

"Do you have a recent picture of Abby that I can have?" Detective Larson asks.

"Yes," Dad says. "I'll get one."

He goes to print one off his computer, leaving Mom and me with the detective.

"When I get back to headquarters, I'm going to enter Abby's data into the NCIC computer system. That's the FBI's National Crime Information Center. We also have a special computer system provided to us by the National Center for Missing and Exploited Children. I can scan the picture you give me into it and generate a flyer that will be distributed to all the departments in the area. We'll also have our patrol officers check out the local parks and other teen hangouts."

"But, Detective," Mom sniffs. "Abby's not a hanger outer. She just . . . isn't. It's not her."

"Mrs. Johnston, we have to investigate all the possibilities, especially until we see what the forensic analysts find on Abby's computer."

Dad comes back with, like, five pictures of Abby, as if he doesn't get that this is for a picture on a milk carton, not a freaking modeling portfolio. Somehow, I don't think being on *America's Next Top Model* was ever part of Abby's plan.

"I wasn't sure which one was best, so . . ."

The detective takes all of them. ·

"Great. We'll figure out which one works for the poster. We'll be interviewing Abby's friends and trying to get a picture of what went on today" — he glances at his watch — "er . . . yesterday . . . and I'll try to see if I can put some pressure on the forensic team to expedite the work on Abby's computer. Unfortunately, they've got a big backlog, so we're always fighting for priority."

He sees Dad open his mouth to argue but he raises his hand and continues. "Believe me, Mr. Johnston, we take missing minors seriously and we'll do everything we can to bring Abby back home safely. In the meantime, you call me if you hear from her or if you think of anything else that might help with the investigation, okay?"

Mom and Dad nod.

The detective's cell phone rings. "Larson . . . Yep . . . Good. I'll be back soon."

He closes his cell and tells us that they've made arrangements to have officers interview Faith at six thirty tomorrow morning since she saw Abby after we did.

"So early?" Mom says.

"Every minute counts," Detective Larson tells her.

Mom looks like she's about to crumple in on herself. I feel like I'm going to throw up, even though we never ate dinner and there's not really anything in my stomach. And Dad . . . I don't ever in a million years want to see that look on his face again.

CHAPTER 16
FAITH ♪ DECEMBER 8 5:45 A.M.

Dad shakes me awake at five forty-five a.m. "Faith, honey, the police will be here at six thirty to talk to you about Abby," he says. "Mom's got coffee on in the kitchen."

I'm totally out of it, but I go take a shower to try to bring myself back into the land of the living. I just can't believe this is happening. It's like some really awful nightmare that I should be able to pinch myself and wake up from, except I am awake and it's real. Abby's still missing and I keep wondering over and over if I could have done something to stop this from happening.

By the time I get dressed and blow-dry my hair, Mom and Dad are sitting at the kitchen table with a guy in a jacket and tie and another in a police uniform.

"Faith, this is Detective Larson," Mom says. "And this is Officer Gans. They want to ask you about when you last saw Abby."

"Can you describe when you last saw Abby Johnston and what she was wearing?" the detective asks me.

I tell him about the bus yesterday. About Abby in the green, fuzzy sweater that matched her eyes, and the fact that she was wearing makeup, when she didn't always make an effort. How she seemed in a good mood, and her backpack seemed heavier than usual. How she lied to me about studying for the math test, but I didn't pick up on it at the time.

"Is Abby a habitual liar?" Officer Gans asks.

"No! Not at all," I protest. "Abby was . . . I mean Abby *is* my best friend. We've always told each other the truth about everything — well, until now, I guess. She has been kind of . . . I don't know . . . moody lately. And she doesn't tell me everything like she used to. Like about this guy she met at the church retreat."

"Tell us more about Abby's friend from the retreat," Detective Larson says.

"That's the thing. I don't really know that much. She was kind of weird about him. Like, I couldn't believe she didn't tell me about him right away when she met him. We always tell each other everything — or at least we used to. But with this guy, it was this big secret. I thought she liked Billy Fisher. She even went out on a date with him. But then, she kept, I don't know, blowing hot and cold on the poor guy. I felt sorry for him because Billy's such a nice guy and I think he really likes Abby. And then, suddenly, out of the blue, she was talking about this mystery guy from the retreat."

"Did she mention a name?" Officer Gans asks.

"No. Until yesterday she never even talked about me meeting him." I see them exchanging glances. "Like, normally we'd be talking about our crushes constantly. But Abby was kind of . . ."

I feel tears welling up, and it's hard to admit this in front of my parents.

"Abby was pulling away from me recently. Like she didn't always sit with me on the bus in the morning and sometimes when I IM'ed her she'd ignore me, even though I could see she was online."

Mom reaches out, puts her hand over mine, and squeezes. Dad hands me a napkin to blow my nose.

"Do you know what websites Abby likes to go on?" Detective Larson asks me.

"Sure," I sniff. "She's on Facebook, and we use MSN to chat. But her favorite's ChezTeen.com."

"That's a new one to me," he says. "Can you spell that?"

"C-H-E-Z-T-E-E-N dot com," I tell him. "It's newish, but it's such a cool site."

"Does it have private chat rooms?" Officer Gans asks.

I nod.

"Do you have to be friends to chat, or can anyone chat with you?"

"Anyone can chat with you," I tell him. "It's like being in a real-life café or at a concert. That's what's so cool about it."

"That's what's so dangerous about it, Faith," my dad says. "I didn't realize you were going on sites like that."

"But, Dad, I don't talk to creepy people. I only talk to people I know, like Abby and Gracie and other kids from school."

"Did Abby talk to people she didn't know?"

"No. I mean, I don't think so. . . . Well . . . maybe . . . once that I know of. It was ages ago, like right before school started. We were chatting about what we were going to wear for the first day and some guy started talking to us about what we were wearing and music and stuff."

"Do you remember his screen name?"

I rack my brain, trying to remember, but I can't.

"All I remember is that he said he was already out of

high school, so I IM'ed Abby on MSN and told her maybe we shouldn't be talking to him because he might be a perv or something."

"Good thinking," Mom says.

"Abby said it didn't matter because it wasn't like we were telling him where we lived or anything, which was true. We were talking about music mostly. I think he and Abby liked a lot of the same music — like it was really weird, their top twenty iPod songs were practically identical. He said they were musical soul mates or something totally corny like that."

My parents exchange glances with the police officer.

"What? Is Abby going to be okay?"

"Faith, there's a possibility that Abby might have gone to meet someone she met online," Officer Gans says. "Does the name Luke Redmond ring a bell?"

I shake my head.

"Luke? Is that the guy from the church retreat?"

"If there *is* a guy from the church retreat," Detective Larson says. "We'll be speaking to the youth director at Abby's church later today."

Did you lie about that, too, Abby? What happened to my friend?

I'm scared for Abby but now I'm mad, too. Mad at her for lying to me. Mad at her for lying to all of us. *Why, Abby? Why?!*

CHAPTER 17

I thought Dad was going to beat the crap out of me last night when he told me the police were coming this morning to interview me "in connection with Abigail Johnston."

"*Police?*" I said, my mouth dry all of a sudden. "Why? What's up with Abby?"

"Well, apparently the young lady is *missing*."

I felt like someone sucker punched me.

"Abby? . . . Missing? . . . Since when?! I saw her in science yesterday and . . ."

She looked so gorgeous in that green, fuzzy sweater that matched her eyes perfectly.

My mother came and stood in the doorway to my room.

"Billy, isn't Abby the same girl who came here for a study date? The one who you went to the movies with?"

"Yeah. Like I said, she's in my science class. I don't understand, she was there yesterday morning —"

She said that it was safer to kiss a dog than a human. Was that a blow-off or just a scientific fact?

"Her mother called earlier to see if she was here," Mom said.

"I thought it was strange, because you haven't seen her or talked about her lately."

"Her *mom* called here? When? Why didn't you tell me?"

Mom shrugged.

Of course my dad started to think the worst of me right from the beginning.

"Son, you didn't . . . force yourself on this girl, did you?"

I would have laughed out loud if I didn't think my dad would have smacked me for doing it. *My own father thinks I raped a girl.* Me, the guy who never even made it to second base.

Mom blew a gasket.

"Will, how can you even *think* such an *awful thing* about your *own son*? Billy would *never* do a thing like that —"

Good to know at least one *of my parents trusts me to do the right thing.*

"Sandy! I asked Billy a question and I want him to answer."

I squared my shoulders and looked my dad straight in the eye.

"No, Dad. I did not *force myself* on Abby. Are you happy now?"

"Don't be fresh with me, kid. I'm just trying to find out why the *police* are coming to investigate *my son*."

"Maybe because I *saw* Abby yesterday? Like, before she went *missing*?"

"That makes sense, Will," Mom said.

Dad seemed to calm down a little. But only a little.

"The police will be here at six forty-five. Make sure you're up and dressed. And brush your hair, for Pete's sake. You don't want to look like a slob in front of the police."

Yeah, because with Abby missing, MY HAIR is the first thing they're going to care about. Right.

"Will do, Dad."

When my alarm goes off at six I want to smash it to smithereens. It was hard to sleep after my little heart-to-heart with Dad. Instead, I hit the OFF button with my fist and drag my tired, sorry butt out of bed and down the hall into the shower.

I keep seeing Abby's face through the steam. The way she looked in the flickering light of the movie we barely watched right before we kissed for the first time. How she laughed at me yesterday morning in science when I made the comment about not eating my own poop or licking my . . . yeah. At least I didn't finish the joke, which was that it wasn't for lack of trying. The private licking part, that is.

Abby, where are you? How could you just be here one day and gone the next?

I'm just heading downstairs to get some breakfast, my hair neatly brushed, when the doorbell rings. I check my watch. Six forty-five on the nose. These guys are prompt.

Mom tells me to hurry up and eat something — she'll get the door. I grab a PowerBar and pour myself a glass of milk.

I hear the guys identifying themselves, showing Mom and Dad their badges, then Mom shows them into the fancy living room, the one we hardly ever use.

Dad comes into the kitchen.

"Hurry up. Make sure you look them in the eye when you answer their questions and call them 'sir' or 'officer.' And tuck in your shirt, for chrissake!"

I follow him into the living room, where Mom stands with the two police officers. They have handcuffs on their belts. And guns. *Holy crap.*

"Good morning, Billy. I'm Sergeant Marr," the taller one says. "And this is Officer Conner."

I make sure to look him in the eye when I say, "Good morning, sir."

"Please have a seat," Mom says. "Would you like some coffee?"

Next thing you know she's going to be cooking these guys breakfast while I'm here shitting a brick.

"No, thanks. We're good," Officer Conner says.

I sit in the chair closest to the door. My leg starts jumping up and down the way it always does when I'm nervous.

"So, Billy, can you tell us about when you last saw Miss Johnston?" Sergeant Marr says, pulling a notebook out of his pocket.

"Uh . . . it was yesterday. Fourth period. In science. We did a lab together. Abby's my lab partner."

"What time is fourth period?"

"It starts at ten after ten and ends at eleven."

"Did anything seem out of the ordinary about Abby's behavior in class yesterday?" Officer Conner asks.

I try to think back to yesterday morning, but all I can think is that Abby is gone. That she's *disappeared*, like those kids on the milk cartons. That someone could be hurting her right now while we're sitting around in my parents' fancy living room, talking. I want to throw up.

"I . . . don't know. . . . I —"

"Take a minute," Sergeant Marr says.

The two officers are watching me intently and I suddenly think, *Holy crap! Do they think I had anything to do with this? Yeah, I have a serious crush on the girl, but we just went to the movies once and then she's pretty much been driving me crazy since then, being friendly but always running away when I try to ask her out again. Does that give me motive? Oh, man. But I HAVEN'T. DONE. ANYTHING.*

I put my head in my hands to blot out the police and my parents, who are staring at me, too, and try to focus on science class yesterday. Abby. How cute she looked in that green, fuzzy sweater; how it brought out the color of her eyes and made me want to rub my hands all over her back. How cold her hands were when I took them in mine, because she said she'd had too much caffeine and she was jittery. And —

"She kept looking at the clock the whole time. All through class. I asked her if she had a train to catch. She said she was hungry because she hadn't had breakfast, and she was counting down to lunch, so . . . I snuck her some of my Snickers bar."

I cast an anxious glance at Dad. "We're not supposed to eat in the classrooms and especially peanuts and stuff, but her hands were all trembling and cold when she got to class. . . . She said she'd had too much caffeine."

Sergeant Marr is jotting stuff in his notebook while I'm talking. I wonder if any of this is important. I'm scared that they think I might have something to do with whatever happened to Abby. *Please let her be okay.*

"Were you close to Miss Johnston?" Officer Conner asks.

Oh, man. Here it comes. I wonder if they're going to do the

Good Cop/Bad Cop thing, like they do in the movies. I'm trying to figure out which one is going to be the Good Cop.

"I don't know if I'd say 'close.' I mean, I really like her and I asked her out. We went to the movies once, and I had a great time and —"

"What movie did you see?" Officer Conner asks.

Despite my nerves, I swallow a laugh, remembering how little we actually saw of it. Laughing would not be at all cool right now. Not cool at all.

"Uh . . . *Zombies vs. Aliens from Outer Space.*"

"Sounds like a great date movie," he says, but it's clear he means the total opposite. "What did you think of it?"

"It was okay." I try to remember something the reviews said, but totally space. All I can think of was how sweet it was when I felt Abby's lips for the first time.

"How long ago was this?"

"Um . . . it was the second weekend of October."

"And did you and Miss Johnston see each other after that?" asks Sergeant Marr.

"Well, yeah. Every day in class. And I was . . . you know, hoping we'd go out on a date again. But . . ."

"But she turned you down?" he says.

Thanks. Rub it in, why don't you?

"Not exactly. The first time I asked her, she was busy. And then . . . it's just . . . I don't know. . . . She always seemed to be distracted or in a hurry whenever I wanted to talk."

Sergeant Marr's face doesn't show any expression, but Officer Conner gives me this look like *Don't you know a blow-off when you see it, dude?* I'm getting the impression he's the one playing Bad Cop.

"Did you ever correspond with Abby online?"

"We're friends on Facebook. But mostly we talked in class."

"Did Abby ever mention anyone named Luke Redmond to you?"

For the second time in less than twelve hours, I get that sucker-punched feeling. *Was Abby dating someone else? Is that why . . .*

"Son, the police officer asked you a question," Dad says.

I didn't realize I'd been blown away into my own little world of total freak-outedness.

"No," I say, shaking my head. "She definitely never talked to me about anyone named Luke."

And looking straight at Officer Conner, I add, "Look, I might be a total moron, but I thought Abby liked me, kinda. I mean, even if she didn't *like* me, like me, she definitely didn't hate me, okay?"

"We're just trying to cover every base so we can find Abby, Billy," Sergeant Marr says. "No one's accusing you of anything."

"Is she going to be okay, Sergeant?"

It's like a stare-off for a minute. I'm the one who looks away first.

"We're doing everything we can to find her, son."

He hands me his card.

"If you think of anything else that might help us, call me. Anytime."

CHAPTER 18
HUNTINGVILLE POLICE DEPARTMENT ♪

AUTOMATED LAW ENFORCEMENT INCIDENT REPORT

Huntingville PD supplemental report case number: 12-11-103898

Date: 12/08/2011

INCIDENT DATA

Incident Type: Missing Person

Date Reported: 12/08/11

Time Reported: 09:45 hrs

Reporting officer: P/O Conner

WITNESS/OTHER

Name: KEENAN, KENNETH H.

Race: Caucasian

D.O.B.: 2/12/86   Age: 26

Occupation: Youth Group Leader

Home Addr: 1487 Mockingbird Lane, Huntingville, CT 06957

Home Tel: 999-578-9374

Work Addr: First Trinity Church, 24 E Elm St, Huntingville, CT 06957

Work Tel: 999-578-1984

NARRATIVE

As a follow-up to the original report of the 14-year-old girl, Abigail Johnston, I interviewed Kenneth Keenan, the youth leader of the First Trinity Church at 09:45 hours on 12/08/11. Mr. Keenan was the adult in charge of attendees from the First Trinity Youth Group to the Youth Directions Summer Retreat attended by Abigail Johnston in summer 2011, at which she claimed to have met her "boyfriend." I was looking to see if Keenan had any pertinent information regarding Abigail.

Mr. Keenan described Abby as a shy girl of above-average intelligence. Although she participated in all the retreat activities willingly, she did not appear to have any close friends. She shared a bunk with the following girls: Dana Lewis, Tricia Frost, Kelly Trotta, other members of the First Trinity Youth Group.

Mr. Keenan is not aware of any liaisons between Abigail Johnston and a member of the opposite sex, platonic or otherwise. He had never heard of anyone by the name of Luke Redmond. The teenagers were supervised by counselors at all times and did not have access to computers or cell phones while at the camp. Keenan had nothing further to add. A criminal history performed on Keenan found nothing.

CHAPTER 19
LILY ⦁ DECEMBER 8 12:30 P.M.

You'd think under circumstances like this I'd get a day off from school but Mom made me go. Like I'm really going to able to concentrate with zero hours of sleep, and everything that's going on. Plus, I feel like I'm wearing this big sign that says: "Freaky sister missing — might have run off with Random Internet Guy." The last thing I need is for Abby's weirdness to rub off on me. You know how it is in middle school. But Mom says my "life should suffer as little disruption as possible." Like, *hello*? What planet do you live on?

Still, I try to pretend like nothing's wrong, even though I can barely keep my eyes open.

"Lily, what is up with you? You look awful!" my friend Dawn says when she catches me at my locker before lunch.

I don't know if I should tell her. If secret-keeping were a class, Dawn would be flunking, and I don't want the whole school to know about Abby. Mom already told the principal, just in case I lose it in school or anything, I guess. But I don't want everyone in the cafeteria staring at me. I don't want to be the girl everyone is whispering about.

"I just had a bad night," I tell her. That way I'm not lying. I'm just not telling her the whole truth.

"I read this thing in *Seventeen* about how you should put cucumber slices on your eyes when you have bags under them and they're all puffy like that," Dawn says.

"Yeah, that'll go down well in the cafeteria. Lily Salad-Face Johnston."

Dawn giggles. "Not here, stupid. At home. It's like giving yourself a relaxing home facial."

Yeah, I don't think there'll be too many relaxing home facials going on at our house any time soon. Like any of us will be able to relax at all until Abby gets home safely. *If she gets home at all . . .*

"Are you sure you're okay, Lily? You just shivered like you've got the flu or something." Dawn puts her hand on my forehead. It feels cool and calm. I want to grab it and keep it there, because it seems to stop my thoughts from racing, but then she'll *totally* think I'm weird.

"It doesn't feel like you have a fever. But if you aren't feeling well, maybe you should go to the nurse anyway. I think there's a lot of stuff going around."

"Yeah," I say, getting an idea. "Maybe I should. Thanks, Dawn."

"No problem. Hope you feel better!"

I watch Dawn head down the hall toward the cafeteria, her blond ponytail swinging, totally carefree. Yesterday, my ponytail was just as carefree. But today, because of fricking *Abby*, it feels like everything in the world has stopped. Not for everyone else, but for me. I can't just keep going to classes and pretending that everything is fine. Because everything is *so not fine*.

I don't go to the nurse. Instead, for the first time ever, I knock on the school counselor's door. Normally, I'd rather die than walk into his office. But today isn't normal.

"Come in," he calls.

His office smells like chicken soup.

"Sorry, I was just having my lunch," he says. "But come on in and have a seat."

He wipes his hands on a paper napkin and holds one out for me to shake.

"I'm Mr. DiTocco. What's up?"

I shake his hand and take a seat next to his desk. The smell is driving me crazy. I'm actually hungry for the first time all day.

"Hi. Um . . . I'm Lily. Er . . . Lily Johnston. My sister . . . Abby . . ."

"Oh, yes," he says. "The principal told me this morning that your sister was missing."

"So, like, have you been expecting me or something? Like, is it normal for someone whose sister is missing to feel like they're totally losing it?"

"Is that how you feel, Lily? Like you're 'totally losing it'?"

His brown eyes are kind and gentle. I end up crying my eyes out all over his packets of saltines.

"I'll take that as a yes," he says, handing me a box of tissues.

"I-i-it's a-all m-my f-fault," I wail.

He lets me cry it out until I'm down to the sniffling and nose-blowing stage before he asks me how, exactly, it is all my fault.

"Because I told on her. And then Mom and Dad were furious, and I think that made her decide to run away with this Luke guy. I mean, if that's what really happened."

"I thought Abby and your mother fought because Abby got a bad grade?"

"Well, yeah. But the thing is, I told. Abby said not to, but I did it anyway. It just made me so happy that Perfect Abby got a D."

"I'm confused. How is Abby's less-than-stellar academic per-formance your fault?"

When he puts it that way, it does sound kind of . . . well, not stupid exactly, but not true.

"Well, it's not. She can't blame me if she spent so much time online that she didn't study. She's the smart one in the family after all."

Mr. DiTocco's fingers dance on his keyboard, then stop as he studies the computer screen.

"I'm wondering why you would say Abby's the smart one, Lily. You made honor roll first quarter." He turns to me and smiles. "Looks to me like you're pretty smart yourself."

"I guess. But Abby's always been smarter. Like, if I get a B-plus, she gets an A-plus. My dad practically worships her. He's totally convinced that she's going to get into Harvard or Yale or Cornell, where he went. I don't even think he *cares* where I go."

"How's your dad holding up right now?"

"He's a disaster. He can't believe Abby might have gone off with a stranger. *His* Abby is too smart for that. Oh, and you should have seen when the police guy asked if Abby was a slut. I thought Dad was going to kill him!"

"The officer asked if your sister was a . . . ?"

"Oh, he didn't actually say *slut*. He used some word begin-ning with *p*, prom-something."

"Promiscuous?"

"Yeah. Which she's not, by the way. She's a weirdo, but not a slut."

"So you and Abby don't get along so well?"

I want to lie and pretend like we had this fairy-tale lovey-dovey sister relationship, the kind that I always wish we had but didn't. But I can't bring myself to do it.

"No. We didn't. We're really . . . different. Well, obviously, because there's no way I'd disappear on my family like this and drive everyone crazy. I'm not that much of an inconsiderate asshole — oops, sorry, excuse my language."

"Language excused, under the circumstances. I hear you are very angry with your sister, Lily, and that's natural. As is the feeling that you're 'totally losing it' when something this traumatic happens."

"I can't do this. Like, how'm I supposed to make any sense of pre-algebra if Abby might be out there . . ."

I break down again at the thought of Abby being, you know. Dead.

"Maybe it's asking too much of you to come to be in school today, Lily. I'm sure your parents were doing what they thought was best, trying to maintain your normal daily routine, but why don't I call your mom and see if she can pick you up?"

"O-k-kay," I say, sniffling. The thought of being able to go home fills me with relief. At least there I'll know right away if anything happens. If Abby calls or better yet, comes home. Or if they get news about anything. I won't be stuck here at school, trying to pretend nothing's wrong and driving myself crazy imagining everything that could be.

"I'll call her from next door," he says, getting up and heading for the door. "You just hang out here for a few minutes and take it easy. Are you hungry? Help yourself to some saltines."

I really want some chicken soup, but I'll settle for a packet of saltines.

"Mr. DiTocco, do you think Abby is going to be okay?" I ask him. "Like, what do you think are the chances of her coming back alive?"

He stops, his hand on the door handle, a pained expression on his face.

"Believe me, I wish I could answer that for you, Lily, but honestly? I just don't know."

CHAPTER 20
TOWN OF LENOX POLICE DEPARTMENT ♪

AUTOMATED LAW ENFORCEMENT INCIDENT REPORT

Lenox PD case number: 12-11-116417

Date: 12/08/2011

INCIDENT DATA

Incident Type: Other Jurisdiction

Date Reported: 12/08/11

Time Reported: 14:30 hrs

Responding officer: Det. Winters

Reporting officer: Det. Winters

WITNESS/OTHER

Name: WHITAKER, CARL J., REV.

Race: Caucasian

D.O.B.: 6/14/59   Age: 52

Occupation: Minister, Retreat Organizer

Home Address: 5098 Willow Lane, Lenox, MA 01240

Home Tel: 999-601-8941

Work address: St. Paul's Church, 144 Walker Street, Lenox, MA 01240

NARRATIVE

Request for assistance from Huntingville, CT, PD. I responded as I am the ICAC affiliate for Lenox. Missing minor Abigail Johnston, age 14, attended Youth Directions Summer Retreat at Camp Mackagow in Lenox, July 16-19, 2011. Told friend, Faith Wilson, that she met a "boyfriend," known as "Luke Redmond," at this retreat. I interviewed retreat organizer Rev. Carl Whitaker, who showed me the list of attendees. Nobody by the name of Luke Redmond attended the retreat. Rev. Whitaker remembers Abby Johnston as a shy girl who did not have many interactions with the opposite sex. All retreat attendees were supervised by counselors at all times, and did not have access to cell phones or computers while they were on the premises. Did a check of the in-house Lenox PD database and did not find any reports on Luke Redmond. Ran an MA criminal history check on the name Luke Redmond and found no record.

CHAPTER 21

"Faith! OMG, is it true?" Grace accosts me at lunch.

"Is what true?"

"Abby. Is it true that she's missing?"

It doesn't matter that I'm in the cafeteria surrounded by all these people. I burst into tears and throw myself into Grace's arms.

"Oh, no," she says, stroking my back. "Oh, Faith."

People are staring, nudging each other, and whispering. Grace pulls me over to a corner and sits me down at a table that someone didn't bother to clean up. I stare at the half-eaten apple and empty yogurt container, the sandwich crust and cookie crumbs, and I wonder if Abby is hungry — like if she's had anything to eat since she's been gone. If the guy who took her . . . or the guy she left with — if that's what actually happened — is treating her okay. I still can't believe Abby would do it — would go off voluntarily with some guy she'd never met. Abby's too smart for that. At least . . . at least I thought she was.

"So have you heard anything? Like do they have any idea where she is?"

"The police came over to interview me this morning. They asked me all these questions about when I'd last seen her and what websites she goes on and . . . I'm so scared, Gracie. What if . . . ?"

I can't bring myself to say the words, and just thinking about it makes me start crying again. Gracie is starting to get all teary, too. It's funny because I always felt like she and Abby were . . . I don't know, that they didn't like each other all that much. It got me down sometimes. But now . . . well, now it doesn't seem to matter.

"I'm sure they'll find her, Faith," Grace says between sniffles. "They have to."

But the thing is, they don't, do they? Like, maybe in the after-school specials they do, but real-life stories don't always have happy endings. And —

"Even if they do find her, Gracie, what if she's off with some creep from the Internet and he's, you know . . . *done stuff*? What if he's hurt her?"

Grace puts her arms around me.

"*Ugh.* That thought freaks me out, too. Totally. It's just too . . . horrible and disgusting and awful. Sick, sick, sick. But try not to think about it, okay? It's not going to help Abby, is it? And it's just going to make you nuts."

"I guess. I just feel so . . . helpless. I wish there were something I could *do*."

The bell rings, signaling the end of lunch. I haven't eaten a single thing. It doesn't matter. I'm not hungry.

"Faith, you have to eat something. Here, I've got a granola bar. Take it."

"It's okay, I —"

Grace doesn't take no for an answer. She pushes the bar into my hand and says, "Just eat it. Starving yourself isn't going to help bring Abby back."

I take the granola bar and force my lips into a smile.

"Thanks, Grace. See you later."

When Mom comes to pick me up, she tells me they haven't heard anything new, but there was a story about Abby missing on the local TV station's lunchtime news with her picture. The police are hoping it'll generate some leads.

"On the *news*? So, like, everyone is going to *know* now?"

I feel a pang of guilt as the words leave my mouth, and it's clear from the look on her face that I'm now officially the World's Worst Sister in Mom's eyes.

"Yes, *everyone is going to know*. That's the *point*, Lily. We need leads if we're going to find Abby."

We spend the rest of the car ride home in silence, broken only when Mom curses out some guy for cutting her off, using language I've never heard come out of her mouth before. And she doesn't even say *Excuse my language, Lily*. It's just another sign that the world as I know it is falling apart. Thanks to my missing sister.

Dad's sitting at the kitchen table, pretty much where I left him this morning. He's got dark rings under his eyes and it's clear he's got a major caffeine buzz going.

"Any news?" Mom asks the minute we walk in the door.

"Detective Heller from the Youth Division called," Dad says. "They've got a lead."

"They do? Heavens, tell me, Rick, what is it? That's good news, isn't it?" Mom says.

"Don't tell me it's good till you hear what it is, Kate," Dad snaps at her. "A woman saw Abby's picture on the news and she recognized her. She told the police that she saw Abby at the Galleria yesterday morning . . . and she . . ."

"What, Rick? She what?"

"She saw Abby getting into a car. With a man."

"Oh, no!" Mom gasps, and she sinks into the nearest chair, her face pale beneath her makeup.

My hands clench into fists.

I can't believe that my sister stole the last freaking Eggo waffle, then walked out of the house like it was any other day, knowing full well that she was planning to wreck our lives. How could she do this to us?

I want, more than anything, for Abby to come back home alive and safe. But when she does, I'm going to freaking kill her for what she's done to Mom and Dad and me. Slowly and painfully.

Detective Heller comes over around four p.m., with a lady officer in uniform named Officer Ball.

"We've interviewed Mrs. Cecelia O'Connell, the woman who last saw Abby," he tells us. "She rode down in the elevator with her from the food court to level two of the parking garage in the Galleria, at approximately eleven forty-five yesterday morning. Mrs. O'Connell remembered Abby because she was interacting with her infant daughter, Samantha."

"Abby's very good with babies," Mom says.

Yeah, yeah, Abby's good at everything. Except being normal.

"When they got to the second level of the parking garage, Mrs. O'Connell saw a blue car waiting near the elevators. She says it was an American-made car, but doesn't recall the make or model or the license plate, although she does remember that it wasn't a Connecticut plate."

"Is there any way to find out from the security cameras?" Dad, the techno geek, asks.

"We're doing that right now," Officer Ball says. "It took a few hours to get the footage from mall security, but we were lucky that we had a specific time frame so we could narrow it down."

"The reason we're here now is because we wanted to let you know that we've called in the FBI on this case," Detective Heller says.

Huh? The FBI? Like Criminal Minds *or* The X-Files?

"What? Why?" Mom asks. "I mean, does that mean you think it's more serious?"

"Mrs. Johnston, we know that Abby was active online, although our forensic team hasn't gotten to her computer yet, so we don't know what she was up to. We also have a witness that saw her getting into a car with out-of-state plates, driven by an adult male. In cases where we think there's a possibility the minor might have been transported out of state, we don't have jurisdiction. The FBI does."

"You think this guy — whoever he is — has taken my daughter out of state already?" Dad says. His face is gray and he looks like he wants to grab his car keys and start driving, somewhere, anywhere, as long as he might find Abby.

"We don't know for sure, but we think there's a good possibility. We really need to get into Abby's computer," Detective Heller tells us. "Another advantage of calling in the FBI is that they have a lot more tech resources than we do, so I'm hoping they can get what we need off Abby's computer more quickly than my guys could. We're totally backed up and the state forensic lab is even more backed up. Their wait time is months, not weeks."

"We subpoenaed Abby's cell phone records, but they didn't yield any clues," Officer Ball says. "We need to get into that computer."

All of sudden, Mom just loses it. It freaks me out because Mom's so together normally. But she just sits there bawling.

"I can't believe this is happening," she sobs. "I can't believe Abby would get in a car with a total stranger."

Officer Ball sits down next to Mom and pats her shoulder.

"Mrs. Johnston, to Abby this man didn't feel like a total stranger. If what we think is correct, she's been corresponding with him for months, and he's been using techniques to gain her confidence — what we call *grooming*. Internet predators spend a lot of time building up friendships with young people. And then they betray that friendship step-by-step, by gradually breaking down barriers, creating isolation, and leading the child to harm."

Leading the child to harm.

Abby is in harm. Being harmed. By some strange Internet Predator Guy. I start crying, too.

Mom hugs me and I feel her tears mingling with mine on my cheek.

"What can we do?" Dad asks. "There's got to be something we can do. I don't understand it. Why isn't Abby's computer top of the pile? She's a young girl in imminent danger. Can't you *do something*, for chrissake?"

"I understand your frustration, Mr. Johnston. Believe me. You don't know how badly I wish we had more resources. I have a daughter myself," Detective Heller says. "But right now, we're doing everything we can. And unfortunately, you have to do the hardest thing of all, which is wait."

CHAPTER 23
FAITH ✦ DECEMBER 8 3:45 P.M.

The last thing I feel like doing is going to stage crew to paint sets. Normally, I love it — being in the theater, joking around with friends, and being with Ted. But it feels so wrong to be going on with life as normal while Abby's missing.

I can't concentrate and I start to paint one of the flats the wrong color and Ted yells at me. I'm so upset I end up throwing the paintbrush at him, spattering paint everywhere, and everyone on stage crew is staring at me like I've gone insane as I run out of the theater to cry in the bathroom.

I've been sitting here in one of the bathroom stalls ever since, thinking about when I met Abby on my first day of school in second grade. We'd just moved to Huntingville from down-state, when my dad bought into the medical practice here. I was sitting in front of this kid Richie Sisbarro. First, he pulled my hair, which was in a long braid. I didn't want to be labeled a tattletale on my first day, so I didn't say anything. Then he kept kicking my chair — too softly for the teacher to hear, but enough to make me want to punch him. I couldn't wait till the bell rang for lunch, so I could get away from him. Abby came up to me right away.

"Richie Sisbarro is such a booger face. In kindergarten, he ripped half the pages out of *Each Peach Pear Plum* when I brought it in for show-and-tell. And that was my favorite book!"

"I love that book!" I told her.

We both started reciting together, *"Each Peach Pear Plum, I Spy Tom Thumb . . ."*

By the time we'd said the whole book together — Abby had memorized it, too — I knew we were going to be best friends.

We've spent so many years knowing everything about each other, liking the same music, the same books, the same movies, the same everything except for ice-cream flavors practically. No matter how many times I think about it, I still can't believe that something this major would be going on in Abby's life and she wouldn't tell me.

But then I'm shrouded by a fog of guilt. I haven't exactly been such a great friend to Abby lately — I've been so busy with stage crew and a lot of the time I would have been IM'ing with Abby in the evenings, I've been on the phone with Ted. And . . . I think this is what makes me feel the worst, like I'm the most terrible person ever . . . she was kind of starting to bug me at times. I feel awful even thinking it with her being missing, but it's true. It's like she wanted everything to stay the same way it had always been, and me . . . well, there's so much new stuff in high school that I want to try and so many new people to meet. It's not like I didn't want to be friends with Abby anymore. I just wanted her to make new friends and try new things, too. I talked to Mom about it and she told me this poem: *"Make new friends, but keep the old, one is silver, the other gold."* She said it was natural to want to branch out and make new friends, but that friendships like mine and Abby's were special and rare, and I should still try to be a good friend to her.

That was when I called Abby and asked her if she wanted to come over for a sleepover. And she said no because she had other plans. I did kind of wonder what she was so busy with all the time — I mean, it's not like she was doing stage crew every day like I was. I was pretty hurt, if you want to know the truth. And then she stopped sitting with me on the bus every day.

I'm such an idiot, because the day she left I was so happy, happy because Abby was talking about double-dating with Ted and me, about finally introducing me to the mystery Church Retreat Guy. It was like she was finally opening up to me again. But she wasn't. She was lying.

I hit the wall of the bathroom stall, hard, because I'm filled with fury like I've never felt before. *Why, Abby? Why did you lie to me? How could you do this?*

There's no answer written in the graffiti on the back of the stall door. There's no answer I can think of. I need Abby to come back and tell me. *I need Abby to come back.*

"Faith? Are you in there?"

Ted calls from the hallway outside. I'm not sure I want to talk to him — or anyone for that matter — but I check my watch and it's time to go home.

"Coming."

I wash my tearstained face, dry it with a paper towel, then go to meet Ted. He's waiting outside the door with my jacket and backpack.

"Do you realize you just spent the *entire rehearsal* freaking out in the bathroom?" he says.

"Yes. *And?*"

"I'm just saying. I mean, I know Abby's your friend and every-thing, but —"

"But what? I should just pretend like everything's normal even though right this very moment someone could be hurting her? Or worse even?"

"But she went off with the guy voluntarily, right? I mean, how screwed up is that?"

Even though Ted is saying some of the things that I've thought myself, I'm mad at him for saying them.

"We don't know that! Maybe she went to meet him and changed her mind and he forced her into the car!"

"Face it, Faith — Abby went to meet some dude she met in a chat room. That's just wrong."

His words make me crazy angry. We've never fought before, but right now I feel like I never want to see him again. I grab my coat and backpack and stomp away down the hall toward the front of school, where I hope Mom's waiting to pick me up.

"Faith, *stop*! Why are you so mad at me? *I* didn't do anything to Abby," Ted shouts at my retreating back.

But he did. He's judged her, just like I've been judging her, just like everyone is going to judge her when she comes back. *If she ever comes back.*

CHAPTER 24
LILY ⚬ DECEMBER 9 9:30 A.M.

I flat-out refused to go to school when I heard the FBI agents were coming this morning. Mom didn't put up too much of a fight. It's not like she's going to work. Only Dad is machine enough to try to get work done while Abby is missing. He actually complained to Mom about this happening so close to the end of the tax year and all the extra pressure that puts on him. I'm thinking, like, there's actually a *good time* for your daughter to run off with some stranger she met online?

Abby definitely takes after Dad. They're both crazy. I'm glad everyone always tells me I'm more like Mom.

I'm watching stupid toddler cartoons when the doorbell rings.

"I'll get it," I yell, but Mom's there before me. She lets in a woman in a pantsuit with her hair twisted up in a bun, and a dark-suited guy with a buzz cut. They flash their badges, and introduce themselves as special agents Saunders (the lady) and Nisco (the guy) from the FBI.

Mom does her Martha Stewart thing but they turn her down. They want to get right down to business. Dad emerges from his study looking even more cruddy than he did yesterday, if that's possible. His eyes are red from lack of sleep and staring at his computer screen trying to figure out other people's tax blunders.

"We wanted to bring you up to speed with where we are in the investigation," Agent Nisco says. "The police brought Abby's computer to our CART guys —"

"That's the Computer Analysis and Response Team," explains Agent Pantsuit. "We're big into acronyms at the FBI."

"Right," Agent Nisco continues. "They were able to get a list of all the sites Abby's visited, and because we have a case of a missing minor, my boss was able to issue what we call an administrative subpoena for all but one of those sites, which allows us to get access to her accounts and see her activity."

"So did you find out where she went?" Dad asks.

"Unfortunately, that's where we ran into problems," Agent Saunders explains. "This ChezTeen.com site that Abby's been active on is relatively new — we hadn't even heard of it."

"Neither had I," Mom says. "I knew about Facebook and MySpace and I knew she had an MSN account, but I didn't know anything about this ChezTeen thing. Did you, Lily?"

"I think I set up an account on there, but my friends are on Facebook mostly, so I never used it."

"Even though it's an English language site, the servers are located outside of the United States, in the Ukraine," Agent Nisco tells us. "So it's out of our jurisdiction. Unfortunately, it doesn't require an e-mail address to register, so we couldn't use Abby's Gmail account to request a password reset."

"It's not that we can't get the information," Agent Pantsuit says, seeing Dad about to blow his top. "It's that we have to go through diplomatic channels, which takes longer, and in these cases, time is something that isn't on our side."

Her words stun us into silence and as if to rub it in, the only sound is the ticking of the clock on the kitchen wall.

Agent Nisco breaks into my scared slide show of all the ways this guy could be hurting Abby, right at this very moment. "We were able to request a password hint and we need you to brainstorm anything you think could be Abby's password," he says. "Make us a list. We know her user name from the police interviews with . . ." He consults his notes. "Faith Wilson. But if we can get that password . . ."

"What's the hint?" Mom asks.

The agents glance at each other. "It's 'Abby loves,'" Agent Nisco says.

"That could be anything from emo music to chocolate to this Luke Redmond guy," I say. "It's no help at all."

"It's not Luke Redmond. We've already tried. That's why we need the help of the people who know Abby best," Agent Nisco says.

"In the meantime, we're following up another lead," Agent Saunders tells us. "We found an e-mail in which Abby exchanged photos with the man we suspect she left with."

Somehow, even more than the lady seeing her getting into the car at the mall, this seems to bring it home to Mom and Dad that Abby actually left home to be with an Internet Creep.

"Oh goodness, Abby, no!" Mom cries.

My father pales. "So you know who this guy is now?"

"Unfortunately, most of these predators are smarter than that," Agent Saunders says, sighing. "They're practiced at avoiding detection. We were able to track the IP address the e-mail was sent from to a computer in a public library in South Boston. Our agents in Massachusetts are investigating."

Dad's shoulders sag, and he looks a hundred years old again.

"But we did get the picture off of Abby's computer," Agent Nisco says, taking a photocopy from the manila folder in front of him.

I lean over Mom's shoulder to look, and see a youngish-looking guy in a Red Sox hat that hides part of his face. He looks so . . . normal. Like an everyday kind of guy you might see on the street or at the mall. I guess I was expecting to see some really old guy with bad teeth and greasy hair, wearing a trench coat or something. Someone whose looks just scream out *I'm a pervert who likes underage girls.*

Suddenly, Dad's fist crashes down on the table, right in the middle of the guy's face, making us all jump.

"The goddamn son of a bitch! I'll kill him! I swear if he harms one hair on Abby's head, I will rip him to pieces!"

I've never seen my dad like this before and it scares me to tears. Mom pulls me onto her lap, even though she usually tells me that I'm too big for that.

She strokes my hair and says, "It's okay, Lily. Daddy's just upset because he's worried about Abby."

But her hand is shaking as it surfs the waves in my hair, which confirms the sick feeling I have in my stomach — everything is so *not* okay. And I don't know if it ever will be again.

CHAPTER 25
BILLY • DECEMBER 9 1:30 P.M.

When I saw the thing about Abby on the news last night, I thought I was going to puke up Mom's chili all over the family room carpet. I can't stand the thought that some guy might be hurting her. And sometimes, I can't help thinking the worst — that she might be . . . dead, and lying somewhere cold and alone, abandoned in some remote place like a piece of trash that someone forgot. That makes me want to scream and punch things and scratch my skin till it bleeds so that people will see how much it hurts.

Because no one gets it. No one understands how it killed me when I got to science and she wasn't there. Call me a sucker, but even when she said no to that date, I was still happier knowing I'd see her again in class the next day. This morning, her empty chair was like a sore that hurt every time I looked at it.

But it's what "they" say that's worse. Who's *they*? Every-*fricking*body, that's who. *Everyone's* got an opinion about Abby, even if they never spoke to her before, and *everyone's* opinion is bad. She's *stupid*. She's a *freak*. She's *easy*. What the hell do *they* know? *They* never went on a date with her. Abby's not like that. She's one of the smartest, prettiest girls I know.

But . . . but . . . BUT . . . then WHY?! *Why the hell did she dis-appear like this?* It's enough to make a guy crazy. It's definitely made this one into a certifiable Grade-A Nut.

I finally catch up with Abby's friend, Faith, in the hallway after lunch.

"Yo, Faith — uh, have you . . . I mean, is there any news about . . ."

Faith looks as crazy as I feel. Like she's barely slept and she's trying to hold herself together through classes that don't make a whole lot of sense when a person you care about is missing.

"Hey, Billy. My mom just left me a voice mail. Abby's parents asked me to come over after school to help them try to think of Abby's ChezTeen password. Something about the FBI not being able to get into her account because the servers are overseas?"

My lunch starts doing the salsa in my stomach.

"The FBI?"

"Yeah, they're involved now. Because some lady at the mall saw Abby getting into a car and it had out-of-state plates. And because of the computer stuff."

Gut punch.

"Wait. She *got into a car*? *By choice*? With who? Was it that Luke Redmond guy?"

The thought makes me want to punch something. Hard. Multiple times. Until I don't feel anything anymore.

"I don't know. And it's making me crazy."

"I just don't get *why*. I mean, I can understand if she didn't want to go out with *me*, but . . ."

Faith's eyes fill with tears.

"Oh, Billy, I wish she'd just gone out with you. I told her she should. I don't understand why, either. . . ."

She's really crying now, and I can't help but put my arm around her. She puts her head on my shoulder and I feel her tears making a wet patch on my sweater.

"And now everyone is saying all this horrible stuff about her, and I'm afraid she won't *want* to come back," Faith sobs.

"We'll just have to make sure Abby knows we're there for her," I tell Faith, even though my own feelings are pretty mixed up right now. I'm still reeling from the thought that Abby willingly went in a car with some stranger. With some other guy. "If she comes back."

I suddenly realize what I said.

"I mean, *when* Abby comes back. Because she has to come back, right? We can't live with it any other way."

Faith hugs me and nods.

"*When* Abs comes back," she says, wiping the tears from her cheek with her hand.

"Well, isn't this cozy?"

This sophomore, who I think is one of the drama geeks, is standing a few feet away with his arms crossed, looking seriously pissed. Faith jumps away from me like I've suddenly developed a contagious disease.

"Oh . . . hey, Ted. We were just talking about Abby. Billy went out with her and he's really worried, like me."

Ted gives us both a *Yeah, right* look.

"So worried that he's hitting on her best friend in the meantime?"

Faith turns bright red and opens her mouth like she's going to bawl him out. But then she just turns on her heel and stalks away.

I look at him and say, "Dude, you have got this *so* wrong. So very, *very* wrong." Glancing at Faith's stiff back as she marches down the hall, I add, "If she's your girlfriend, you owe her an apology. A *really* big one. And if I were you, I'd give it to her *PDQ*."

CHAPTER 26
FAITH / DECEMBER 9 3:45 P.M.

I told Grace to give my apologies for missing stage crew. Even though I know "the show must go on," if there's something I can do to help find Abby, I've got to do that first. People — and in "people" I'm including Ted, who I can't *believe* was such a Grade-A jerk about Billy — will just have to understand. No matter what they think about Abby's decision to go off with some Internet guy.

I can't believe the difference in Mr. Johnston when I walk into their kitchen. He looks like Abby's grandfather instead of her father. Mrs. Johnston isn't looking so hot, either. I don't even think she's wearing makeup. Abby would laugh so hard at that. She always jokes about how her mom doesn't even get up to go to the bathroom in the middle of the night without makeup. *See, Abby? Look what you've done? You've even managed to make your mom forget to put her face on.*

Lily rushes over to hug me. Lily, who normally just thinks of me as her weird older sister's weird friend. I wrap my arms around her and squeeze her tight, just like I would Abby. Now I *know* the world is completely upside down and back to front.

"Do you want anything to eat?" Mrs. Johnston asks. "We've

got plenty of leftover Chinese. I guess we weren't as hungry as we thought we were."

"No, we ate," Mom says. "In fact, I made you these cookies to keep you going."

"Oh, Elaine, you didn't have to," Mrs. Johnston says. But then she hugs Mom and starts to cry.

"Kate, honey, Abby will be okay," Mom says, hugging Mrs. Johnston and swallowing her own tears. "We've all been praying for her, and I just *know* that she'll come home safe."

Lily sits on a kitchen chair, kind of hunched over, looking so scared and miserable that I forget how normally she's such a pain in the butt and I rub her back just the way I would Abby's.

"You sit down, Katie," Mom says. "Let me make you a cup of tea. Rick, do you want one? Lily?"

Mrs. Johnston sinks into the nearest chair and rests her head in her hands.

"So what can we do besides make tea?" I ask. "You need us to try and think of what Abby's password might be?"

"We've been trying for what feels like *forever* and had total Password Fail," Lily says, passing me a yellow pad covered with word and number combinations that have been crossed out.

"No offense, Lily, but seriously, Abby's bound to pick something *you* wouldn't be able to figure out," I tell her.

I was afraid Lily would be upset, but she actually half smiles.

"Yeah. Too right."

"We thought that if anyone might be able to guess, it would be you, Faith," Mr. Johnston says. "You're Abby's best friend."

Not that I've been such a great friend recently.

The guilt almost crushes me, especially sitting here at Abby's kitchen table with her parents and Lily.

"I'll try my best."

Mrs. Johnston explains how the ChezTeen.com servers are in the Ukraine so it's going to take the FBI much longer to get access to the critical information that they think is in Abby's account than it would be if everything were in the United States. Unless . . . unless, we can figure out her password.

I slide the pad across the table toward me and ask Lily to pass me a pen.

"So how do we do this? Do I make a list and then you give it to the FBI? Or do we try them?"

"We've been trying them," Mr. Johnston says. "One of us has been writing down the password and another's been typing it in."

"Okay. I'll start writing if you want."

"Let's do it," he says, grabbing one of Mom's cookies and pulling his laptop toward him.

An hour later, every single thing I've thought of has failed and I'm struggling to think of anything else.

"Why don't you take a break, Faith?" Mrs. Johnston says. "You've had a long day and you look tired." She looks at my mom. "I know Faith has school tomorrow, Elaine, and homework. Whenever you think she needs to go home, just say the —"

"NO!" I protest.

Mom gives me a look, like, *Who's the Mom around here?*

"I mean, *please*, Mom, I really want to stay longer. I want to help. I *need* to help. I'm sure I'll figure this out soon. I just . . . Maybe . . . maybe if I go look in Abby's room, it'll give me some ideas."

I stand up and head for the stairs.

"We'll stay for another hour, Faith," Mom says. "I know you

want to help, but you do have school tomorrow. And you've got homework, honey. Getting behind on your own schoolwork isn't going to help Abby."

Would Mrs. Johnston make Abby go home in an hour if *I* were missing? Or does Mom not think I can do this? Or is she just lying to Mrs. Johnston because really she thinks this is all hopeless and Abby isn't coming home at all?

It's so strange to be sitting in Abby's room. I've been here, like, a zillion times before; I know it almost as well as my own. But to be here without Abby, not knowing where she is or if she's even . . . alive and okay . . . that makes me start crying again. I lie on Abby's bed, my head on her pillow, and when I breathe in I can just catch her familiar smell. *Abs, please, where are you? Come back. I promise I'll be a better friend if you'll come back safely.*

This isn't helping Abby. I've got to pull myself together.

I grab a tissue from the box on Abby's bedside table and wipe my eyes. Okay, I'm going to start from the bed and walk around the room, looking at everything to see if it jogs my memory about things that Abby has said or done, anything that she might have decided to use as a password.

Her closet is so neat compared to mine. Abby always gives me a hard time about how messy I am. My mom jokes that we're like the two guys on this old TV show, *The Odd Couple*, where Felix was a neat freak and Oscar was a slob. After that, sometimes I'd call Abby Felix and she'd call me Oscar.

I write down *Felix, Oscar* and *Odd Couple* on the yellow pad. Abby signed up for ChezTeen before everything started going weird between us. Maybe, just maybe, it was our friendship she loved. It's a long shot, but we might as well try everything.

Abby's desk is as neat as her closet. I open and close drawers, feeling like a snoop. Nothing strikes me. There's a bulletin board above her desk with pictures of us pinned up from as far back as second grade. Abby and me dressed as salt and pepper shakers on Halloween in third grade. The two of us winning the three-legged race on Field Day in second grade. We practiced so hard for that, racing up and down the backyard with our legs tied together, falling over constantly at first until we got our rhythm, but giggling as we lay on the grass to catch our breath, looking for shapes in the clouds overhead.

She's saved the ticket from the first time our parents took us to New York City to see a Broadway show, *The Lion King*, the movie ticket from when we saw *Lord of the Rings* — Abby loved Viggo Mortensen as Aragorn, but I was crushing on Orlando Bloom as Legolas — and the one from when we went to see The Fray in concert. I hear their music in my head:

> *Where did I go wrong, I lost a friend*
> *Somewhere along in the bitterness*
> *And I would have stayed up with you all night*
> *Had I known how to save a life*

My heart thuds heavily in my chest. I don't care what Mom says. I'll stay up all night if that's what it takes.

OMG, Abby, I just hope I know how to save your life.

I have fifty-nine more ideas written on the pad when I go back downstairs to the kitchen.

"Here goes nothing," I say, handing them to Mr. Johnston.

"We really should go," Mom says. "I've got the other kids at home and you have school tomorrow."

"Mom, please," I beg. "Let me at least see if any of these work. It's not like I'm going to be able to concentrate on homework anyway."

She exchanges glances with Mrs. Johnston.

"Okay," Mom sighs. "Fingers crossed, Rick."

Mr. Johnston starts typing in passwords. As they're rejected, he crosses them off the list on the pad.

My heart sinks as more and more words get crossed off. I start praying. *Please, let one of them work so we can find Abby. Please, please, please . . .*

Lily's half asleep at the end of the table, her head resting on her arms. Mrs. Johnston stares at the light fixture. I can't even imagine what's going through her head.

"Holy . . . Faith, you did it!" Mr. Johnston shouts. "We're in!!"

Lily wakes up and rubs her eyes. Mrs. Johnston jumps up and looks over his shoulder.

"What one was it?" I ask.

"Aragorn," he says. His eyes are bright, suddenly, instead of tired and dull, and you can see the hope radiating from him. "Kate, get the FBI on the line."

I want to stay. I don't want to move from this kitchen until Abby walks back through the door. But after Mr. Johnston talks to the FBI, he explains that they have to go through the chat logs on Abby's account and start tracking down this Luke guy she's gone off with.

So Mom makes me go home. But I lie in bed all night thinking about Abby, until I see the dawn light through my window shade.

CHAPTER 27

Agent Pantsuit called my parents at eight a.m. and said that she and Agent Nisco were on their way over.

Mom comes in and wakes me up to tell me, even though I normally sleep late on Saturday morning.

"I thought you'd want to know," she says. She hugs me. "And you, sweetheart. How are you holding up?"

"Like crap. Kind of like you and Dad."

I know Mom's a complete wreck because she doesn't even tell me to watch my language.

"I really hope they have some good news for us. I'm not sure I can take it if it's bad news," Mom says. She sighs. "I better get the coffee going. And some breakfast, even though none of us seem to have an appetite. We're just living on caffeine and nerves at the moment. Your father's going to have an ulcer by the time this is over."

"Can you make French toast?"

I've barely been hungry the last few days, but right now I crave sweet, gooey comfort.

"Sure, baby. Set the table quickly, because the FBI will be here soon."

Mom and I are clearing up the breakfast dishes when the agents arrive. Dad lets them in and Mom pours them mugs of coffee.

"We've been able to move ahead on multiple fronts," Agent Saunders tells us. "We were able to get a read on the license plate from the mall security cameras. The car is registered to an Edmund Schmidt, from South Boston, Massachusetts. We've put out an APB on the car and on Schmidt."

"Thanks to Abby's friend, Faith, we've been able to track down the IP address of this Luke Redmond that Abby's been chatting with. It's the same address in South Boston that Schmidt's car was registered to," Agent Nisco explains. "Because we have the chat logs linking him to Abby, and an eyewitness who saw Abby getting into Schmidt's car, we had probable cause for a search warrant. Our guys went in about an hour ago. Schmidt wasn't there but his mother was. He's thirty-two years old, works at Starbucks as a barista, and lives with his parents."

"Mrs. Schmidt gave our agents permission to access the family computer, and just on a preliminary scan we found more than a thousand images of child pornography in a hidden directory," Agent Saunders says. "We suspect that Abby's not the only minor he's been grooming."

Dad crumples up his napkin into a little ball. I bet he wishes it was Luke/Edmund's, or whatever-the-creep's-name-is, head.

"So what happens now?" Mom says.

"Unfortunately, it's more of the same," Agent Saunders says, her eyes warm and sympathetic. It's the first time I see her act like a real-life person, instead of just an agent in a pantsuit. "Waiting. With the APB on Schmidt's car, hopefully we'll track them down sooner rather than later."

*   *   *

News trickles in throughout the morning. Apparently, Schmidt's mother confirmed that the picture of "Luke" from Abby's computer was her son, Edmund. Although he has no previous record, when confronted with the fact that he had child porn on the family computer, Mrs. Schmidt crossed herself and told the investigators that there had been "some unfortunate business" several years ago when her eldest daughter accused Edmund of doing something inappropriate with his niece, her granddaughter, Camilla. Mrs. Schmidt didn't know who or what to believe and it caused a huge family rift — Edmund and his eldest sister, Mary, haven't spoken in over five years and it's just about broken her heart. She lights a candle every week and prays for their family to come together in love and Christ.

Yeah, like that's going to happen now. NOT.

But then Agent Saunders says that Mrs. Schmidt told investigators that she wonders if Edmund's "problems" have anything to do with "that business with the priest back when he was an altar boy."

Wow, I think. No wonder he's screwed up.

Agent Pantsuit tells us that it's quite common for people who have been sexually abused as kids to become abusers themselves.

That sets Dad off big-time. "Are you trying to get me to feel *sorry* for this guy?" he shouts, a slow flush burning its way up his face. "Because I have no sympathy for the man who preyed on my daughter. None at all. I'd like to see him strung up from the nearest tree."

"Rick, calm down," Mom says.

"I will not calm down! My daughter is out there in the hands of some pedophile and you expect me to listen to sob stories about this creep's traumatic childhood?"

Dad pushes his chair back so hard it falls over, and he doesn't even bend to pick it up. He just starts pacing back and forth.

"I bet he'll get some bleeding-heart lawyer and they'll use that to try and get him off," he says, spitting out each word like it tastes bad.

Agent Nisco puts his hand on Dad's shoulder and tells him maybe they should go take a walk and get some fresh air.

"Let's find Abby first before we start getting worked up about Schmidt's trial strategy, okay?"

Dad's shoulders slump over as he nods his agreement.

Agent Nisco gets the call at two thirty p.m. I'm busy trying to do the homework that Mom forced me to look up online, while she stood over my shoulder, making sure I didn't pull an Abby. But it's near impossible because my brain's jumping around like popcorn in a microwave.

His phone doesn't ring, it buzzes.

"Nisco," he answers.

We all stop what we're doing and listen, like we do every time his phone buzzes. I'm holding my breath, afraid to let it go.

"Okay . . . and they're moving in soon? Great, keep me posted. Thanks."

For the first time, Agent Nisco's craggy face breaks a smile. "Schmidt's car has been spotted by New York State Police, just north of Plattsburgh, and there are two people in the vehicle. They're moving in to apprehend."

I release my breath in a loud whoosh of relief.

"Oh . . . oh, thank the Lord," Mom says, bursting into tears. Dad puts his arms around her and rubs her back. I go and hug them both. We stand there, our arms entwined, as if that will hold our family together until Abby can join it again.

We spend the next hour watching the second hand tick on the kitchen clock. When I'm not staring at the clock, I'm gazing at Agent Nisco's jacket pocket, willing his phone to buzz again with someone on the other end saying that Abby is safe and well and that she's on her way home.

When he stands up and reaches into his pocket, we all start.

"Nisco . . . Yep . . . Good." He listens for a while and I can't tell from his face if what he's hearing is good or bad. They must teach that at FBI school or something. "Where are you taking her? . . . Okay, we'll get the parents up there, stat. Yeah. Good work. Bye."

"They got her?" Dad asks. "Is Abby okay?"

"New York State Police apprehended Edmund Schmidt at approximately three ten p.m. Abby is now safely in police custody."

I burst out crying, huge sobs of relief. Abby might be a complete pain-in-the-ass freak, but I've never been happier about anything in the world than I am to know that she's alive and safe. Not anything ever. Even when I got that Juicy Couture hoodie for half price. Or when Mom got me third-row Taylor Swift tickets.

Mom and Dad both have tears streaming down their cheeks.

Mom hugs Agent Pantsuit, saying, "Thank you, thank you, how can we ever thank you?"

Dad sits down heavily on the kitchen chair, like his legs won't hold him up anymore.

"Did he . . . is she . . . ?"

He can't say the words out loud, but we all know what he is trying to ask. Did Luke Redmond, Edmund Schmidt, or whatever you want to call that freaky Red Sox hat–wearing perv do IT with Abby?

I really try hard to push that thought out of my brain. It's just too gross and scary to think about.

"They'll be taking Abby to the police station first," Agent Saunders says. "That's where we'll meet her. Once you're there, we'll go over to the nearest hospital, where she'll be examined by what we call a SANE nurse."

"What, as opposed to a crazy nurse?" I ask.

Agent Pantsuit gives me a brief, lips-only smile. "Like I said, we're big into acronyms. It stands for Sexual Assault Nurse Examiner. They specialize in doing forensic exams on women who might have undergone sexual assault."

Her voice is all steady and calm, but it kind of feels like she's trying to prepare us for the worst.

Dad is gripping the edge of the table so hard his knuckles are white.

"Maybe Lily should stay here," Mom says. "With a friend. I could call Elaine Wilson."

"Why?" I protest. "I want to see Abby, too!"

"I think it's probably a good idea," Agent Saunders says. "Just to give Abby a little breathing room before she's surrounded by too many people."

She sees me opening my mouth to protest and says, "Lily, we're going to be asking Abby a lot of questions, and you wouldn't be allowed in the room. It would get very boring."

"But it's not fair, I —"

"Lily, you're staying here, and that's final," Dad decrees. "Kate, call Elaine Wilson. We should get on the road as soon as possible. I need to see that Abby is safe with my own eyes."

Like I don't?

My eyes well up with tears as Mom reaches for the phone. It's always all about Abby as far as Dad's concerned. I wonder if she'd stayed away forever if anything would have changed.

Mrs. Wilson says she'll be here in ten minutes to take me over to their house.

"Before you see Abby, there's something you should know," Agent Nisco says. "When the suspect, Edmund Schmidt, was apprehended and he was being led away in handcuffs, Abby was extremely concerned about what was going to happen to him. She shouted out to the police, 'Don't hurt him!'"

Mom and Dad look at each other, like WTF? I can't believe it either. You'd think that after being trapped with that creep for all this time, Abby would just be, "Yay, the police are here to rescue me, woo-hoo!" But instead she's trying to *protect* the dude?

I always knew Abby was a freak, but this is even beyond her usual level of freakdom.

"It's not unusual for the victim of an Internet predator to identify with him, very strongly in fact," Agent Saunders says. "Otherwise she never would have run off with him in the first place."

"But . . . how could she . . . He's a . . ." Dad sputters.

"I know it's hard to understand," Agent Nisco says. "But these guys, they really convince the girls that they're in love with them."

Dad shakes his head, as if to say, *No, not my Abby.*

"The grooming process is an insidious seduction, Mr. Johnston," Agent Saunders says. "And it's between players of very unequal skills. Here's a grown man and a young, inexperienced girl, who is used to dealing with the boys at school."

"Yeah. Remember what our romantic skills were like in high school?" Agent Nisco says. "On a scale of one to ten, I probably ranked a two. And that's being generous."

"So then this guy comes along who knows all the right things to say to make a girl feel good about herself — it's very powerful."

"But Abby's too smart to fall for that," Dad says.

Excuse me, Dad, there's an urgent call for you from 1-800-DENIAL.

"Rick, honey, I think it's pretty clear that Abby fell for it, for reasons that none of us can understand," Mom says. "Which is why we need to see her and talk to her."

She turns to me, like she suddenly remembers I'm here.

"Lily, go pack an overnight bag, just in case. I don't know how long this will take us. Rick, I'll go pack one for us. I want to be ready to go as soon as Elaine gets here. Abby needs us."

I head up to my bedroom to pack, thinking, *Don't I need you, too?*

PART III

CHAPTER 28
ABBY • DECEMBER 10

This morning when I woke up in yet another grungy motel room, Luke was already dressed and sitting in the chair by the window.

"Come on, lazybones," he said. "Let's get moving. Just get dressed. You don't have time to take a shower."

There was no kissing or cuddling like there had been the previous mornings. Or any of the other stuff. I can't say I minded that. But it worried me because he seemed kind of, I don't know, distant. Like my dad gets when he's thinking about work.

I jumped out of bed, grabbing a towel to wrap around myself. Not that the towels in that place covered very much. That's one thing I've learned about cheap motels. The bath towels are the size of the washcloths in the kinds of hotels Dad takes us to.

Another thing I learned is that you don't want to walk on the carpet in bare feet. I bet if Billy and I did one of our petri dish swabs in this place, it would grow all kinds of scary stuff.

Don't think about Billy. Don't think about home. Keep this in a box totally separate from everything else.

I grab my jeans and shirt from the floor and get a clean pair of panties from my backpack. I'm running out of clean clothes and wonder about asking Luke if we can stop at a Laundromat. Or maybe he'll buy me some new clothes. Didn't he say *"Only the best for my girl"*?

Is this crappy motel with the ugly, orange polyester bedspread and brown shag carpet punctuated with cigarette holes his idea of the best?

We go to a drive-thru McDonald's for breakfast. Luke pulls his hat brim way down over his forehead, like he does whenever we're somewhere with people around. I order a Bacon, Egg & Cheese Biscuit and a milk, and he gets an Egg McMuffin and a large coffee. When he pulls out his wallet to pay, he says, "I'm gettin' low on cash. Do you have any?"

Guess I'm not going shopping for new clothes.

I dig into my backpack and hand him twenty dollars from my babysitting money. He keeps the change after he pays.

Luke's moody and distant all morning as we hit the highway heading north. I keep asking him what's the matter and he snaps, "Nothing." I stare out the window at the barren trees, wondering what's changed and why I'm in the car with him when he doesn't even want to talk to me. I can't help myself from thinking about home and I suddenly miss Mom and Dad so bad it hurts. I want to be back in my own room, sleeping in my own bed. I want everything to be just like it was before.

But it's never going to be like it was before. Not since that first night in the motel room.

"Tell me how much you want it, baby." His hot breath, panting in my ear.

A tear escapes from my eye and rolls down my cheek to

the corner of my mouth. Luke glances over before I can wipe it away.

"Don't tell me you're bawling again, Abby. Maybe I should just put you on a bus and send you back to Mommy and Daddy."

That just makes me cry harder. My parents are probably beyond mad about me taking off with Luke, and now Luke doesn't even seem to *like* me.

"D-don't you l-love m-me anym-more?"

He sighs heavily and pulls the car over to the side of the road.

"Of course I do, baby," he says, putting his arm around me. "You're my girl. Right?"

"R-right," I say, sniffling.

"So are we done with the tears?"

I swallow hard and take a deep breath, making a big effort to stop crying. I don't want him to be mad at me anymore. "Okay."

"Right. Let's get back on the road. I want to try to make it to Canada by nightfall."

When Luke sees the police lights and hears the sirens, he swears. Then he turns to me and says, "Abby, they're going to tell you we're wrong and this is wrong, but remember, I love you. You're my girl. Whatever you do, don't you forget that."

I start crying again then, uncontrollably.

"I won't, Luke. I promise."

Luke is forced to pull over. State troopers surround our car with guns drawn. I've never had a gun pointed at me before and I'm scared to death. One of them approaches Luke's window. Luke rolls it down. The trooper asks Luke if he's Edmund J. Schmidt of 282 Tudor Street, South Boston, Massachusetts. I wait for Luke to tell him that this is a case of mistaken identity and this is all a big mistake, that his name is Luke Redmond. But he just nods, and before I know what's happening, the trooper points his gun at Luke and yells at him to get out of the car and put his hands up.

"Luke, what's going on? Why don't you tell them your real name?" I cry as he opens the car door. He ignores me.

The policeman practically throws him against the car, frisks him, and slaps on handcuffs.

I open my door and get out to tell them they've made a mistake, but one of the troopers puts his hand on my shoulder and asks me if I'm Abigail Johnston of Huntingville, Connecticut.

"Yes, I am, but —"

"Don't worry, honey," he says. "You're safe now."

I don't have time to tell him that I was safe before, that Luke would never do anything to hurt me, because I see them leading him away to a police car, his hands cuffed behind his back, a policeman on either side of him, each grabbing his arm roughly.

"DON'T HURT HIM!" I shout, tears streaming down my face.

Luke turns and looks back at me over his shoulder with the saddest smile. I wonder if I'll ever see him again, and it feels like my heart is breaking.

The police take me to the station, where they put me in a room that has bars on the window, cold plastic chairs, and a table. A female police officer, Officer Domuracki, gets me a cup of hot chocolate. I wrap my hands around the Styrofoam cup. The warmth is the only thing anchoring me to reality. It feels like this is all happening to someone else.

"Your parents are on their way," she says. "But it'll take them a while to get up here from Connecticut."

The thought of my parents coming comforts and terrifies me at the same time.

Officer Domuracki sits with me for a while trying to make small talk, to get me to tell her about myself, about my family, about what happened. But the only person I want to talk to right now is Luke, and no one will tell me where he is or what's happening to him or what's *going* to happen to him. Finally, she gives up and leaves me in the room with some boring magazines.

I'm half asleep with my head on the cold Formica of the table when I hear my father's voice.

"Abby! Thank heavens you're safe!"

I raise my head and he and Mom are standing in the doorway — Mom has tears streaming down her face. I get up and run to them and they both envelop me tightly in their arms, so tightly I can barely breathe.

"We were so worried, Abby," Mom sobs. "You have no idea. . . ."

My father's shoulders are shaking. I look up at his face and feel gut-punched to see he's crying, too. I've never in my whole life seen my father cry, ever. Seriously. Dad doesn't do tears.

If I wanted to teach them a lesson like Luke said, then it looks as if they are well and truly schooled.

"Where's Lily?" I ask.

"She's with the Wilsons," Mom says. "Faith sends her love. If it weren't for Faith, we might not have found you."

"That's right," Dad says. "Faith is a real hero. She helped the FBI figure out the password to your ChezTeen account so we could track that son of a bitch down."

Son of a bitch? I realize Dad must mean Luke.

I guess Luke was right. He knew people wouldn't understand about us.

"Daddy, you've got it wrong. Luke's not . . ."

"Don't talk to me about that monster, Abby," Dad says, stiffening, as he takes his arms from around my shoulders. "And his name isn't even Luke. It's —"

"I think it's best if we save that conversation for later," says a woman in a dark pantsuit.

She introduces herself to me.

"Hi, Abby. I'm Agent Saunders of the FBI."

Her handshake is firm, her fingers cool. I wonder if she's ever, like, shot someone.

"Abby, it's important that we get you to the hospital, now that your parents are here."

"The hospital? What for? I'm fine. Honest. There's nothing the matter with me. Look at me."

Agent Saunders does look at me. She looks me straight in the eye.

"We need to take you to the hospital, Abby, so that a specially trained nurse can do what's called a forensic exam. She'll take evidence that can be used in the event of a trial."

Evidence? A trial?

I can't meet her gaze. I look at the wall above her right shoulder.

"He didn't hurt me. Luke loves me."

His hand gripping my hair so hard it felt like it would come out by the roots. *"Tell me you want it, baby. Tell me you want it right now."*

"Are you *insane*?" my father explodes. "How can you think that monster *loves* you?"

His anger flows over me like hot volcanic lava, and I stand there paralyzed. Separate. It only works when I keep them separate. And now the two worlds are colliding in one huge painful explosion that makes me want to crawl inside my own skin and hide.

Agent Saunders exchanges glances with Officer Domuracki, and the policewoman goes over to Dad and quietly suggests that maybe he should accompany her out of the room for a while to calm down, because him shouting at me isn't in my best interest right now.

"I'm her father. I have every right to be here," I hear Dad say in an angry undertone.

I just stare out the barred window and let the voices flow around me while I picture the sad smile on Luke's face as the policemen led him away in handcuffs. *Where is he now? What are they going to do to him? Does he still love me? Is this all my fault?*

"Abby," Agent Saunders says, bringing me reluctantly back into the room. Dad's no longer here. It's just the FBI agent, Mom, and me. Mom's face is pale and pinched with worry. "This might not seem important now, but later on, you might feel differently. We have to harvest whatever evidence we can while it's available. Did you shower this morning?"

Why does she care about that? Do I smell or something?

"No. I didn't have time. Luke said he wanted to get on the road."

"That's good. How about we head over to the hospital now and get this over with, so that you and your parents can head home?"

"But —"

"Abby," Mom says. She takes my hand, gingerly, like she's almost afraid to touch me. "I know this is . . . unpleasant . . . but you *have* to do it."

I continue staring out the window and try to crawl a little deeper inside my skin.

"Whatever."

I'm picturing Luke's smile as I lie here on the hospital bed in a stupid paper gown. Agent Saunders keeps trying to get me to talk about him, but I don't want to talk to her. She doesn't believe what I say anyway. I told her that Luke didn't hurt me, that he loves me, but she and Mom say I have to have this stupid exam anyway because it's "standard procedure."

So I just stare at the fluorescent light overhead as I wait for the SANE nurse to come and do whatever it is she's going to do to me. SANE, that's a joke. It stands for Sexual Assault Nurse Examiner, but SANE is about the last thing I feel right now. I had to take everything off. Everything.

Mom is sitting on a chair beside the bed. Every so often she strokes my hair but then she drops her hand like she's afraid I'm going to give her the cooties.

There's a knock on the door, and it opens. A pretty Asian woman in a white coat comes in accompanied by the nurse in pink scrubs, the one who made me wear this stupid paper gown "opening to the front, please."

"Hello, Abigail. I'm Nurse Wong. I'll be performing the rape exam."

"But Luke didn't rape me — he . . ."

"Just lie back, Abby, and put your feet in these stirrups. Relax if you can. I'll try to get this over with as quickly as possible."

I can't believe this is happening to me. I stare up at the fluorescent light overhead, trying to pretend this isn't me, not my body, not my pubic hair that's being combed. Not my inner thigh that's being photographed because there's a bruise high up on one of them near my privates. Not my left breast that's being photographed because Luke left a huge hickey on it, or my right shoulder where there's a bite mark.

"I'm sorry, Abby, this will be a little cold," Nurse Wong says, picking up this metal contraption and moving between my legs.

Ow, that hurts! "*Relax, sweet girl, and take it. Take it all. I'm gonna fuck you so good, baby girl. Damn, you're tight. I'm gonna give it to you harder, baby. Oh, yeah, that's so good.*"

"Please, Abby, you need to keep your knees open. I know this is uncomfortable, but it'll be over more quickly if you can just take a deep breath and try to relax," the nurse says.

My eyes are closed, but I feel my mother's hand grab mine and squeeze it tightly. I cling to hers until the nurse takes the cold metal thing out of me and covers me with the paper gown again.

When I open my eyes, there are tears streaming down my mother's face.

"*Stop bawling, Abby, and look like you enjoy it, for chrissake!*" *His fingers on my chin turn my face toward the camera.*

My own eyes are dry.

*　　*　　*

They won't even let me have my underpants back when it's over. The nurse picks them up with tweezers and puts them in a plastic bag for "evidence." They give me these stupid paper panties to put on. Mom says they're the same kind they give you in the hospital after you have a baby. Oh, yeah, speaking of which, I have to take a pregnancy test, too. And get tested for sexually transmitted diseases. When I'm dressed (with my paper panties, which are really uncomfortable) the nurse talks to Mom and me about how in a few weeks time I should get tested for HIV. Just in case.

I pretend to sleep on the five-hour car ride home so I don't have to talk to anyone. But I keep thinking about what Dad said. That Luke's name isn't really Luke.

"Are you Edmund J. Schmidt, of 282 Tudor Street, South Boston, Massachusetts?"

Why didn't Luke tell them the truth? Why didn't he say no?

The foundations of my life are crumbling and I'm about to be buried under the wreckage. My head spins, just like when I was in the motel room that first night, drunk on vodka and cranberry juice, until I finally fall asleep for real in the backseat, exhausted.

The FBI lady, Agent Saunders, is sitting across from me in our living room. There's also another lady from the FBI, Maura, a "victim support specialist," who says she's there to help me. Because, apparently, I'm a victim. Mom is next to me, holding my hand. Dad's hovering by the door, like he half wants to be here but half doesn't, in case he hears something about his little Abby that will upset him.

It's too late, Daddy. I'm not your little Abby anymore.

I reach down inside for the ice-cold numbness that I feel whenever I think of Luke and pull it over me like a security blanket. Numbness is what I want more than anything right now. I just wish everyone would leave me alone so I could stare at a blank wall and not think or talk about anything.

"Abby, I need you to tell me everything you can about Edmund J. Schmidt," Agent Saunders says.

"I would if I knew who the hell you were talking about."

"You know damn well who it is!" Dad exclaims from the doorway. He looks at me like I'm some kind of alien from the planet Filth. Which is kind of how I feel when I'm around him.

"Edmund J. Schmidt is the actual identity of the man known to you as Luke Redmond," Agent Saunders says.

"But —"

"He's thirty-two years old, from South Boston, Massachusetts. Lives with his parents: Joseph, an auto mechanic, and his mother, Anna, a retired secretary."

"Are you Edmund J. Schmidt of 282 Tudor Street, South Boston, Massachusetts?" the state trooper had asked. And Luke never told them anything different.

"No. You've got the wrong person. Luke's twenty-seven and he's from New Jersey. Toms River."

"What were you thinking running away with a man more than twice your age, Abby?" my father bursts out. I disgust him. I've spent my whole life trying to make him proud, but by going off with Luke, I blew it. Forever.

Maura gets up and talks quietly to Dad, but I think I get the gist of it. Basically, she's telling him to get lost because it will be easier for me without him there. Maybe she *is* there to support me, even if I'm not really a victim.

Dad opens his mouth to argue but when he looks at Mom for help she mouths, "Go." He heaves a sigh and splits, leaving just us girls for this merry little inquisition.

After he's gone, Agent Saunders pulls a piece of paper out of her file and hands it to me.

"We had this faxed to us from Boston. Do you recognize this man?"

It's a photocopy of a Massachusetts driver's license belonging to Edmund Joseph Schmidt. And although I don't want to admit it, the guy in the picture looks exactly like Luke.

"I'm not sure. Maybe."

"We obtained a warrant to search the Schmidt house, and took the computer used by Edmund Schmidt as evidence. Our experts are going over it right now. The IP address corresponded to some of the communications that you received on your computer."

I don't say anything. I'm trying to take in the fact that Luke isn't Luke. That Luke is Edmund. But I know one thing. No matter who he is, he loves me. I'm still his special girl, the one he loves more than anyone.

"I need to talk to Luke. I'm sure he can explain all this."

I feel Mom stiffen next to me.

"I'm afraid that's not possible, Abby," Agent Saunders says. "And even if it were, I'm sure Schmidt's lawyer wouldn't allow it. Nor would I advise it."

Hearing that Luke has a lawyer brings home to me even more how much trouble he's in. All because of me.

"How did you first meet this man?" Mom asks.

But I know the question she's really asking: *Where did Dad and I go wrong?*

"It was the website I go on all the time, ChezTeen.com. I talk to all kinds of people on there. That's the whole point of the site, to talk to people."

"I thought you only chatted to people you actually know in real life," Mom says. "That's what they tell us you should do in all the PTA talks about safe use of the Internet."

I roll my eyes.

"But, Mom, this site is different from, like, Facebook. They have the latest movie trailers, new music videos, and virtual concerts and things like that, and you can talk to other people about all that stuff."

"And it's geared to teens, and whenever a site brings teens, it attracts predators, unfortunately," Agent Saunders explains with a sigh. "We try as hard as we can to keep up, but new sites pop up constantly, and teens migrate to them." She looks at Mom. "And as you saw in this case, when the servers aren't in this country, we have a real problem getting timely access to the information we need to protect a child from harm."

"Luke would never harm me!" I protest. "You don't understand him. He really cares about me. He . . ."

I'm about to say "he loves me" but both Maura and Agent Saunders are looking at me with pity in their eyes like *You poor gullible kid, that's what they all think.*

Well, fuck them. They're wrong. I know they are. I need Luke so bad. I want to call him, but they've taken away the cell phone he gave me as "evidence." I can't e-mail him because they took away my laptop as "evidence," too. I might not ever get it back, even. How much does *that* suck? And there's no way in hell Mom and Dad are ever going to buy me another one after this. They've taken my underpants as "evidence." I'm surprised they haven't stuck me in one of their stupid plastic bags and marked me as "evidence," too.

Agent Saunders takes out another piece of paper from her folder, and hands it to me facedown. "Abby, does this look familiar?"

I turn it over and the bagel I ate for breakfast threatens to come back up. It's a picture of me, topless, in my bedroom. It looks like . . .

"Where did you get this?"

"Our agents downloaded it from a child porn site. Edmund Schmidt uploaded it, along with several other pictures of you. The 'Abby series' is being discussed in pedophile chat rooms."

She waits while I stare at the picture. I wrap my arms around myself and rock back and forth, as if the motion can bring me back to being a baby, before all this happened.

"I'm afraid it gets worse, Abby," she says.

Worse? What could possibly be worse? No . . . No . . .

"*You're so beautiful, baby. I need to capture the moment when every sweet inch of you finally belongs to me. . . .*" — *fingers hard on my chin, turning my face toward the video camera* — "*Stop bawling, baby, and look like you enjoy it!*"

The next morning, he leaves me in the motel room while he goes to buy breakfast, and he takes the camera with him "in case I accidentally push the ERASE *button on the best moment of his life, ever."*

He wouldn't. Not Luke. He loves me. He said it was just for him, for us, because I was so beautiful.

Maura comes and sits on my other side as Agent Saunders takes out a small laptop and opens it. She pushes PLAY and there I am naked, on that ugly plaid bedspread in that crappy motel room, my legs spread wide, and Luke is saying all the things he's going to do to me. The video Abby says something — it's hard to tell what because my words are so slurred — and Luke laughs and holds my head while he gets me to drink some more. Then he . . .

"STOP IT! Make it stop!"

I feel dizzy, because the floor has just collapsed under my world. *Luke* did this? *My* Luke, who said he loved me? Luke, who said I was his special girl? He put pictures of me on the Internet, on porn sites, for *perverts* to see? He put *that* video up for everyone and anyone to see under the caption: VIRGIN PUSSY GETS SLAMMED SO HARD SHE CRIES.

This isn't real. This can't be happening. It's a bad dream and I'm going to wake up and it'll all go away and life will be normal again.

Mom's hand covers her mouth as she stares at my image frozen on the screen, like she's trying to hold in the guts she's about to puke out from the sight of her oldest daughter losing her virginity for everyone and anyone to see.

Then it's like she visibly tries to put on her Mom Face.

"Are you okay, honey?" she asks. "You look pale. Do you want some tea?"

She can't look at me. She can't wait to escape from my presence; she needs some excuse to be away from me, because what she's seen disgusts her so much.

No, I'm not okay, Mom. No, I don't want tea. I just want to be Abby again, not some Internet porn star with my own "series."

"This has got to be an awful shock for you, Abby," Maura says. "And it must feel like a terrible betrayal."

"Can you . . . take it . . . take them . . . down?" I ask, my voice shaking. The thought of all these perverts out there looking at me, looking at pictures of me that were meant only for Luke, makes me want to go run to the shower and scrub my skin until it hurts.

"We will make attempts to get these images and the video taken off the servers," Agent Saunders says. "But the problem with most of these child porn sites is that they're not located in the United States, so we have no jurisdiction."

"That's the same problem that we had when we were trying to find you, Abby," Mom tells me. "The server thing. If it weren't for Faith being able to guess your password, we might not have found you in time."

Faith. How did she guess? Well, duh. I suppose if anyone was going to be able to hack my account, it would be Faith. She knows the way I think better than anybody. Except for Luke. But I bet even Faith couldn't imagine me being an Internet porn queen.

What happens if people at school find out about this? I might as well just die now.

I reach deep inside for my numbness blanket but it's gone. I'm forced to feel and what I'm feeling is so overwhelmingly awful that I wish I could rip my skin off. Maybe that would make me feel less dirty.

Agent Saunders starts asking me questions about Edmund Schmidt again. I still feel like she's talking about a different person, that it's this horrible Schmidt guy from Boston who took the pictures of me and put them online, not my boyfriend, Luke, the one who loves me, who tells me I'm his special girl.

"You weren't the only girl he was chatting with, Abby," Agent Saunders says. "Schmidt had chats going with at least four other girls, from the ages of twelve through fifteen, from all over the country."

Her words shatter me like a plate-glass window. I don't know what hurts me more — the pictures and videos of me being posted online or the realization that if Agent Sanders is telling me the truth, then everything Luke said to me is a lie. Which makes me the world's Biggest Fucking Idiot, as well as someone whose half-naked photos are being gawked at — and probably worse, gross — by a bunch of perverted weirdos. And whose loss of virginity is now a major motion picture of the porn world.

How could you do this to me, Luke? You said you loved me, that I was your girl. Is that what you were saying to all these other girls, too?

I don't realize that tears are streaming down my face until Maura hands me a bunch of tissues.

"Abby, we realize this is incredibly difficult for you," Maura says. "But the more you can tell us about him, it'll help us to make sure that he doesn't do this to anyone else."

I don't care about anyone else right now. I just want to go to bed and pull the covers over my head and never have to face anyone ever again. I just want to never have to feel anything, ever. I just want to be numb. Forever.

"Maybe we should take a break," Mom says. "Are you sure you don't want anything to eat, sweetheart? Or to drink?"

I just shake my head, covering my face with my hands to try and block them all out. To block everything out. To try to find the comfort of nothingness again.

CHAPTER 30
FAITH ♪ DECEMBER 12

"So, what happened with Abby? Did, like, she get raped or something?"

If another person asks me that, I'm going to scream. It's been like this all day. I told two people, Gracie and Billy, that Abby had been found and was home, and all of a sudden it's like the whole school knows and turned it into "Abby got raped."

The thing is, I don't even *know* what happened to her. Mom's taking me over to see Abby after school, but she said I shouldn't ask her, that if Abby wants to speak about her "traumatic experiences," she will, in her own time. But I'm her best friend and if it weren't for me, they wouldn't have found her. She *has* to tell me.

This whole Luke thing — I can't believe it all happened in the first place, that she would be stupid enough to run off with this guy. Abby's usually so smart about everything, way smarter than me. How could she fall for a creep like him?

"It's none of your business," I tell anyone who asks what happened to Abby.

They all probably heard on the news that the police arrested Edmund Schmidt, age thirty-two, of Boston, Massachusetts. They've all probably seen Abby's eighth-grade yearbook picture, the one she hated, on their TV screen. But it's not like any of them were such good friends to her before.

When Nick Peters and Amanda Armitage come up to me in the hallway and start peppering me with questions about Abby, I finally blow.

"What do you care?" I shout at Nick. "You couldn't even remember her freaking name, you moron!"

I burst into tears and run for the bathroom. Gracie follows me.

"OMG, Faith, you should have seen Nick's face," she says, laughing. "I don't think any girl has *ever* called him a moron before. And Amanda . . . she looked like she just drank a diarrhea milk shake."

"It's not as if they even *like* Abby," I say, grabbing some toilet paper to blow my nose. "Amanda's been a total witch to us for as long as I can remember. They just want gossip, that's all."

"Can you blame them, Faith?" Grace says. "Seriously. This is the biggest thing that's happened at Roosevelt High ever. There are *TV cameras* outside."

"But . . . can you imagine what it's going to be like for Abby to come back to school? I can barely stand it today and it's not me that it's happened to."

Gracie looks away.

"Look, Faith, you're probably going to be really mad at me for saying this, but I'm going to say it anyway. Maybe Abby should have thought about that before she ran away with that Internet creep. I mean, seriously. What was she thinking?"

I feel this rush of anger at Grace, but when she meets my eyes, finally, it fades away because the truth is, I'm wondering the same thing.

CHAPTER 31
ABBY · DECEMBER 13

Mom and Dad still aren't letting me out of their sight, other than to shower and go to the bathroom. Faith came over last night to bring me homework. At first it was really awkward. Like, I know she wanted to ask me what happened and did he do stuff and all the gory details, but how can I possibly tell Faith about how I'm now the star of a "series" of naked pictures on a child porn site? About how the video of me losing my cherry is being watched by perverts around the world.

I feel like the dirtiest filth on earth and I love Faith too much to contaminate her. *She's* still a normal girl. That's something I'll never be, ever again.

But then she just looked at me and said, "Oh, Abby, I was so scared!" and she threw her arms around me and hugged me and I felt her shoulders shaking.

Did I say dirtiest filth on earth? I meant in the universe. I'm this awful scum of a person who has let everyone down, especially the people who are closest to her.

"I'm sorry, Faith," I said, starting to cry myself. "I'm so, so sorry."

She lifted her head, tears tracing the freckles on her cheeks.

"You don't know what it was like, not knowing . . . and imagining . . . You hear all these stories of girls being tortured in basements or getting cut up in wood chippers and —"

"Look, I'm here and unchipped, okay?"

"Okay. I'm so glad you're safe, Abs."

She looked like she was about to start crying again so I asked her how things were going with Ted. Turns out that wasn't such a good idea.

"Not so well. We . . . kind of broke up."

"What? I thought things were going so well?"

"They were," Faith said. Suddenly, she couldn't meet my eyes. "But . . ."

"But, what?"

There was this awkward silence, in which it seemed like Faith was trying to figure out what to say, but then she finally just looked me straight in the eye and said, "The thing is, Abby, when you ran off with this guy without telling anyone, I felt so awful, because before you never would have done something like that without telling me. And if you had told me, maybe I could have talked you out of it."

I opened my mouth to try to tell her that no one could have changed my mind about going to meet Luke, that it was like my destiny or something, but she held up her hand and continued.

"But I was so wrapped up with the play and Ted that I wasn't there for you."

Tears flooded her eyes and she grasped both of my hands.

"Ted . . . Well, he said stuff about you and we had this huge fight and broke up."

She shakes her head as if to erase the memory.

"But . . . I'm just . . . I'm so sorry, Abs. I'm sorry for being such a bad friend."

Guilt doesn't even begin to describe what I felt right then. Faith was so happy with Ted and now they've broken up because of me and she's apologizing to me for it? Lily's right. She was happy to see me when I got back, but it didn't take too long afterward before she proceeded to tell me how badly I've screwed everything up for everyone.

"You're not a bad friend, Faith. You're the best."

I hugged her and even though I'd felt angry at her before I went away with Luke, I felt closer to her then than I ever had.

"So . . . what are people saying about me?" I asked.

The flush on Faith's face told me that whatever people were saying, it probably wasn't anything I wanted to hear. But I need to know the worst. At some point, I have to go back to school.

"I don't know. . . . I . . ." She didn't meet my eyes.

"Come on, Faith. Just tell me. I'm going to find out sooner or later."

Faith took a deep breath and looked straight at me.

"People keep asking me if he raped you and stuff. I told them it wasn't any of their business. But people want to know . . ." She swallowed. "But *I* want to know how you could go off with some creep from the Internet that you never met before in your life. How someone as smart as you could do something that stupid."

Each word felt like a needle, piercing my skin. But Faith wasn't done.

"What I really, really need to know, Abs," she said, tears welling in her eyes, "is why didn't you tell me? Maybe if we'd talked . . ."

"You were busy," I mumbled, feeling like the biggest piece of shit in the world. "With the play and everything. Things were different and I . . ."

"But we're still best friends, right? And best friends tell each other stuff. Especially important stuff like they're thinking of running off with some guy they met over the Internet."

"It wasn't like that, Faith. You don't understand. Nobody does."

"So explain it to me, Abby. Make me understand."

I took a deep breath and tried to figure out how to begin.

"Like I said, you were busy and I guess I was feeling, I don't know, lonely and . . . like . . . well, Luke listened to me. It was like he knew me better than anybody, and understood exactly what I was going through."

I could tell Faith was upset at the "knew me better than anybody" thing. I guess I could see why. We were always the ones who knew each other better than anybody.

"But couldn't you see he was just pretending?" Faith asked. "You know, whatever they call it . . . 'grooming' you?"

"It wasn't like that," I told her. "It really felt like . . ."

The loss hit me suddenly, and I was crying hard over the loss of something I never really had.

"It felt like he loved me, Faith. But he didn't. He was telling all these other girls he loved them, too. I'm just an idiot. A dirty, brainless idiot, who's screwed up everyone's lives."

Faith was hugging me and our tears mingled where our cheeks touched.

"Oh, Abs, you're not dirty. And you haven't screwed up everyone's lives."

But Faith doesn't know the half of it. She doesn't know that I'm the star of the "Abby Series" on all these child porn sites.

She doesn't know that I'm a "celebrity" just like Paris Hilton now, with my own personal sex tape. She doesn't know about the stuff that happened in those dingy one-star motel rooms while I was away with Luke.

"What about you and Ted?"

She sighed.

"I guess it wasn't meant to work out. It's pretty awkward still being on stage crew with him. But, whatever."

"I'm scared to go back to school, Faith. I mean, it was bad enough before, but now . . . "

"I'll be there for you, Abs. I'll always be there for you. And this time, don't forget it."

CHAPTER 32
ABBY ⁄ DECEMBER 15

"Do you want me to walk you in?" Mom asks me as I sit with my hand on the door handle, afraid to open the car door and get out.

If you thought the first day of high school was bad, try going back after you ran away with some guy you met online who turned out not to be the loving person you thought he was, but was actually a creep and a perv who was chatting up lots of other girls.

I feel breakfast coming up the back of my throat.

"Can't I stay home another day? I really don't think I'm ready."

"Honey, you've already missed over a week of school and the end of the marking period is coming up. Maura said you should try to get back into a routine. We've talked to the counselor at school. You can always go see her if . . . things get . . . difficult."

Difficult. Everything is *difficult* at the moment. Sleeping is difficult because I keep having horrible dreams. Waking up is difficult because I can't sleep. Looking in the mirror is difficult because I hate the person I see. But the worst part is seeing the reflection of myself in my father's eyes. That's worse than any mirror.

When I make no move to get out of the car, Mom says, "Come on, Abby, let me just walk you inside."

"Mom, I'm in high school, not nursery school, okay? I can manage to walk up the stairs by myself."

She gets that hurt, "I was only trying to help" look and I feel bad. I spend pretty much all of my time right now feeling bad.

I squeeze her hand. "Don't worry, Mom. I'll be okay."

Mom kisses my cheek and whispers, "Good luck." She tells me she'll be there to pick me up after school. She's rearranged her whole work schedule so that she can be my personal chauffeur/jailor. My parents don't trust me to be unsupervised anywhere. I guess I can't really blame them. But I didn't realize how much I enjoyed my freedom until it was gone.

Heart pounding and stomach churning, I open the car door and get out. I hear someone go, "OMG! There's that girl, Abby Johnston! You know, the one who . . ."

I don't hear the rest because the voice drops to an undertone. But I can fill in the blanks for myself: *Was stupid enough to run off with an Internet predator. Was foolish enough to believe he was in love with her. Was such a moron that she sent him revealing pictures of herself that he went and posted on a child porn site. Was drunk and ended up having her virginity taken in what is now a downloadable online video.*

More than anything I want to dive back into the car and tell Mom to drive me home so I can go to bed and bury myself under the comforter. But Mom has to get to work. I've already screwed up everyone's life enough. So I slam the car door behind me and force myself to start walking up the steps toward the front door of school, running a gauntlet of whispers and staring eyes. No one talks *to* me. They just talk *about* me. I guess I've really made a name for myself here at Roosevelt High.

I keep my eyes on the ground as I walk down the hall to my locker, trying to wrap myself in indifference, to tell myself that none of this matters. But it doesn't work anymore. It's not like I'm going to be able to go home and talk to Luke about my crummy day at school. He's being held on remand in some prison upstate. *And his name isn't even Luke. It's Edmund. Eddie? Ed? I wonder what he called himself when he talked to all the other girls he was chatting with. The other girls he was telling how beautiful and special they were. The other stupid idiots like me.*

"Abby! How *are you*?"

Gracie swoops across the hall and envelops me in a hug.

"I'm *so* glad you got back safely," she says. "We were so *worried* about you. Faith was a *complete* basket case."

I was kind of jealous of Grace before, but the fact that she's being nice to me now, when I'm a social leper, brings me close to tears.

"Are you okay? Do you want me to walk with you to your class or anything?"

"You won't think I'm totally lame?"

She gives me a sympathetic smile.

"No, I won't think you're totally lame. This has got to be pretty awful, huh?"

I nod, not trusting myself to speak without bursting into tears.

"Come on. Let's get your stuff out of your locker, then I'll take you to homeroom."

*   *   *

She's as good as her word. Not only that, during homeroom she talks to Faith and the two of them come to walk me to my next class. And the one after. It's not like having them on either side of me stops people from staring and talking and whispering. It's not like I don't hear people pretending to cough, but really saying "slut" after I walk by. But at least I don't feel totally alone, like I did when I was walking into school. Their friendship feels like some kind of . . . protection.

"Aren't you guys going to get in trouble for being late to class?" I ask them.

"Gracie went to talk to the principal," Faith says. "He gave us both passes."

I guess Faith was right about Gracie all along. I really underestimated her. I really underestimated them both.

"Thanks, you guys . . . it . . . really means a lot to me."

I'm doing reasonably okay until it's time for science and I realize that I'm going to see Billy. It's bad enough that all these other people think that I'm a stupid, crazy slut, but Billy . . . I'm not sure I can face seeing the disgust in his eyes.

"I don't want to go to science, Faith. Maybe I can pretend I'm sick and go to the nurse."

"What, because of Billy?"

"I don't want him to hate me. It's bad enough that everyone else does."

Gracie opens her mouth like she wants to say that everyone doesn't hate me, but I'm looking her straight in the eye so she shuts it. There's no point lying.

"Abs, you shouldn't worry about Billy," Faith says. "*He*

really cares about you. You should have seen him when you were missing. He was really freaked out. And not just because the police went to his house and asked him questions, either."

"The police questioned *Billy*?"

"Well, yeah. Because you'd gone out on a date with him and stuff. And because he was one of the last people to see you before you disappeared."

"That just gives him *more* reason to hate me."

"But he *doesn't*. That's the point," Faith says. "Just go to class. You're going to have to see him sooner or later. And like I said, *he cares about you.*"

Unlike Luke, who just said he did but lied. Like he lied about everything else.

People stare at me when I walk into science. But then everyone turns away like they've got something really important to do. I'm not sure which is worse — everyone staring, or knowing that they're desperately trying not to. I wonder if things will ever be normal again, if I'll just be plain old Abby who nobody notices.

I sit down in my usual seat at the lab table and pretend to look at my notes as intently as everyone else is pretending that everything is normal in my life. I hear the sound of Ms. Forcier's heels tip-tapping over in my direction and I feel her hand on my shoulder.

"Welcome back, Abby," she says just loud enough for me to hear. "I'm so glad you're safe."

I'm afraid to look up at her, in case I see judgment in her eyes, so I keep my eyes lowered. She puts some handouts on my desk.

"Here's what you missed while you were gone. The midterms are next week, so you've got some catching up to do. Let me know if you need any extra help."

"Okay."

"I can help, too."

Billy. I'm afraid to turn and face him.

He cares about you, Faith said.

So did Luke. But he lied.

But Luke was really Edmund.

And Billy isn't Luke.

I turn and face Billy, expecting to see the kind of look I've been seeing in the hallway: the scorn, the sneering, the judging. But there's none of that. It's just . . . Billy. Billy, with a tentative smile, like he's just worried about how I'm feeling.

"Hey, Abby," he says.

"Hey, Billy."

"It's about time you got back, you slacker. It sucked having to do the labs by myself."

I can't believe he's joking with me like nothing happened. Like everything's normal. Like *I'm* normal. Doesn't he realize that I'm . . . this stupid person who did this awful thing? But hearing him tease me like this feels like the greatest gift anyone has ever given me. Because, for a second or two, I almost feel like old Abby again. Enough that I risk joking back.

"Well, it's about time you did some of the work, Fisher. Typical guy, expecting the woman to carry the load all the time."

That gets me a real smile, just as Ms. Forcier starts class.

I'm taking notes and trying to concentrate on everything she's saying, because I know I've missed stuff while I've been gone, but I'm really aware of Billy. Then I see his hand edging toward mine out of the corner of my eye, passing me a note.

U scared the crap outta me, Abby. Do me a fave and stick around, k?

I'm not glad I scared him. But I am glad that even though I'm . . . who and what I am now, he still wants me to stick around. *But will he be so accepting if he finds out everything?* Probably not. So I might as well enjoy this for the short time that it lasts.

K. Will stick. Like glue.

He passes the note back.

Glue too messy. Double-sided tape maybe? ☺

I can't hide a smile, but right then Ms. Forcier turns around from the board so I tuck the note in my pocket and turn my full attention back to science.

Billy walks with me out into the hall, where I wait for Faith and Gracie to escort me to math.

"How come you're not running away?" he asks. "Usually you're in such a hurry to get to your next class."

I flush, thinking of all the times I used that excuse because I didn't want him to ask me out again. Now I wonder what would have happened if I'd stayed still long enough to listen to what he had to say. Maybe I would have gone out with him again. Maybe I wouldn't have become so obsessed with Luke. Maybe I would have "made better choices" as my parents would say. Somewhere, in a parallel universe, there's an answer to that question. But where I live, I'm stuck with who I am and what I did, and I have to live with it. I just hope it's not forever.

"I'm waiting for Faith . . . and Grace. They're going to walk me to my next class."

"What, you've been gone a week and you already forgot the way?" he says, a teasing light in his eyes.

Can't he see the looks? Doesn't he see how everyone is staring at me like I'm some putrid creature that just crawled out from under a very dirty rock?

"No . . . it's just . . . well . . ." I can't look him in the eye.

I see Grace and Faith coming down the hall and wish they'd hurry so I wouldn't have to explain. It feels so good to pretend to be Real Abby again with Billy that I don't want to shatter the illusion, because I know that once it's gone, it's gone, and it'll be back to my suckfest life of "living with the consequences of my actions."

"Wait —" Billy says, eyes narrowing. "Are you taking crap about what happened? Are people hassling you?"

Well, *duh.*

"What do you think? That I'm being welcomed back with open arms and smiles and a parade?"

"But —"

"Hi, Abs!" Faith says. "What's up, Billy? Sorry to interrupt, but we have to get Abby to her next class."

"Abby, we need to talk," Billy says.

I'm not sure I want to talk, because I'm afraid of what he's going to say to me. But I guess I kind of owe it to him.

"Okay. But you'll have to call me. I'm not allowed to IM at the moment for —" I feel myself blushing. "Well, for obvious reasons."

He blushes, like the subject embarrasses him, too.

"Yeah. Well . . . I'll call you tonight."

Gracie and Faith don't say anything until we turn the corner of the hallway and then they freak out on me and are all, *OMG, Abby!*

"So what's going on with you and Billy?" Gracie asks.

"Nothing," I say. "Nothing's going on with me and anyone, and that's the way it's going to stay. It's just . . ."

"Just what?" Faith says.

"It's just . . . he teased me."

"That jerk! How could he be so insensitive?" Grace says.

"*No!* Not like that. Like in a good way. Like I was still me."

I can see they don't get it. Faith's got that little crease between her eyebrows.

"But, Abby, you *are* still you," she says. "Of course you are."

They don't understand. They can't understand because they don't know what happened in the motel room. They don't know about the pictures and the video. They don't know that I have to wonder every minute of every hour if some creepy guy somewhere is looking at pictures of me naked, or downloading that video of Luke doing it to me. They don't understand how that changes you.

We get to the door of my math class.

"Faith. I can't tell you how much I wish I *were* the same me." My voice catches. "But I'm not. And I don't think I ever will be again."

Well, one good thing's come out of this. Nick Peters actually remembers my name.

"Hey, *Abby*," he says, flashing me his perfect teeth when I walk into class. "Welcome back."

Amanda gives me this fake look of concern.

"How *are* you? Is everything *okay*?"

"Um, thanks. I'm fine," I lie.

I sit down and focus on the board, trying to ignore the stares of my classmates.

"You look great, Abby," Nick says. "Really *fine*."

The guy sitting next to him snickers.

I don't get it. Nick's never said anything about my looks before. He's never even paid me much attention other than to copy my homework. I glance back at him briefly. He's looking at me intently and grinning.

"Uh, thanks."

I turn around and take out my pencil.

"*Slut!*"

It's said quietly and as a half cough, but it's definitely the word. Someone sitting near me. I think it's Amanda. I'm afraid to turn around and look, especially because Mr. Evans is starting class.

Tears well up in my eyes but I can't let them fall. Instead, I take myself away, so it's as if I'm watching the scene in a movie and real Abby is somewhere else, somewhere she can't be hurt by the sting of their words or the scorn of their glances.

"*Whore!*"

The same low half cough, but this time it's from the other side and a guy. I feel sorry for the girl sitting in the math class, but she's not me. I'm just an observer. The comments go on for ten minutes or so, until Mr. Evans remarks that there seems to be a lot of coughing going on and offers cough drops to anyone with a tickly throat. That shuts them up for a while, and lets the girl concentrate until the bell rings to signal that class is over.

Nick nudges me as I'm getting my books together and passes me a folded piece of paper with a smile and a wink. I still don't get why he's suddenly being so nice to me, especially now.

Slowly, I unfold the note and when I see what's on the paper I'm drawn back into myself by the horror of it. I hear snickers and laughter and the half-coughing "slut" and "whore" but I've shrunk so far back within myself that it sounds like it's coming from a great distance. Staring straight ahead, being sure not to make eye contact with anyone, I crumple the paper in the palm of my hand and walk to the classroom door. Faith and Grace aren't there. Instead of waiting for them, I run the gauntlet of staring eyes and whispering mouths until I get to the nurse's office, where I tell her I have an awful migraine and I need to go home.

Because on the paper Nick passed me was one of Luke's pictures of me naked. Because now I realize that everybody knows.

CHAPTER 33
LILY • DECEMBER 15, EVENING

They're shouting again. I turn up my iPod so I won't have to hear Dad asking Abby over and over how could she, how could she go off with *that man* and Abby crying and crying and Mom telling Dad to shut up and leave Abby alone. It's like Dad's obsessed with it — which if you ask me is sick, but nobody is asking me anything. It's like I don't exist. Except Mom says I have to go to therapy, too. We *all* have to go so we get over the "posttraumatic stress," blah blah. I don't know why I have to go. I'm the only normal person in this house. You don't see me running off with pervs I met online, do you?

But no, just because Abby was an idiot, I'm getting pulled along on this crazy train, too.

And school sucks because of her. Everyone's been looking at me like I'm some kind of freak ever since my sister was on the news; first as an AMBER Alert and then when the police arrested Edmund/Luke/Pervert Face/Whateverhisnameis. Whatever social cred I had is shot. Permanently.

It's not that I'm not happy Abby's home safe and everything. I am. Even though life has been one great big suckfest ever since she got back — I'm like the Invisible Kid in this house while everyone focuses on Abby, Abby, Abby.

But I wouldn't trade places with Abby, not for a zillion dollars. Dad can barely look at her, and when he does he has this expression on his face like he just stepped in a big pile of dog poop. It makes *me* feel bad, so imagine what it feels like for Abby. Mom's afraid to let Abby out of her sight. She even changed her work schedule so she can drive Abby to school and pick her up. Guess who still has to take the bus?

Everyone's walking on eggshells all the time, trying not to make things worse, except for times like now when Dad can't help himself and he starts off on Abby about *how* and *why*, and then the whole cycle starts over again.

The weird thing is, Abby's not fighting back like she would have before. She just sits there and takes it like a rag doll. It's so not the pain-in-the-butt sister I normally know and hate.

I hear her come up the stairs, crying, and the door to her room closes. It doesn't even slam like it used to. And that's what makes me want to go to her, even though it's probably stupid, Lily, stupid.

It would be so much easier to just stay in here and listen to my tunes. It's not like Abby ever wants to talk to me anyway. But I hear her crying even over Beyoncé. Whatever. I rip off my earphones and go to her room. I don't knock when I open the door, and you know things are seriously bad with Abby because she doesn't even yell at me.

She's curled up on the bed, sobbing.

I don't know what to say or do. It's not like Abby and I get along, even. But I hate to see her like this, even if she has made my life suck. So I lie down on the bed next to her and put my arm around her.

"Are you okay, Abby?" I ask, even though I know that's probably the Stupidest Question Ever.

"D-d-dad h-hates m-me," she sobs. "He th-thinks I'm a s-sl-ut."

"Dad doesn't hate you, Abs. You should have seen him when you were . . . you know, missing. He was, like, a total wreck. Mom was in way better shape, and she was pretty much a basket case, too. We all were."

"He c-can't even l-look at m-me. L-like he j-just l-looks over m-my h-head."

I don't know what to say. I mean, Dad's seriously screwed up, that's a fact. But then I see Abby's perfectly neat desk and her totally organized bookshelf.

"Face it, Abs, you were Dad's perfect little Abby Angel. You're smart, you get good grades, you're totally obsessively organized just like him. You're almost his Dad clone but a girl. But you did this thing now that he doesn't understand. I don't understand either, Abs. And Dad can't handle it."

"Everyone at school looks at me l-like I'm the biggest freak that ever walked the p-planet Earth. I'm like the ebola virus — p-people want to stay as far away from m-me as possible."

"I know how you feel."

She sits up.

"What, they're doing that to you, too?"

"*Duh!* My sister ran off with an Internet perv. It was all over the papers and on TV. Do you think they're, like, electing me student body president?"

Abby starts crying again.

"It would have been better for everyone if Luke had killed me and chopped me up with a wood chipper like Faith said."

Now *that* ticks me off. Big-time.

"Oh, shut up!" I shout at her. "Like *that* would have been so great for me and Mom and Dad?"

I came in here to make Abby feel better, but right now I'm just mad, so mad I can't help myself.

"And his name isn't *Luke*, dammit. It's *Edmund*. Edmund Schmidt. *He lied to you, Abby!* It was all one *great big lie* and you were stupid enough to fall for it and ruin everything for everyone."

Abby just lies there, curled up like a baby, sobbing, and I feel like the Worst. Sister. Ever.

"I'm sorry, Abby. I suck. I didn't mean —"

"*What on earth* is going on in here?"

Mom stands in the doorway, glaring at me like she's just caught me torturing puppies.

"Lily, out of here. NOW."

"I was just . . ."

"I don't want to hear it. *Go to your room!*"

I look back at Abby, wanting to make it right, but she's still crying into her pillow.

I don't know if there's a way to ever make things right again.

CHAPTER 34
ABBY / DECEMBER 17

The therapist's office is modern, with fern plants and one of those little Zen waterfall things that's supposed to make you relaxed. I was expecting a real shrink couch, where I could lie down and pretend to go to sleep so I wouldn't have to answer her questions. Instead, I have to sit across from her in a funky black leather armchair that I keep sliding around in. I have to take off my shoes and sit cross-legged to get comfortable.

My mother is outside in the waiting room. I hope that white-noise thing works, because I don't want her to hear. Not that I'm planning to say anything, but . . . whatever.

"Hi, Abby. I'm Dr. Binnie. What brings you here?"

Like she doesn't already know.

"I thought my parents told you."

"I'd like to hear what you have to say."

I don't want to say anything. I don't want to talk about Luke or about what happened. I want it all to go away. But she's just sitting there, staring me out, waiting for me to open my mouth. It's like a game of chicken — which of us is going to break the silence first?

It's me.

"I met this older guy online and I ran away with him. Now I've screwed up everyone's lives, my dad and my sister hate me, and my mom thinks I need a jailor."

"Why do you think your father and sister hate you?"

"Because they think it's all my fault. Because I was stupid enough to run away with Luke."

I give this grim half chuckle.

"It's not like they're the only ones. Everyone at school thinks so, too. Except Faith. And Grace. And well, Faith and Grace might think so, but they at least stick up for me when everyone else is being a jerk."

"Faith and Grace are . . . ?"

"Faith's my best friend. Since second grade. I just met Grace this year. Through Faith. At first I was kind of jealous of her, 'cause I kind of felt like, I don't know, maybe Faith would . . . end up liking her better than me. But she's been nice to me since . . . it all happened. Oh, and so has Billy."

"Tell me about Billy."

"He's a guy in my science class. We went on a date before . . . you know . . . and I liked him . . . but then when I got all wrapped up with Luke, it got too confusing."

I told u, I'm the jealous type. No. I can't think of Luke.

"The funny thing is, Billy has every reason to hate me, but he's one of the few people who still likes me. He calls me a lot — like almost every night — just to see how I'm doing. I mean, he said he still doesn't understand what made me do it, and he says he really hopes someday I can explain it to him, but it doesn't stop him from joking with me in class like I'm the same smart, normal Abby I was before. Not the stupid 'ho' that everyone thinks I am now."

"And what do you think? Do you think you were stupid?"

Silence, except for the sound of the Zen waterfall, which now that I think about it sounds more like there's a dwarf peeing in the corner.

"Well, *duh*. I mean, like, Luke told me he loved me and I was stupid enough to believe him. Meanwhile he was telling all these other girls that he was in love with them, too. So, yeah, I guess I pretty much should get the Stupid Idiot of the Year Award."

"Do you think you deserve everyone at school being a jerk to you?"

"I can't blame anyone. I would think the same thing about me if I were them. I mean, Luke's name isn't even Luke. It's Edmund. He even lied about his name. And his age. And where he lived. And it's not like we haven't had all those Internet Safety talks at school a zillion times. I just . . ."

I pick at a stray thread that's fraying at the bottom of my jeans.

"He didn't seem like a creep. I thought he really cared about me."

Tears well up in my eyes, and I reach for the box of tissues on the table next to me.

"I think that's what hurts the most. Almost as much as my family hating me and everyone at school being mean. That it was all a lie. I ruined *everything* because of one great big huge lie."

"Abby, it's important for you to realize that these predators are highly skilled at manipulating young people," Dr. Binnie says. "It's a process we call 'grooming.' It's all about winning your trust for the sole purpose of sexual exploitation."

I feel my cheeks fire up when she says *sexual exploitation*. I wonder if she knows about the online pictures, about the video, that I'm Abby the Teen Porn Queen. Imagine how that will look on my college application.

"You are the victim here, Abby. A victim of a crime. Did you make some bad decisions? Yes. But you are still the victim of a felony crime, and you shouldn't let anyone make you forget that."

"But it's not like he stole me off the street and kept me in a shed for eighteen years like that girl," I say. "She really *was* a victim. I left by myself. Like, that's what Dad keeps going on about. How could I have gotten into the car with Luke? What was going through my head? Dad's totally blaming me for it. He doesn't think I'm a victim at all."

"We'll be having some family therapy sessions to work through that, Abby. But what's important is for *you* to recognize that you were a victim here."

I try to absorb what she's saying, but all I can hear is my dad's voice: *How could you get in the car with that monster, Abby? How could you be so stupid and irresponsible? I don't even know you anymore.* Or Lily: *It was all one great big lie and you were stupid enough to fall for it and ruin everything for everyone.*

"Yeah. I guess."

"You don't believe me."

"I don't know what to believe anymore."

"Luke won your trust, and then he violated it. I'm not surprised you're having problems trusting and believing. But I hope we can work on that together."

She smiles at me for the first time, and I want to believe her, to believe that maybe I'm not this total piece-of-crap person and that maybe life will be okay again someday. I want to believe her so badly.

But all I feel is tired. Tired and afraid to believe in anyone or anything. And wishing like hell that I never had to go back to school ever again.

CHAPTER 35
FAITH ⚈ DECEMBER 18

It takes all my powers of persuasion and best-friend blackmailing guilt-tripping to get Abby to agree to come see the final performance of *A Midsummer Night's Dream*. She doesn't want to be anywhere near school unless she has to, and I can't say I blame her. People are being such . . . jerks. Someone scratched *Slut* on her locker. I tried to cover it with a Post-it note before she saw it, but it was too late.

I would have cried, but Abby just got all quiet, opened her locker, and got her books to go home, like nothing happened. I was like, "Come on, Abby, we have to go report this to the principal!" but she just shook her head and said, "What's the point?"

It's almost like she feels like she deserves it. Kind of like Ted said she did.

I miss him so .much. Why did he have to be such a jerk about Abby?

He's standing a few feet away as we wait for the houselights to dim before the performance. I want to go over and put my head on his shoulder, to run my fingers through the dark curls at the back of his neck. But I can't. We've barely spoken since that day we fought. I hoped he would call me or something. But nothing.

I peek from behind the curtains into the audience and see Abby sitting with her parents and Lily. My parents and my brother and sister are next to them, and right behind them is Billy Fisher. Billy is leaning forward and whispering to Abby. I actually see her smile, something I haven't seen her do since . . . the whole Luke thing. She told me Billy has been calling her practically every night, just to talk and see how she's doing. She seemed so surprised by that.

"You know he really *likes* you, Abby," I told her.

"But I . . . really treated him kind of badly before and now . . . well . . ."

"Now, what? You should walk around wearing the scarlet letter for the rest of your life?"

"Yes. No . . . I don't know."

I'm really glad Abby's started seeing a therapist. She totally needs one.

The lights in the auditorium dim and the curtains open. The play starts and as always I'm caught up in the story. Until I sense Ted standing a few inches behind me. I'm so aware of him I can't concentrate on the dialogue. I just want to lean back against his chest. Then I feel his hand on my shoulder, rubbing the spot where he knows I always get tense. I hold my breath, hardly able to believe that I'm feeling the warmth of his fingers.

"Breathe," he whispers, his words tickling my ear. "You can't relax unless you breathe, Faith."

I take a deep breath in and out, and lean back against him. He rubs my shoulders for a few minutes more, then folds his arms around me.

"I've missed you so much," he whispers.

"Ditto," I whisper back.

I wish we could go somewhere to talk, to figure out what happens next. But there are scenes to change and props to move. So I just stand there, watching Puck sprinkling love-in-idleness juice on Titania's eyelids onstage, but feeling the real magic offstage with Ted. For this moment, that's enough.

CHAPTER 36
LILY · JANUARY 3

Whoever invented family therapy was meaner than a middle school gym teacher. It's serious torture. We're all sitting around the shrink's office — and guess who gets the least comfortable chair — and then we have to talk about how we're *feeling.*

"I'm feeling that I would rather be home watching *Degrassi,* because it's not *me* that ran off with some perv," I say, earning myself dirty looks from Mom and Dad.

Abby just stares at the little fountain in the corner. She does a lot of that recently. Just zones out of whatever conversation. I feel like waving my hand in front of her face and shouting, *"Yo, Abs, it's because of you that we're stuck in this place!"*

"I sense that you're angry with Abby, Lily," Dr. Binnie, the shrink lady, says. "Are you?"

"What, just because I'm a total social reject because of her? And my parents are fighting, like, nonstop? Why would I be angry at *poor, wittle Abby?*"

"I understand your anger, Lily, and you have a right to feel angry. But you need to remember, Abby was a victim here."

Yeah, yeah. It's always about Abby.

"Like how? She got in that freak's car by herself. It's not like he kidnapped her."

I know Dad's on my side, because his head is nodding the tiniest bit, and this is the same thing I've heard him yelling at Abby over and over.

But boy, do we get schooled. Dr. Binnie gives us this whole lecture about Internet predators and how they "groom" kids and how we shouldn't be blaming Abby so much because she was a victim of a devious manipulator who spent all this time gaining her trust just so he could abuse her. And how now we're abusing her all over again by blaming her for it.

I feel about an inch tall by the time she's done. I look at Dad for moral support, but he's just staring at the pattern on the rug.

Abby is sitting in a black leather armchair, her legs tucked up under her, like she wants to curl up into nothingness. I guess I don't blame her. Even if she did go with the guy willingly, maybe, just maybe, it's time for us to start cutting her a little slack. Especially since she's been getting all this flack at school, too.

I look over at her.

"I'm sorry, Abs."

She doesn't look at me. "It's okay."

"No. It's *not* okay. I've been mean to you. Get mad at me. Be a beeyotch like you normally would."

"*Lily!*" Mom snaps.

The shrink puts up her hand, to shush Mom up.

Abby finally looks at me.

"Why should I? You guys are right. I *did* get in the car with Luke. I *did* mess up everyone's life."

"But it's like the shrink — I mean, Dr. Binnie — said, right? Perv Face was a manipulating, grooming liar. He *made* you think you were in love with him."

"I should have been smarter than that," Abby says, her voice beginning to tremble, a stray tear rolling down her cheek. "I'm a straight-A student, after all. Right, Dad?"

Dad still can't meet her gaze. I want to shout at him, *Look at her, you jerk!*

"I don't understand it, Abby. I still can't get my head around it," he says. "We talked to you about using the Internet safely. You had assemblies about it at school. But you did it anyway. And you . . . *exposed yourself* . . . and . . . I don't think I'll ever understand as long as I live how *my daughter* could do something like this."

OMG. The way he says "exposed yourself." No wonder Abby feels like dirt.

"Mr. Johnston, right now it's not necessary for you to *understand* Abby," says Dr. Binnie. "What's important is for you to *accept* that she's a victim in this, and treat her as such."

I look over at Abby and she's gazing at Dad's averted face with pleading eyes, tears streaming down her cheeks.

Look at her, Dad. Come on, look at her.

"Rick. He was a predator. He preyed on Abby," Mom says. "These people . . . have websites where they give each other tips on how to do it. Agent Saunders gave me some links and I've been doing research." It's true. I don't know if it's because she feels guilty about not knowing what Abby was up to, but Mom's in serious danger of turning into some kind of crazy Internet Safety Guru. "You can't believe the things they —"

"F-forget it, Mom," Abby sniffs, her eyes downcast, her body starting to curl up into itself again. "J-just f-forget it."

"No, don't," I say. I get up and stand right in front of Dad, where he can't help but look at me. "Dad. Look at Abby. Look at her. It's not her fault. Stop blaming her."

No one speaks. Abby's weeping mingles with the tinkling of the fountain in the corner.

Dad still can't bring himself to look at my sister. I want to take his head and yank it in her direction.

"Do you want to know w-why, Dad?" Abby says suddenly. "D-do you want to know w-why it was so easy for L-luke?"

"His name is Schmidt," Dad snaps. "Edmund Schmidt."

"Whatever." Abby sighs. "The man I knew was Luke Redmond. And the reason I went off with him, the reason I thought I loved him was because . . ."

She breaks off and blows her nose, and takes a deep breath and continues.

"The reason I thought he loved me, and I loved him, was because he *listened* to me. Do you hear me, Dad? *Because he listened to me!*"

Abby's practically shouting at him, and he finally turns and looks at her. *Go, Abs.*

"And you're saying I don't?" Dad asks. "That this is all *my* fault?"

"No! But . . . high school's been really hard and it's not like you've been around all that much since you started the new business. And things were getting weird with Faith, like she was making all these new friends and I wasn't and I was . . . lonely."

"So you had to make friends with a pervert?"

Sometimes parents are so freaking dense.

"Mr. Johnston, I think what Abby's trying to tell you is that she was lonely and the predator was very clever in sensing her needs and trying to fill them in order to manipulate Abby for his own ends," Dr. Binnie says. "That's how the grooming process works."

"Why couldn't you just talk to *us*, honey?" Mom asks. "Why couldn't you just *tell us* you were lonely?"

"Yeah, right," I say. "Like *that's* going to happen."

"What's that supposed to mean?" Dad says, all mad at *me* now. I don't care. As long as it takes some of the heat off of Abby.

"Seriously, think back to the prehistoric era when you were teenagers," I say. I see Dr. Binnie raise her hand to her mouth to hide a smile. She seems okay for a shrink, not that I actually know any other shrinks except for Mr. DiTocco, the counselor at school. "Would *you* have told *your* parents that you felt like a total loser with no friends?"

I glance at Abby.

"No offense, Abs."

And believe it or not, I really didn't mean any.

"None taken, Lily," Abby says.

She's still facing Dad with that sad, pleading expression. His gaze jumps from her to the floor to the tinkling fountain to the ceiling and finally settles on a spot on the wall to the right of Abby's head.

"When I think of him . . . touching you . . . I just . . ." Dad's hands clench into fists. "It makes me . . . I want to kill . . . I —"

Suddenly, he covers his face with his hands, and his shoulders slump over. And then he's making these awful sounds, like a dying walrus. Mom puts her arm around him and murmurs, "Rick, it's okay, it's okay."

And then Abby uncurls herself from the black leather chair and crosses the carpet. She stands in front of Dad and goes to put her arms around him, then stops, like she's afraid, like she's worried that he won't want her to because she's too dirty 'cause she's been contaminated by that freakazoid perv she ran off with. So she just touches his shoulder, lightly, with her fingertips, enough to let him know she's there but without risking giving him perv cooties. And Dad uncovers his face and looks at her. Really *looks* at Abby. He sees her eyes, which are bright red from crying, and the look on her face that's begging him to still love her, even though she fell for that creep's lies and did all the crazy, stupid things she did.

"Christ, Abby, when I thought you were dead, it almost killed me," Dad says, pulling Abby into his arms.

Okay, I'm crying now, too. Who wouldn't be? Yeah, the shrink, but that's because this is all in a day's work to her, I guess.

I know school's still going to suck — it's not like this family therapy crap is going to magically change my status as a social leper with a crazy sister. But I guess this was worth missing *Degrassi* for, if it means maybe our family has some remote shot at being normal again someday.

CHAPTER 37
ABBY / FEBRUARY

"Abby, wake up! You're having another nightmare," Lily says, shaking me.

She looks pale in the golden light of my bedside lamp.

"That must have been a really bad one," she says, handing me a tissue to dry my tears. "You were crying and you shouted 'Help me!' in this really pathetic voice."

"At least I didn't wake up Mom and Dad," I say. "I'm . . . really sorry I disturbed you."

"It's okay." She squeezes my leg gently. "Really."

There are so many ways I screwed up by getting in Luke's car, but for some strange reason, once she got over her initial pissed-offedness, this whole thing seems to have made Lily and me closer. I mean, I don't think we'll ever be the sharing-clothes-and-makeup kind of sisters. We're still very different. But somehow we seem to have found a way to talk without fighting. At least some of the time anyway.

"Abs . . ." Lily says. "What . . . what is it that you're dreaming about when you freak out like this? Is it what HE did to you?"

Lily refuses to call him Luke. She'll only call him Schmidt or Perv Face or HIM. In a way she's right because there is no such person as Luke Redmond. But it's hard for me to give him up so easily, because of what he meant to me. Or at least what I thought he meant to me.

I think back to my nightmare and a shiver passes through me. Wrapping my arms around my shins, I curl up tight and rest my chin on my knees.

Don't get coy with me now, Abby. You know you want it. You've wanted it all along.

Lily's looking at me, her sleepy eyes filled with love and concern. I don't want to pollute her dreams with the filth inside my head. But she's waiting for an answer, and knowing Lily, she won't leave until she gets one.

"Some of it's . . . what happened. But then . . . it's like . . . I dream . . . that he's going to . . . kill me. That I'm going to . . . die . . . in that room . . . without ever seeing Mom or Dad . . . or you . . . or anyone . . ." My voice catches and I can't stop the tears from starting again. "I dream I'm going to die . . . without seeing any of you . . . ever again."

Lily's eyes glisten and she suddenly throws her arms around me.

"Oh, Abby!"

She rocks me gently, and rubs my back, like *I'm* the baby sister.

My mother finds us curled up next to each other in my bed the following morning. She doesn't say anything, but her mouth is a compressed line of worry.

"Another nightmare, Abby?"

I hesitate before telling her the truth. "Yes . . . A really bad one this time."

"Why didn't you wake me up?"

"It's okay." I look at my sister breathing softly on the pillow next to me. "Lily was here."

The victim support specialist at the FBI calls us periodically to update us on the investigation. They found all kinds of sick stuff on Luke's computer — not just the pictures of me, but videos of really young girls, like as young as five even, having sex with older guys. I ran to the bathroom and threw up when Mom told me that. I can't believe that I thought I was in love with someone who was capable of something so incredibly sick and gross.

But I wasn't in love with that guy, really. It's like there are two separate people. There's Edmund Schmidt, this perverted pedophile Internet predator who had disgusting porn on his computer and was busy "grooming" several girls besides me. Then there's Luke, the guy I was in love with — or at least who I thought I was in love with. Luke, who listened to me, who seemed to understand me better than anyone else. But the thing is, Luke isn't real. Luke is just a fictional character that Edmund Schmidt made up to trick me.

Dr. Binnie has been trying to help me understand how predators work so I will stop blaming myself so much.

"The predator's greatest tool is listening, Abby," she told me. "That is how Luke was able to gain your confidence and your trust . . . and ultimately, your love. Because he listened to your problems and reflected them back to you, but without any genuine empathy."

"Yeah, that's what hurts so much, I guess. And what makes me feel . . . like such a first-class idiot. I've always thought of myself as smart. Everyone always *told* me I was smart. Being smart is the one thing I'm supposed to be good at and now I'm not even good at that."

"Abby, there's a difference between academic intelligence and emotional intelligence. Clearly, you're a very bright girl. But you're also fourteen, and emotional intelligence develops as you mature. That's part of the reason your age group, young adolescents, are the group at highest risk for being targeted by predators."

"Great. So I'm just another statistic."

"I didn't tell you that so you could feel like another statistic. More so you could understand that there's a good reason predators like Schmidt are on the lookout for boys and girls your age. Because they know you're at a point where you're starting to explore your own identities. And you're also trying to be more independent from your parents, and that, as you know from experience, causes conflict. When kids argue with their parents, it gives the predator an opening, one that they're expert at exploiting."

I remember how Luke always took my side when I complained about my parents. How he took my side about everything. How it felt so good to have someone who agreed with everything I said, instead of telling me that I was being negative, like Faith.

Faith, the one who has stuck by me through all of this, defends me to the people who bad-mouth me, and calls me every night to make sure I'm okay.

"I guess . . . I guess *real* friends tell it like it is, even if you don't want to hear it."

Dr. Binnie nods.

"*Especially* when you don't want to hear it. But they do it in a kind, loving way."

We're both silent for a moment. The ever-present waterfall tinkles in the background.

"What if I have to testify at his trial?" I ask. "I don't know if I could handle seeing him again, knowing that everything he said to me was a lie just so he could . . . do stuff and . . . put it online."

"Is that a possibility? Has anyone spoken to you about it?"

"No. But, like, they did that forensic exam at the hospital. And when the FBI questioned me, they recorded everything and warned me that it might be used in a court of law and stuff. They still have my computer and my underwear as evidence."

"The victim support specialist can probably tell you more about the likelihood of having to testify," Dr. Binnie says.

"I guess. I'll ask her, the next time I speak to her." I take a deep breath. "Maura says the FBI can notify me whenever they arrest someone who's downloaded the 'Abby Series.' I don't know what to do."

"What would be the advantage of knowing?"

"I guess that some other creep has been arrested and won't be able to do what Luke did."

Dr. Binnie nods.

"Can you think of any drawbacks of knowing?"

Can I ever.

"Well . . . it's like sometimes I have nightmares about people all over the world watching me naked. Like millions of computer screens all filled with that video of Luke . . . you know . . . doing it to me."

I take a tissue out of the box on the table next to me, not because I feel like I'm going to cry, but because I need something to fidget with while I'm talking.

"I wake up and tell myself that it's only a dream. Then, sometimes for a day or two, I can forget about it."

I roll up the tissue and twist it into a pretzel shape.

"But, like, if they tell me they've actually arrested someone for downloading it, then it's not just a dream, is it? It's real. And it's like it's happening all over again."

"That's a good point, Abby. It's important whatever choice you make, that you protect yourself and allow yourself the space to recover from the trauma you've been through."

I start shredding the tissue into small, neat strips. Dr. Binnie just sits there observing me, her pen poised above her notepad, the fountain tinkling away in the corner as if to say, "Ask, Abby, ask." It's not until I've totally decimated the tissue that I finally take a deep breath and pose the question that's really on my mind:

"Dr. Binnie, do you think I'll ever be, like, normal again? Or am I going to be 'That Girl Who Ran Off with the Internet Skeev' for the rest of my life?"

She doesn't answer me right away, and I get this sinking feeling like, *Oh man, I'm doomed forever.*

"I'm not going to lie and say your life will go on as if this never happened, Abby. A trauma like this can take years to overcome. But can you go on to have a happy, productive life? I certainly hope so. That's the goal of therapy. Talking about what happened certainly will help. But it's definitely not going to happen overnight and you shouldn't expect it to. Take it in baby steps and realize that there will be times that for each step forward you'll take a few steps backward. And remember, by helping to put Schmidt behind bars you are preventing him from doing this to other girls."

Preventing him from doing this to other girls.

That's got to be a good thing because I don't want anyone else to have to go through this. Ever.

CHAPTER 38
FAITH / APRIL

Ted's over at my house watching a movie when Abby calls. I think about letting the answering machine pick up, but I don't. I already lost Abby once by ignoring her for Ted, and I'm not going to make that mistake again.

"What's up, Abs? I'm watching a movie."

"I'm sorry. I can call back if you want."

"It's okay. We paused it."

"We? Is Ted there?"

"Uh-huh."

"Did I tell you I'm so psyched you guys got back together?"

"Only about fifty times."

"Okay, okay. So I've been thinking . . ."

"Alert the press!"

"Shut up! Seriously. I've been talking about it with Dr. Binnie, too, and Agent Saunders. I'm going to do a talk about Internet Safety. Like for schools and stuff. Telling kids about my experiences so that maybe they won't get suckered by a predator like I did."

"Wow," I say. "That's really brave, Abs. And a great idea. Except . . ."

She so excited about this — it's the most happy and positive Abby's sounded for the longest time, definitely since . . . IT happened. I wonder if I should rain on her parade or just shut up. But after what happened at the auditions, I figure someone's got to say it, and that someone probably better be me.

"Abs, I'm really proud of you for wanting to do this and all, because I don't think I'd have the guts after everything you've been through. But . . . how are you going to get up in front of all those people?"

Crickets. Ack. I *knew* I should have kept my mouth shut.

"I know, I know. Every time I think about doing it I feel sick to my stomach. But I feel like I've got to face my fears. Like if I can beat this, then I've won. Schmidt hasn't ruined my life. At least not all the way. I'll still be a social reject, but at least I'll have done something good."

Personally, I doubt she's going to be able to pull this off, but I'm not about to tell her that. Right now, Abby needs my encouragement, and if that's what my best friend needs, that's what I'm going to give her.

"I'll help you practice. Maybe Gracie can help, too. She's really good with projecting and all that, you know, because she's been to drama camp and stuff."

"Why don't you and Gracie come over for a sleepover next weekend? I'll start trying to figure out what I'm going to say before then."

"Okay. It's a date. And speaking of that, I'd better get back to mine."

"Oh, I'm sorry. Tell Ted I say hi."

"I will. Bye!"

Ted's finished all the popcorn by the time I hang up. He follows me into the kitchen to get some more Coke while I go to make more.

"So what's up with Abby?"

"She's going to do a talk at schools about Internet Safety and what happened to her. To try and warn other kids."

Ted snorts Coke out through his nose.

"So attractive," I say, handing him a paper towel.

"You have *got* to be kidding me. Are we talking about Abby 'I fainted at my auditions' Johnston?"

I glare at him, even though he's only saying the same thing I thought.

"We have to support her. What she's doing is really brave."

"Look, I'm not disputing that it's a brave idea . . . in *concept*. But come on, Faith. In reality, it's kind of crazy when that girl has the worst case of stage fright, like, ever."

The microwave beeps, but I ignore it.

"Then we have to help her figure out how to get over it," I tell him. I throw my arms around his neck and look up into his eyes. "She *needs* this, Ted. Abby really needs to do this. And somehow, I have no idea how, we have to help her make it happen."

He smiles down at me.

"You are possibly the awesomest person in the universe, Faith Wilson. Do you know that?"

"Only *possibly*?"

He kisses me.

"Totally, definitely, positively."

He lets me go and takes the popcorn out of the microwave.

"Against all my better judgment, I promise to do everything I can to help you coach Abby for what is destined to be a disastrous presentation. Now can we watch the rest of the movie?"

"Only if you let *me* hold the popcorn this time, you pig."

CHAPTER 39

LILY / MAY

I'm starting to think my dorky sister has more friends than I do.
How sad is that? It seems like every other day there's a group of
people over here, helping her to practice for this Internet Safety
presentation.

Dad was totally against it at first. I think he wishes we could
just sweep this all under the carpet and forget it ever happened.
He definitely doesn't like anything that reminds him of *That Man*
and Abby. Like every time the FBI calls to update us about the
case, he gets angry all over again and goes into a funk. Mom has
to remind him that if Abby is trying to get her act together and
move on, he has to try and get over it, too.

But when Abby got this idea that she wanted to, like, talk
about the whole thing in public, Dad went totally nuclear. He
made like it was all about protecting Abby, but I think it was
more because he doesn't want to hear it, or want the world to
know that this happened to us. To his perfect daughter. Yeah,
Dad. Like it's some great big secret after it was on the news and
in all the papers.

We had this whole family therapy session about it. Abby totally
surprised me, because she stuck to her guns, even though Dad

was all over her to drop the idea. I guess doing this really means something to her. She said that if talking about it means that one other person doesn't fall for some creep like Edmund Schmidt — she's started calling him that now instead of Luke — then it will be worth the terror of getting up onstage in front of people.

I was like, "I'm fine with it, as long as you don't come to my school. I mean, no offense, but, you know, things are hard enough already."

Mom gave me one of her "Shut up, Lily" looks — it feels like I get those practically every time I open my mouth at the moment — but Abby was cool with it.

"It's a deal, Lily. I won't come to your school," she said. "Anyway, I'm not even sure I'll live through doing it at *my* school without passing out. It's not like I have such a great track record with being onstage."

I couldn't help it. I remembered Abby passing out at the auditions and I giggled. I covered my mouth with my hand, but the more I tried to stop, the more I wanted to laugh. Mom, Dad, and Dr. Binnie were all looking at me like I was some kind of lab specimen, but then it happened . . . Abby laughed, too. And then the two of us were in that shrink's office cackling like a pair of hyenas, while the grown-ups looked at us like we were crazy.

Maybe we are. But we get on better now than we did when we were normal.

"*Breathe*, Abby! You have to *breathe*. Otherwise, you *will* pass out, I guarantee it!"

I stick my head into the family room. Abby's standing in front of the television, holding her speech. Her hands are shaking so much I don't know how she can read the thing. Faith and Ted are on the sofa, and Abby's friend Billy, who's actually kind of cute in a geeky kind of way, is in the armchair. Gracie is directing from the sidelines. I slide onto the sofa next to Faith.

"How's she doing?" I whisper.

Faith sighs.

"That good, huh?"

"My hands are shaking so much I can't even read what I'm supposed to say," Abby wails. "I'm *never* going to be able to do this!"

"You *will*, Abby," Grace says. "Think positive!"

Billy goes and stands next to Abby. He takes her hands in his and steadies them.

"Here. Just pretend I'm your podium."

Abby blushes. She so has a crush on Billy, even if she tells me she's not ready for any of that stuff and, anyway, who would want to go out with her after what happened? I may only be in seventh grade, but *duh*, I'm not blind. Billy still wants to go out with her, despite the whole Creepy Freak thing. I guess she'll figure that out sooner or later. Hopefully sooner.

"Okay, Abby. Take it from the top," Gracie says.

Abby starts again, and this time she actually manages to get through the speech. Her voice is shaky and she sounds like she's going to start crying any minute, but at least she's still vertical by the end of it.

I stand up and clap wildly. "Go, Abby! You rock!"

Faith's jumping up and down doing a really lame imitation of a cheerleader. I hope she never gets it in her head to try out for the squad, because they'd laugh her off the face of the planet.

Abby's got this dopey smile on her face, like she can't believe she actually pulled this off — managing to read a speech in front of all of, let's see, five people. None of us have the heart to remind her that the auditorium holds, like, this number times a hundred. But I guess you crawl before you walk or whatever.

Later that night, after everyone's left, I walk by Abby's room and I hear her practicing. It's so crazy because alone in her room, she's a different person — she sounds so strong and passionate about what she's saying, like she really means it and she never, ever, wants anyone to go through what she did. I stand outside her door listening until she's finished, and then I knock and go in.

Abby looks at me like I'm some weird space alien.

"What?"

"Did I actually just hear you *knock* before you came in? Who are you and what have you done with my bratty sister, Lily?"

"Shut up!"

I plop myself on her bed.

"You sounded great. Seriously. I was listening just now from outside the door."

"Wow. I'm glad I didn't know. The minute I know I have an audience is when I start losing it."

"So . . . why can't you . . . like, pretend that there's no one there? You know, *visualize* or whatever?"

"I know. That's what Gracie says. But . . . they *are* there. I'm not that good at pretending."

"There's got to be a way. Maybe we can look up stage fright on the Internet or something."

Abby rolls her eyes.

"Yeah, in the five minutes a day 'only for homework and while an adult is watching' time I get on the computer?"

"Well, I can look it up then. And an adult is *always* watching now that Mom and Dad have put that monitoring software on the computer. It's like totally Big Brother. What happens if I want to complain about them to my friends?"

"The Internet isn't a right, it's a privilege," we both say together. And then we crack up.

"Jeez, Abs, you know you've totally screwed things up for me. Now, I'm never going to be able to IM my friends that Mom's the most embarrassing person who ever walked the face of the earth without her knowing."

She sighs. "I know. And if I'm ever allowed real computer privileges again, what if a guy — like a guy my age, who I actually know, IM's me to ask me out or something. Is Dad going to e-mail him back to give my answer?"

"Maybe we should discuss our *feelings* about this in family therapy," I tell her. "Like maybe Dr. Binnie can help us come up with some rules like they can read our stuff but they can't say anything about it. Seriously, we've got to have some privacy, right?"

"According to Mom and Dad, I *forfeited my right to privacy.*"

"Well, *I* didn't."

"No. And I'm sorry that I've messed everything up for you."

It feels good to hear her say that. It's not like I want Abby to go on feeling like crap about what happened, I really don't. But it does something for me to hear her say she's sorry.

"It's okay. I'll live. And I'll make you pay, by stealing your clothes or something. Well, I *would* if you actually had any clothes worth stealing. But all your clothes are f-u-g-l-y."

Abby laughs.

"Okay, now I know the *real* Lily's back."

"Seriously, Abby, your speech is great and, you know, it's going to be way more real to people than the boring Internet talks they give us at school. So I was thinking . . . like, if you could kick that stupid stage-fright business, maybe you could come and do it at my school, too."

She stares at me with wide eyes that are suddenly glistening.

"For real?"

I nod.

"Oh, Lily!" she cries, throwing her arms around me.

I hug her back, inhaling her Abby smell of shampoo and body lotion. Then I push her away.

"Okay, jeez, enough with the mushiness! Now read that whole stupid speech while I'm sitting here. You can do it. I know you can."

CHAPTER 40
BILLY / MAY

I catch a lot of crap from guys who wonder how I could still crush on a girl who voluntarily got in a car with a perv. People tell me she must be royally screwed up, that I must be some kind of masochist, that I'm just asking for trouble by even hanging around with her.

My parents are some of those people. They hate that I'm over at the Johnstons' so much, trying to help Abby with her speech, after one date with the girl got me an interview with the police, like I could have been a suspect or something. I keep trying to tell them that she's not that girl. Well, okay, she is that girl, but that's not all she's about.

I want to kill that guy Schmidt. Every time I think about him touching Abby it makes me want to puke and punch things at the same time.

Did it almost send me postal when those pictures of her started circulating around school? Hell, yeah! I wanted to beat the crap out of the kids who were passing them around. And the ones who were looking at them. And especially the assholes who were sniggering and making comments to Abby when she walked down the hall. No one dares to do it when I'm with her, because they know my fist would end up in their face. The suspension would be worth it. My parents might not think so, but I do.

I get so angry that people can't look past all this stuff with Schmidt to how Abby's an honor student, one of the smartest girls I've ever met. They don't understand how good these perverts are at manipulating people, and how easily it could have been their girlfriend or their sister or the girl next door who was sucked in by that dude's lies. And nobody seems to appreciate how incredibly freaking brave Abby is — how she has to put up with all this crap from the other kids at school day after day, but she's still going ahead with the idea of doing this talk. Even though the one time she tried to get up on stage to audition she passed out.

I wish everyone could see how hard she is working at overcoming everything she's been through and facing this stage-fright thing. We're over at her house again, Grace, Faith, and me. Even Abby's sister, Lily, is helping out these days. But Abby's still shaking, even just speaking to the four of us.

"So, Abby, how come when you answer a question in science class you don't get all freaked out like this?" I ask her. "Because, like, there's at least thirty kids in that class and you answer the question just fine."

Abby stares at me: So do all the others.

"I don't know," she says. "I never thought of that."

"Neither did I," says Faith. "That's a really good question. It's true, Abs. You answer questions in class just fine. It's only when you have to stand up in front of everyone to do a presentation that you freak."

"So what's the difference?" asks Lily.

Abby sinks onto the sofa.

"I don't know . . . I guess . . . well, when I answer a question it's like . . . I don't have all the scary thoughts because . . . I know I've studied . . . and I know the answer."

We let that sink in and then Grace pipes up.

"Well, think about it, Abby. No one knows this subject better than you. Because it happened to you. You can't have a wrong answer because *it's your story.*"

"That's so true!" Faith exclaims. "It's the Abby Johnston story. No one else's."

Abby doesn't look entirely convinced. She's still shaking her head, like she can't do this.

"I did some research about stage fright," I tell her. "Online. And one person who had it really bad said it got better when he started thinking about it as talking to just one person. Like, instead of thinking about the whole auditorium, just pick one person in the audience and imagine you're talking to them. You can switch people — like, move from one person to another. But you should just keep thinking of it as a one-on-one talk between friends."

"You did research?" Lily says. She gives me this look like maybe I'm not so bad after all. "Well, I've been doing some, too. One thing said you have to believe in the value of your message. Which you so totally do, Abs, right? And *we* all do or else we wouldn't be wasting so much time helping you instead of chillaxing and watching *Degrassi*, which is what we'd rather be doing. Or at least *I* would anyway."

"Yeah, speak for yourself, Lily. I can think of a lot of things I'd rather be doing than watching that garbage for drama llamas," I tell her.

"Who are you calling a drama llama?" she retorts.

"Okay, guys, I get it," Abby says, intervening before Lily and I get into a full-fledged drama llama debate. "I'll try again. Let's see. . . . Think I know my stuff. Value of my message. One-on-one."

"You got it," Grace says.

"Go, Abby!" Faith tells her.

Abby takes her place in front of the TV. Then she notices her mom standing in the doorway.

"Mom, do you have to listen?"

"Abby, think one-on-one," Lily says. "Just ignore her. I always do."

"Don't I know it," Mrs. Johnston sighs.

"Okay, here goes," Abby says.

She takes a deep breath and she focuses on one person in the room. And that person is me. She looks me straight in the eye and tells me the whole story, as I gaze straight back at her, hardly able to breathe because she's just so freaking . . . incredible. She nails that sucker. Even though I've heard this speech, like, fifty-something times before, I've got goose bumps on my arms when she talks about getting in the car with that asshole creep. *I'd like to kill that mofo loser if I ever get my hands on him.*

By the time she's done, all the girls are wiping their eyes, and I'm so proud of her I want to throw my arms around her, pick her up, and kiss her. Except I can't do that. Abby's freaked out about all the physical stuff since . . . IT all happened, and she's asked me to take things slow this time. Which isn't easy, but I'm trying. So I just give her a really big smile and say, "Abby, you sure aced that one."

She looks like she just won the lottery.

"You know, guys, for the first time, I think maybe I can really do this," she says.

"Are you telling me we've been sitting around here for weeks helping you and you were thinking of *bailing* on the idea?" Lily's looking like she's ready to commit fratricide, or sistercide, or whatever.

"No . . . I was always *going* to do it. It's just that I never believed I really *could*. But now . . ."

She goes to Lily and hugs her, and then she hugs Faith and Grace. I'm holding my breath, wondering if this is a girl-only thing, but then she comes over to me. She hesitates for a moment and then she puts her arms around me and hugs me. And it feels *good*. Her hair smells like fruit shampoo and I breathe it in quickly before she lets go.

"Thanks, Billy," she says, giving me a shy smile that threatens to push the needle off the Cuteness Scale.

"Anything to help, Abby. Seriously."

"So . . . can you sit in the front row when I talk at school? It kind of helped to feel like I was talking to you."

"Done deal."

She goes to talk to Faith and Grace. It's been so frustrating because I wanted to help Abby deal with all this stuff she's been through, but I didn't know how. But now I feel ten feet tall because she needs me, even if it's just to sit there like a dummy while she talks to an auditorium full of people.

Lily sidles over to me.

"You *so* have a crush on her."

How does Abby live with this kid?

"Yeah, so? What's it to you, drama llama?"

"So, she totally crushes on you, too."

Sometimes I kind of get that impression, but it feels good to have it confirmed.

"How do you know?"

"Trust me. Little sisters know. We have ways."

"I'm not sure I want to know those ways."

"No. You totally don't."

"So you really think I'm not wasting my time . . . I mean, that Abby might, you know, be okay with this again soon?"

Lily glances over at Abby, who's over with Grace and Faith, all laughing and animated, so pumped from having kicked that speech's butt.

"Dude, how am I s'posed to know if it's going to be soon? But she's doing a lot better. Dr. Binnie — that's the shrink lady we see — she says that Abby's being *remarkably resilient*."

"That sounds pretty good."

"Yeah. But she also said it can be like ten steps forward and five steps back."

"So I should just be patient, is what you're telling me?"

"If you think Abby's worth it, yeah."

I look over at Abby. She catches my eye and smiles at me.

"Yup, she's worth it," I tell Lily. "A thousand times worth it."

"Now if we could convince Abby of that," Lily says, sighing.

CHAPTER 41
ABBY / JUNE

I'm standing backstage listening to the hum of voices as students file into the auditorium for the Internet Safety talk that Agent Saunders is going to give them. That after months of practicing in front of my friends and my family and Dr. Binnie, *I'm* actually supposed to be giving with her. Mom is in the audience and Dad even took off from work so he could be here to see me. They wanted to be backstage in case I freak out, but I told them I'd be okay, even though I'm totally not.

The audience sounds like a swarm of bees. Angry killer bees. Deadly, angry killer bees that can deliver fatal stings.

"How am I supposed to get up and speak about this in front of all these kids when the last time I was onstage and the place was almost empty I passed out?" I feel my heart start to race, and my breathing is getting fast and shallow. "I must have been *crazy* to think I could do this!"

Faith puts her arm around me and gives me a hug.

"You *can* do it, Abby. Seriously, after all the stuff you've been through, you can do *anything*."

"You know what I do if I'm nervous?" Grace says. "I just imagine everyone in the audience naked."

Luke naked in the motel room, holding a camera. His thing sticking straight up like a hockey stick, even bigger and redder and scarier in real life. I close my eyes again.

"Touch yourself, baby. Like you do on the webcam."

I shudder. Faith glares at Grace.

"OMG! I'm *soooo* sorry, Abby, that was just . . . crazy dumb of me. How about . . . you imagine everyone in the audience wearing . . . I don't know, Dora the Explorer underwear?"

"What, even the guys?"

Grace nods, smiling. "Especially the guys. Especially the guys on the football team."

The thought makes me giggle, and once Faith sees that I'm over my posttraumatic blast from the past, she relaxes and starts laughing, too.

"Okay. I'll think Dora the Explorer underwear. . . ." I say.

"And Mickey Mouse ears!" Faith suggests.

"Yes! I love it!" Grace says. "And what about fluffy bunny slippers!"

"Stop, you guys! Otherwise I'm going to be laughing so hard at the image of these ridiculously dressed football players, I'm not going to be able to talk."

"Seriously, Abs, remember other things we talked about, too. You're not talking to the whole auditorium. You're talking one on one. Billy will be in the front row," Faith says.

"And you believe in the value of your message, right?" Grace says.

"Do I ever," I tell her.

"How are you doing, Abby?" Agent Saunders comes over. She's wearing, surprise, surprise, a pantsuit. I wonder if her entire closet is filled with dark-colored pantsuits or if she ever gets to wear jeans or a skirt or a dress or anything girly.

"I'm okay, I guess. Just nervous. You know. Stage fright."

"Yeah, I get nervous, too, before I have to do these things."

Say what? She looks as cool as a cucumber. She must have magical powers sewn into that pantsuit or something.

"You look surprised," she says.

"Yeah."

"You don't *look* nervous at all," Faith says. "You seem totally relaxed."

"Part of it's practice," Agent Saunders says. "I've done this talk so many times I could probably give it in my sleep. But it's also because I'm so passionate about getting this message out to kids. I confront this stuff every day in my work and I see how oblivious most young people — and, I hate to say it, their parents — are to the dangers. You kids know your way around the technology so much better than us oldies. But there's this attitude I sense when I'm talking that *this will never happen to me.*"

"And I'm living proof that it can, aren't I?" I say.

"That's why you giving this speech is so important," she says. "And brave."

"I don't feel very brave right now."

Agent Saunders puts her hand on my shoulder.

"It's your story, Abby. No one can say you got it wrong. Just go out there and tell it."

Principal Mullins comes and asks Agent Saunders if she's ready to start. Then he goes out, silences the angry killer bees, and introduces her.

She's got this whole PowerPoint presentation talking about how predators can track you down and stalk you through pictures and info you put on your Facebook profile or innocent remarks you make about what you're doing in chat rooms. I know what the kids are thinking, because not so long ago, I was one of them. I was one of the kids in the audience thinking, *I would never be that stupid* or *No way that would ever happen to* me.

I hear Agent Saunders talking about some Internet predator cases. Other cases, not mine. Cases where the kids weren't lucky enough to come home safely like I did. She talks about one where this predator met a teen girl at a mall and then strangled her while they were having sex in his car. Later, he just dumped her body in a ravine. That was right here in Connecticut. She was a year younger than me. There's another case in which a seventeen-year-old girl was talking to a guy on Facebook who was supposedly sixteen. She went to meet him and ended up dead in a field. And it turns out the "teen" she was chatting with was actually thirty-two. That could so easily have been me. I guess that's why I still wake up in the middle of the night in a cold sweat several times a week. But at least I'm waking up, and for that I'm thankful every single day. Even on the crummy ones.

Eventually, Agent Saunders introduces me, which means it's time to go out onstage and face them all.

She whispers, "You can do it!" before she walks offstage, leaving me standing there all by myself facing the spotlights.

I look out into the darkened auditorium. A million eyes burn into my skin and my heart is an anvil, pounding against the wall of my chest. I feel myself getting dizzy but *I will not faint.* I grip the podium where Agent Saunders's laptop rests. She's already set it up to the first slide of my PowerPoint presentation, since I don't have a laptop anymore. Mine's still "evidence" in the trial of *U.S. v. Edmund Schmidt*, and chances are I'll never get it back. Mom and Dad sure aren't in any hurry to get me a new one, either.

I search past the spotlights for Billy, and catch a glimpse of him in the front row. He's there, just like he said he'd be, giving me a smile and a thumbs-up. I take a deep breath, knowing that I can talk to him, one-on-one. Then I hear Faith's and Grace's voices in my head: *Dora the Explorer underwear . . . Mickey Mouse ears . . . Fluffy bunny slippers . . .*

A faint smile playing on my lips, I lift my head, take another deep breath, and begin:

"Hi. I'm Abby Johnston and last year I was the victim of an Internet predator. Like most of you, I didn't think it could happen to me. I bet, like me, you think this kind of stuff only happens to other people. Stupid people. People who don't know any better. Well, I'm here to tell you that it doesn't. It can happen to anyone. Each and any one of you who is sitting here in this auditorium. But by telling you my story, I hope that I can help to prevent that from happening."

I know some people are waiting to hear the gory details — like did Luke rape me and stuff like that — but this isn't the *Jerry Springer Show*, so, too bad, they're not going to get that.

Instead, I tell them about a guy named "Luke" and how he gradually became my "friend."

"It's not like he contacted me and right away I jumped in a car with him. What I've learned is that one of the best tools people like Edmund Schmidt have is listening. They listen to us talk and mirror back our interests and hopes and fears so it sounds like they're just like us and understand us better than anyone. The person I knew as Luke tricked me, seduced me, kind of, into thinking he was a better friend to me than my real friends, and that he cared about me more than even my parents and my sister. Which is ridiculous when you think about it. But when you're arguing with your parents and you feel misunderstood — which seems to happen a lot in high school — and then there's this person who's telling you that you're right and everyone else is wrong and they understand what you're going through . . ."

It's so dark and quiet in the auditorium I have no idea if people are bored, or think I'm an idiot, or are waiting to throw paper airplanes with *Slut* written on them. I look over at Billy and he nods and smiles, so I take another deep breath and carry on.

"The thing is, Schmidt told me the things that I wanted to hear, not the truth, like a real friend would. I was always right and my parents were always wrong. He made me doubt my best friend, Faith, the person who has stood by me since second grade and who continues to stand by me today. And of course, he flattered me and told me that I was beautiful and hot and that he was in love with me, which is very seductive when you're feeling kind of insecure, or down, or maybe a little bit lonely.

"What I didn't know was that at the same time, he was telling several other underage girls what they wanted to hear, too. And that he was going on child porn message boards to compare notes with other predators about techniques for tricking us or 'grooming' us, so that we'd do the things he wanted us to do."

I show them a slide of my bedroom.

"I felt safe because I was at home in my bedroom. When he first started asking me questions that seemed a little . . . weird, like 'What's your bra size?' I figured it didn't matter if I told him because it wasn't like I was ever going to meet him. It was just online. It wasn't real. The thing is, if some guy in class asked me that question, I wouldn't answer. I'd want to slap him. But for some reason, it was different on the Internet — because the person wasn't in front of me and I was in my pj's, in my house, in a place that I felt safe. But it's not safe.

"It might *seem* different. You might *feel* safer doing stuff because you're in the safety of your own home. But you aren't. Anytime you chat with someone you don't know, you're taking a risk. Because even if they seem nice . . . even if they seem like they're your best friend and they care about you and understand you better than anyone else in the whole wide world and they love you . . ."

I feel a lump in my throat and I have to swallow hard, because I'm determined to get through this without crying.

"Well, they *tell* you they love you, anyway. The thing is, you really don't know them at all. And the reason they're listening to you, and being so understanding, isn't because they're real friends. It's because they're getting you to rely on them and trust them so they can take advantage of that trust and . . . hurt you."

I look beyond the spotlight for Billy, because I need a friendly face for what I'm about to say.

"I know a lot of you think that I was stupid. Or that I'm some kind of slut. That whatever happened to me I deserve because I got into the car with this guy. Believe me, it's something I've punished myself for over and over and over again. But

I've learned that I'm a victim of Edmund Schmidt, even though I was dumb enough to get in that car. I'm just grateful that thanks to the hard work of the police and the FBI, I came home safely and I'm alive to tell you this story, unlike the other kids Agent Saunders told you about.

"And I don't want any of you to ever have to go through what I've gone through. Never. Ever. Which is why, despite having sworn I would never get up onstage in front of people again after passing out and making a fool of myself at the drama auditions, I'm here standing in front of you now. It's just that important. So, please — be careful. Be safe. Strangers on the Internet aren't your friends, no matter how well they seem to know you or you think you know them."

I take a deep breath and look out into the darkness. At everyone. At all the eyes that are watching me and probably judging me and maybe still thinking that I deserve what I got.

"Al Franken, a comedian who's now a senator from Minnesota, said: 'Mistakes are a part of being human. Appreciate your mistakes for what they are: precious life lessons that can only be learned the hard way. Unless it's a fatal mistake, which, at least, others can learn from.' I'm really lucky because my mistake didn't turn out to be fatal, when it really easily could have. But I hope that, like me, you can all learn from it. Thank you for listening."

It's really quiet after I finish, and I think that I've done the impossible — I've bored an entire school assembly to death. But then a few people start clapping and then more and — I can't believe this — people are standing up and applauding me. Actually giving me an ovation. I'm getting cheered in the same school where, for the last six months, I've been getting cold-shouldered in the halls, and whispered about, and where someone scratched *Slut* on my locker.

I'm not going to cry, but boy, are my eyes getting watery.

Principal Mullins thanks me, and I get to go offstage, where Faith and Gracie envelop me in a massive great big group bear hug, and Agent Saunders gives me a big grin and tells me I was awesome.

"Anytime you feel like coming with me to a school, you just let me know," she says. "Hearing it from you makes a big impact."

"Let me wait till my legs stop shaking from doing this talk before I think about doing any more," I tell her.

"No problem," she says. "Well, I've got to get my stuff and get back to the office. You take care of yourself, Abby."

"I will . . . and thank you. For everything."

"Just doing my job."

I know she is just doing her job, but it's more than that. She really believes in what she's doing. In trying to keep kids like me safe from creeps like Edmund Schmidt. Which is pretty cool, if you ask me.

Edmund Schmidt is in jail awaiting trial. I still see him in the nightmares that continue to haunt me, but at least I won't have to see him in real life. The district attorney's office said they have enough evidence from the chat logs and all the porn they found on his computer. The forensic evidence that the SANE nurse took during that humiliating exam should be enough to convict him of statutory rape.

I'm just glad I'll never have to come face-to-face with him again. If I did, I'd want to ask him one question: WHY? But I also know that there would be no point asking it. Because everything he ever said to me was a lie.

Billy passes me a note during science the following week.
Do you want to go to see a movie this weekend?
I write back:
It depends. Are we actually going to WATCH the movie?
He has to smother a snort.
It depends.
On what?
On how good the movie is, duh!
This time I'm the one who half snorts, half coughs. Ms. Forcier turns around and looks in our direction, like *What is going on with you two?*
He grabs the paper from me, writes, then passes it back and looks at me sideways from under his hair.
Soooooooo? What's the verdict? Yea or Nay?
I think for a moment — am I ready for this? Billy's been so amazing to me. He doesn't treat me like I'm this defective, freaky girl because of what happened — even if that's how I feel myself sometimes. And that's the problem. I'm just afraid that if he kisses me that I'll think of Luke. Or Edmund as I make myself call him now. That I won't be able to stop those thoughts coming into my head. I've talked about this in my individual sessions with Dr. Binnie a lot — like, am I going to be freaked out about this kind of stuff forever and never be able to live a normal life? She

reminded me that recovery is going to be a long, hard road, and that I'll have good days and bad days. But if I give up, then Edmund Schmidt has won, and I'm not going to let that happen. Never ever. Not on your life.

Yea, I write in big, bold letters, and slide the note back to Billy.

When he reads it, he turns to me and smiles.

Baby steps.

ACKNOWLEDGMENTS

I'm often asked where I get the inspiration for my novels. The answer in this case is an Internet Safety presentation at my son's school. Supervisory Special Agent Tom Lawler of the New Haven office of the Federal Bureau of Investigation told me a true story, which sparked a question to which I felt compelled to write the answer. I am indebted to both SSA Lawler and Marybeth R. Miklos of the New Haven FBI office and Linda Wilkins in the Office of Public Affairs at FBI Headquarters, for their extraordinary assistance with the research for this novel.

I'm deeply grateful to Detective Sergeant (retired) Jim Marr, Sergeant Mark Zuccerella of the Detective Division Special Victims Section, and Police Chief David Ridberg of the Greenwich Police Department for helping me to ensure that the early stages of the investigation and police reports were portrayed as accurately as possible.

I owe many refreshing beverages and tasty snacks to Karen Ball, Justine Domuracki, Maura Keaney, and Dr. Amy Zabin, who gave me excellent feedback on various phases of the manuscript.

My apologies to my beloved critique group, led by the ever amazing Diana Klemin, and including fellow scribes Susan Warner, Bill Buschel, Dr. Alan Shulman, Gay Morris, Steve Fondiller, and Tom Mellana (to whom I am a groupie for life for coming up with the title) for all the sleepless nights suffered after our critique group sessions. I promise to write a funny novel about rainbows and fluffy bunnies someday. Well, maybe fluffy anime bunnies.

Team Scholastic rocks my socks. My amazing editor, Jen Rees, has been a great champion of this book, despite the creepiness factor, because she "got it" right from the beginning. Joy Simpkins, Susan Jeffers Casel, and Starr Mayo were fantastic copyeditors, finding things that I never would have thought of and sparing me serious (and I mean *serious*) embarrassment. Phil Falco blew me away with the perfectly chilling book design. I'm still waiting to find David Levithan's kryptonite, because he really IS Superman. Thanks to Lauren Felsenstein and Tracy van Straaten and everyone in publicity, production, sales, and marketing for helping this book make its way out into the world.

Super Agent Jodi Reamer is living proof that one should never underestimate persons of diminutive size, because they can, quite literally, kick your butt. Thank you for putting up with my periods of authorly angst and reminding me to just keep on writing.

My kids, Josh and Amie, inspire, teach, and amuse me every day. My sincere apologies for all those creepy books on my bedside table during the research phase. Smooches, my darlings. I love you to the end of the Universe and back again.

Hank, I love you and am infinitely grateful for so many things, not least for lending me your convertible to take for a spin and blast Led Zeppelin when I need to clear my head and get inspiration, and for reading this manuscript early enough to catch potential plot flaws. "Whole Lotta Love," babe.

For more information about Internet Safety, visit:
http://wanttogoprivate.com
http://chezteen.com